I0602658

Duchesses Don't Cry

BARBARA RUSSELL

All rights reserved.

No part of this publication may be sold, copied, distributed, reproduced or transmitted in any form or by any means, mechanical or digital, including photocopying and recording or by any information storage and retrieval system without the prior written permission of both the publisher, Oliver Heber Books and the author, Barbara Russell, except in the case of brief quotations embodied in critical articles and reviews.

NO AI TRAINING: Without in any way limiting the author's [and publisher's] exclusive rights under copyright, any use of this publication to "train" generative artificial intelligence (AI) technologies and/or large language models to generate text, or any other medium, is expressly prohibited. The author reserves all rights to license uses of this work for the training and development of any generative AI and/or large language models.

PUBLISHER'S NOTE: This is a work of fiction. Names, characters, places, and incidents either are the product of the author's imagination or are used fictitiously. Any resemblance to actual persons, living or dead, business establishments, events, or locales is entirely coincidental.

Duchesses Don't Cry 2025 © Barbara Russell

Cover art by Dar Albert at Wicked Smart Designs

Published by Oliver-Heber Books

0 9 8 7 6 5 4 3 2 1

one

London, 1886

Isabella wasn't superstitious, but getting stung six times in a row by the firethorn's spikes was bad luck.

She was wrestling with the overgrown bush in the conservatory, wincing every time a thick, spear-like thorn stung her fingers through her useless gloves.

And they said firethorn didn't grow well in England. The darn plant should be used as a weapon; it had tough armour, speed in growing, and an attitude to match its fierce appearance.

"You win, you bloodthirsty beast." She tossed the pruning shears on the workbench. "I've had enough."

The sunlight glinted off the glossy green leaves, making them look as if the plant were celebrating its victory. She removed her leather gloves. Ruby drops of blood trickled down her fingers.

"My lady!" The alarmed voice of Lawson, the lady's maid, coming from behind her, made her jolt.

"What is it? Have the seedlings of my orchids arrived?"

"No, my lady. Your mother is waiting for you in the sitting room. The Dowager Duchess of Gloucester is here. Your presence is urgently requested upstairs."

"But Mother said she didn't need me today. She said I had the afternoon for myself."

"The Dowager wants to see you as well. Honestly!" Lawson shook her head. "You should be ready anyway."

After removing her pinafore, she wiped her hand on a cloth and patted her curls as Lawson waved her out of the conservatory.

"Quickly." Lawson brushed off a few leaves from Isabella's skirt as they walked along the hallway. "Heavens, you ruined all the work I did for you. The skirt is wrinkly and has drops of mud on the hem, just like when you were five years old."

"I'm sorry. I got carried away with the firethorn. It keeps growing in the wrong shape, no matter what I do. And it's overtaking the whole corner. I read about some gardening techniques in the notes of Lancelot Brown that—"

"Yes, yes, fascinating. Now..." Lawson stopped in front of the closed set of double doors opening to the sitting room. "Leave gardening behind and turn into the younger daughter of an earl for the next half an hour."

"I will, but the Dowager isn't here to see me. She wants to talk to Helen."

"It doesn't matter, my lady." Lawson straightened Isabella's collar and brushed more dirt off her skirt. "The Dowager is curious to meet you. Remember to smile." She plastered a smile on her face before opening the doors. "Your Grace, Lady Isabella."

"Finally," Mother said in a disapproving tone.

"Oh, the young one." Her Grace Eve, the Dowager Duchess of Gloucester, narrowed her emerald gaze on Isabella as if assessing her qualities, which shouldn't be many, judging by how quickly the matron looked away.

Isabella curtsied. "Your Grace."

Mother shot her an incendiary glare that promised a long, private conversation, and her sister, Helen, seemed to have swallowed a lemon. But seriously, Isabella had no idea she would meet anyone today.

"What were you doing?" Helen asked, perched on the armchair with her back perfectly straight and her gown neatly pressed.

"The firethorn won another battle. Look." She showed her pricked fingers. "That plant is a menace. My fingers are swollen and hurt. I don't think I can type any articles tonight."

Helen gave her the slightest shake of her head, her black eyes widening with fear.

Mother touched the bridge of her nose.

"Articles?" The Dowager put down her cup of tea somehow without making the cup clink against the saucer.

"I support—"

"Isabella has a passion for gardening," Mother said, silencing her. "She spends hours in the conservatory. But more on that later. Sit down and have a cup of tea, Isabella." The words were sweet; the tone was a commanding one.

Isabella did as told. She guessed no one was interested in hearing how she supported the movement of women determined to obtain the right to vote. Not that she did much aside from volunteering to typewrite articles, letters, and leaflets, or attending marches. Other women risked being imprisoned or beaten by the police every day for their ideas.

She managed to pour herself a cup of tea without spilling a single drop despite her aching fingers. If that wasn't an accomplishment, she didn't know what it was.

"So when can Helen meet His Grace?" Mother asked. "We would love to have tea together."

The Dowager's frown smoothed when she angled towards Helen. "Since my grandson graduated from Sandhurst, one of the best students in his year, of course, he has travelled through the kingdom, but he's now in London. I'm eager to see him settled and married. I'm not young, and after the untimely death of his parents, I'm worried about him." Her voice remained surprisingly flat.

"I'm sure Helen and His Grace will discover they have a lot in common." Mother patted Helen's hand.

Helen gracefully nodded her head in a gesture that could mean anything.

Isabella wondered why the Dowager had summoned her here. The conversation didn't regard her. The Dowager had only shown interest in Helen as the future bride of her grandson—thank goodness—and Helen was the eldest, receiving more pressure about finding a good match.

"Helen is such a lovely lady." The Dowager's green eyes twinkled. "You speak three languages, play the piano and the violin, sing, paint, and are an expert in mediaeval history. How fascinating."

Helen blushed but not too much, because too much blushing was vulgar, as Mother always said. The way Helen could control the amount of blushing was an art Isabella hadn't mastered yet.

Helen bowed her head gracefully. "Thank you, Your Grace."

The Dowager's smile vanished. "And what about this young lady?"

"Isabella received the same education," Helen hurried to say. "She's very accomplished."

Accomplished? The sip Isabella was swallowing went sideways, and she coughed into the napkin. Accomplished wasn't the word Helen used in private conversations.

"Apologies." She wiped her mouth.

"Do you speak three languages as well?" the Dowager asked.

She glanced around. Mother stared at her with an expression that said, '*Don't embarrass me.*' Helen's right eyebrow twitched as it happened whenever she had to lie.

Isabella swallowed again. "*Oui.*"

And that pretty much summed up all the French she knew. Well, aside from croissants, crêpes, and soufflé. Because French delicacies were too delicious not to be remembered. Voilà!

But then again, Helen had always dreamt of being the perfect wife of a lord—and a duke was interested in marrying her—and had studied hard to achieve her dream.

Isabella, on the other hand, preferred botany, dancing, and philosophy to languages. Besides, while she would be happy to find a husband she liked and start a family, her mother never pressured her to marry as highly as possible. That burden had always been on Helen's shoulders.

As a result, Isabella had received more freedom. Freedom she'd used and abused to do as she pleased—mostly gardening.

"Excellent," Mother said in an over-enthusiastic tone before the Dowager could investigate further Isabella's linguistic skills. "We must organise an afternoon tea or a dinner party then."

The Dowager nodded. Her hair was styled in an old-fashioned coiffure—ah! Another French word—that hadn't been seen around in a few decades with a hairnet made of crochet yarn and tight backward rolls.

"Absolutely," the Dowager said. "We're organising a celebration for my grandson's return in Dockerly Castle next week. Something to cheer up the family after our recent losses. You're welcome to join us."

"Next week?" Isabella whispered.

Helen let out a ladylike gasp.

Mother beamed and put a hand on her chest. "We'll be delighted."

Not Isabella. If she weren't waiting for the precious orchid seedlings to arrive, she'd be happy to spend a few days in a castle. But unless she took care of the seedlings and planted them herself, left unattended, they might rot, and orchids were terribly tricky to grow. Not to mention they cost a pretty penny. Pennies that came from her purse. It'd taken her months of savings to buy the seedlings.

Surely, Mother didn't want her to come, anyway. Her motto when it came to Isabella's behaviour was *'don't embarrass me.'* Mother wouldn't risk taking her to a darned castle with a duke.

Yes, Isabella would surely be left home.
Problem solved.

two

I f Grandmama said the word 'lovely' once again, Anthony would pack his things and return to Sandhurst to shoot with a rifle for another year.

"...a true English rose," she said. "So well-educated. Among all the young ladies I've met and considered as the future Duchess of Gloucester, Helen is the best. Who would have imagined the daughter of an earl could be so perfect? I thought Margaret, the daughter of the Duke of Bradford, would have been my only choice, but goodness, she's as interesting as a rock and just as bright. Helen is lovely."

There again.

His brother, Patrick, hid a grin behind his cup. "Lovely."

"Grandmama." Anthony put down the ironed copy of *The Times* he'd been trying to read for the past half an hour. "I appreciate your efforts, but we agreed I would have the last word on the choice."

"Of course. I simply spared you the long and tedious affair of searching for a suitable match." She sipped her tea, gazing at him over the rim of her cup. "I interviewed over fifteen young ladies.

Not a simple task, I must say. But it was worth it. I won't allow an unprepared girl to tarnish the impeccable—"

"Name of our noble and ancient family," Anthony and Patrick said together.

Grandmama huffed. "You two have no manners."

The Indestructible Duchess, they called Grandmama because she'd survived two cholera pandemics, a mine explosion, and a shipwreck. To him, she was a second mother. Oppressive at times but always caring.

"Why are you complaining, brother?" Patrick said from the other side of the table. "You have to do nothing but marry a beautiful lady. I wish Grandmama did the same work for me."

"All in good time." She turned serious. "Anthony comes first, and you already have too many ladies chasing you, and vice versa." She shot a glance at the ceiling. "In my time, ladies never, ever showed any interest in a gentleman. We scorned every word the gentlemen said, and if one of them persisted, then we considered him as a possible suitor."

"Charming," Anthony muttered, pushing aside the newspaper.

He'd inherited the title for almost a year, but he was already tired of the ridiculous amount of responsibilities dropped on him. Least of all the pressure of marrying and producing an heir.

"You might show some enthusiasm." She gave him a disapproving look.

"I'm busy, Grandmama. Between the meetings in Parliament and reading the reports from my stewards, I don't have time for social calls. I'd rather be in my garrison than in the House of Lords."

"Anthony." Grandmama put her hand on his. "I understand your plans have abruptly changed, but you're the duke now, and you can't escape your responsibilities."

As if he didn't know that.

He slid his hand out of hers. Guilt soured his mouth.

Three years ago, Father had died of grief after Mother's death and never had the chance to be the duke. Grandfather had grieved too deeply to prepare Anthony for his ducal role.

Then, less than a year ago, Grandfather had died as well, and Anthony had suddenly become the most unprepared duke of the House of Beaufort with enough duties to choke him.

Silence dropped for a few moments. If only they would leave him alone to work.

"Well, you'll meet Helen soon," Grandmama said. "Helen's sister is a shockingly uninspiring woman. If you marry Helen, we'll have to deal with Isabella as well. But anyway, I invited them to Dockerly Castle."

"Why didn't you tell me?" He controlled his tone of voice.

She stiffened. "I'm telling you now."

He was the duke, and he wanted to be the one making the decisions.

They stared at each other until Patrick cleared his throat.

"Please don't kill each other here. The blood would ruin the carpet."

He and Grandmama turned towards him with matching frowns.

Patrick held up a hand. "It was a joke. A silly joke, but still a joke."

Anthony sipped his tea. At least he would have the last word on the choice of his bride. He wanted a woman who was ready to share the burden of his work and who wanted to support him. A pretty wife who thought only about attending dinner parties wouldn't be happy next to him.

"Naturally," she said, "if that stubborn Austrian von Gruner hadn't proved to be nothing but a fool, we would celebrate in our manor on Maiden Hill instead."

"Naturally," he said, "if you hadn't called him an imbecile buffoon, he might have been more inclined to negotiate with us."

She narrowed her eyes. "Von Gruner insulted your father."

"And you replied in kind. I received a letter from von Gruner last week," Anthony said. "Needless to say, he has no intention of meeting me. He hasn't replied to any of my letters since then."

"It's a miracle he sent you a letter at all." Patrick chuckled nervously. "I would call it progress. We didn't manage to extract a single word from him in months of negotiations."

"Von Gruner enjoys playing with us," Anthony said. The lack of progress with the Austrian was another failure in his ducal career.

Grandmama twitched her mouth. "He didn't even send us his condolences."

"I would love to try to negotiate with him," Patrick said. "And I fancy a trip to the Continent."

Anthony shook his head. "No, you'll stay here, behave, and avoid causing trouble."

"It sounds dreadfully boring."

"Why are you complaining, brother?" He rose, but Grandmama stopped him.

"So do you approve of celebrating in Dockerly Castle with Helen and her family?"

"You've already decided."

Ignoring her scowl, Anthony headed for his study.

Another uncomfortable night of troubled sleep had left his neck muscles sore. At his desk, before opening the correspondence, he checked his personal diary. His physician had told him to write down everything that made him happy or smile each day. An exercise to remind him that there were many good things in his life worth celebrating—or so the physician had said.

The previous entries for the past weeks didn't have a long list of words. Some records were empty. The last annotations reported only the word 'family.' Or what was left of it.

After having returned home from the war and his parents' deaths, he found it hard to make sense of his life. He had a title he wasn't ready to hold, politics he didn't understand, an Austrian count who refused to negotiate the return of his parent's beloved estate, and nothing to look forward to.

Now he even had to get married as soon as possible. But after Father and Grandfather's premature deaths, the family was short of heirs, and producing one was his duty, as Grandmama reminded him every day.

Duty. All his life had been nothing but duties, and they were cold, empty companions that sucked all his energy and gave nothing back.

And he was supposed to share his shadow with a young woman and ruin her life, too.

UNFAIR. Unjust. Unreasonable. Unwarranted.

Isabella searched for all the un-words describing her undeserved situation.

Mother had dragged her on the trip to Dockerly Castle right when her precious orchid seedlings were about to arrive. She'd protested, pointing out she would be only a dead weight no one was interested in talking with, but Mother hadn't listened.

We're a family, and we're going together, Mother had said.

The fact the Dowager had expressly asked for the whole family to come had decided Isabella's fate.

So here she was, in the middle of nowhere in the English countryside, being rocked to and fro in a crowded travelling coach.

"Stop sulking." Helen patted her shoulder as they drove on among bumps and jolts. "We're visiting a new place. I mean, it's in the country, which is too wild, muddy, and generally unkempt. But unlike me, you adore the wilderness. You should be happy."

"Absolutely excited," Isabella muttered, her chin on her closed fist.

Father was sound asleep, snoring softly with his head resting on the wall.

"Sit properly." Mother swatted her shoulder. "You're all bent forwards, and close your legs. You aren't riding a horse. Benjamin, wake up for heaven's sake." She shook Papa.

"I agree, I agree," he said, blinking.

Isabella laughed but stopped when Mother scowled.

"To what are you agreeing?" Mother asked.

Father ran a hand through his dishevelled hair. "To whatever you said, darling." He winked at Isabella.

She grinned and composed herself although the drive made her muscles sore and her mood gloomy.

Helen, instead, was radiant, seemingly already enamoured with His Grace Anthony Beaufort, the eighteenth Duke of Gloucester. The greater the number, the more prestigious the family...the more intimidating the person, in Isabella's opinion.

She tried to find the view of the endless barley fields engaging, but they paled in comparison with the colourful flowers in her conservatory.

"Just a few days," Father whispered. "Then we'll be back to our lives."

"I'm worried about the orchid seedlings. They're from Guatemala." Isabella huffed. "The seedlings might rot if they aren't planted properly."

"Stop this fuss. Our gardener is excellent." Mother waved a dismissive hand. "He'll do a good job. As for you, I believe this experience will help you widen your horizons and meet new friends. Exclusive friends. And after this visit, Helen will be more famous than Lady Mary." She harrumphed. "I got heartburn from how many times I heard Lady Mary being referred to as the Swan of London."

"I haven't seen her in a while," Isabella said.

Mother smirked. "The swan must have migrated somewhere else. I don't care where she is as long as she isn't Helen's rival in marrying the duke."

"It's not a competition—"

"The castle!" Helen gestured out of the window. "Look!"

"Crikey!" Isabella gazed up at the ridiculously tall turrets and the imposing fortress looming from the top of a hill.

Dockerly Castle cast a long shadow on the green fields, with its battlements, a curtain wall, and a portcullis. With its stonewalls and sharp gables, it looked like a set of fangs coming out of the ground as if a giant dragon were about to burst out. The rest of the country seemed tiny compared to it.

Admittedly, the trip had just turned exciting.

"Stop staring at everything as if you were stunned," Mother said. "At least for the next few days."

Father exhaled. "Leave her be."

"Stop defending her. It's because of your lack of discipline she's become such an unrefined lady."

"She's spirited, that's all, and she has her own interests."

Mother pressed her lips together. Father yawned, ending the conversation. Isabella smiled fondly at him, and he squeezed her hand in reply.

"We've arrived." Helen pointed at a tall stone arch marking the entrance of the Beauforts' estate.

"Finally." She admired the neat row of cypress trees lining the road and the trimmed hedges.

The groundskeeper had to work hard.

Ten minutes later, the coach was still driving along the longest driveway in history. Acres upon acres of green hills and mowed grass surrounded the castle.

"The duke must own half of England." Isabella stuck her head out of the window.

"Thirty estates," Helen said like a well-prepared student. "The Beaufort family is one of the most ancient in the kingdom."

Mother exhaled. "Don't remind me of that. Just the thought makes me worry." She gripped Helen's hands. "Darling, we're so lucky, so blessed, and you're going to be a well-respected duchess."

"Hopefully, happy as well." Father took Helen's hands, too. "I know marrying so high has always been your ambition, and I know you studied hard, but if you have the tiniest doubt about marrying the duke, if you think you'll be miserable next to him, don't marry him."

"Don't listen to him." Mother removed Father's hands from Helen's. "We're talking about the eighteenth Duke of Gloucester. Whatever doubt you have about him will be gone the moment you take tea with Her Majesty."

Helen beamed so widely Isabella could see the back of her mouth. "Yes, I mean, Mother has always said that a duke would be perfect for me...and I believe her." Her eyebrow twitched. "It would be wonderful."

Mother and Helen hugged each other among giggles and sobs. If Isabella had to meet the queen for tea, she would have a fit of anxiety.

She was the first to jump out of the carriage, thrilled to see the castle. An army of servants gathered around her. There were gardeners, maids, footmen, and stable hands—more workers than she'd ever seen.

Footmen and maids rushed to take their luggage and welcome them.

"That's what I mean when I say the Beauforts are powerful," Mother said in awe, hooking her arm through Helen's. "The next duchess will have all the grounds at her disposal, meet the queen and foreign monarchs on a regular basis, wear the most expensive jewels and gowns."

Father frowned. "A duchess's life isn't just tea parties and holidays. Helen would have duties, too, some of them difficult. She would represent Her Majesty outside of the kingdom. She would need to show her support to the army, and during Trooping the Colour—"

"Helen would be prepared for all that," Mother said.

"Yes, but you make it sound like being a duchess is something easy and enjoyable when it's not." Father lowered his voice. "Not to mention she might dislike the duke completely."

"Shush." Mother glanced around, worried.

Isabella avoided commenting. Besides Helen's tense expression proved Papa's words weren't a waste of breath. While Helen was certainly prepared to be a duchess from an educational point of view, she knew little of a duchess's political role and even less of the duke. Isabella didn't envy her.

"Oh, impressive." Helen put a fluttering hand on her chest when they entered the cavernous hall.

Real suits of armour lined one side of the entrance, alongside tapestries and portraits of the previous dukes and duchesses.

"One of the duke's ancestors fought in the Battle of Stamford Bridge next to King Harold," Helen said with awe.

Isabella was impressed. Even she knew the Battle of Stamford Bridge had happened centuries ago when the Britons had fought against the Vikings.

"Don't wander around." Mother took her hand, preventing her from inspecting a suit of armour closely. "It's not polite to go around like a nosy person."

"Lady Montrose, Lord Montrose, Lady Helen, Lady Isabella, welcome." The butler bowed, somehow without creasing his shiny suit. "I'm Rogers. Her Grace is waiting for you."

He barely finished saying that before the dowager duchess walked down the sweeping stairs, wearing a high-necked, long-skirted gown that gave Isabella a choking sensation.

"Welcome." The Dowager fit perfectly in the entry hall. With her tall stature and regal posture, she was as intimidating and imposing as the castle. "I trust you had a pleasant journey." She glanced over at Isabella without lingering but smiled at Helen.

"The journey was lovely, Your Grace." Mother bowed her head.

"Lovely? It was completely—ouch!" Isabella winced as Helen poked an elbow into her side.

"We're fine, Your Grace," Helen said. "Happy to be here."

Isabella frowned. She'd promised not to cause trouble, but now she couldn't even make a general comment on the journey? She wasn't going to say anything embarrassing, for Pete's sake. A bit of trust in her would be nice.

Father bowed. "Thank you for your invitation, Your Grace."

The Dowager smiled at Father but kept her gaze on Helen. "Mrs. Stamell will show you to your rooms, and I'll see you later after you've freshened up. My grandson is busy at the moment, but he's eager to meet you all." She headed for the other side of the entry hall, giving orders to the butler.

Isabella gazed around as she went up the stairs. What did this famous duke look like? Did he resemble one of the serious men in the portraits? Or was he like his grandmother—auburn hair and green eyes? Some of the people in the portraits had frightening expressions. Others wielded swords or rifles. Some showed smirks that made them look like murderers.

The corridor was wide, cold, and so long that it had to reach Scotland. She squinted but couldn't see its end.

"Isabella!" Mother and Helen chorused.

"Stop staring like that," Helen whispered.

"Sorry." Just a few minutes in the castle, and Mother and Helen had become two executioners.

They talked in hushed tones, but she overheard the words *perfection* and *demure* a few times. Frightening. Speaking of which, she hoped the castle was haunted. A ghost would cheer up the chilly atmosphere.

"Your room, Lady Montrose." Mrs. Stamell opened the door to a wide room. "The earl's room is on the left while your daughters have the rooms next to yours."

"Thank you, Mrs. Stamell." Mother gave them a pointed look. "Refresh yourselves and have some rest, girls. I'll see you later."

Father bussed Helen and Isabella on their cheeks before going to his room.

Isabella's room was so big and wide that her voice echoed off the walls. She jumped on the four-poster bed, and Helen followed her, instead of going to her bedroom. They tumbled backwards in a heap of clothes and pillows, laughing.

"I understand your excitement. This room is amazing," Isabella said, lying next to Helen.

"I knew you would love this place." Helen spread her arms and touched the brocade curtains. "It's like a fairy tale. A duke, a castle, and more luxuries than I've ever imagined."

Isabella propped herself up on an elbow. "Do you want to marry a man you've never met?"

"I met him briefly years ago when I went to the opera with Mother. Anthony and his brother, Patrick, were there. Their parents were still alive. The duke is...serious."

"Is that all? One brief encounter, and you're happy to marry him?"

Helen tugged at the golden tassel of the rope holding the curtain. "He's a duke, you ninny, and not just a duke, but a duke of an ancient family. Of course, I'm happy to marry him."

"What does he look like? Is he handsome?"

"I remember his dark Sandhurst uniform and intense green eyes. He was so grave and scary I barely spoke to him. Alas, he isn't handsome. Quite rough to be honest. Patrick, instead, is a fine and handsome gentleman, and he didn't stop chatting. He's very charming."

"Serious and scary. Not the adjectives I would want for my husband."

"It doesn't matter. I'm so happy." Helen sighed, staring at the blue canopy and not sounding happy at all. "I've studied so hard to become a proper lady. Years of dance lessons, languages, and music. Now I could be a duchess!" Her black eyes gleamed. "Be part of this prestigious family. I can't believe I'm going to be the eighteenth Duchess of Gloucester. And I'm absolutely ready." She gripped Isabella's hand. "This is what I want, what I've always wanted."

"What mother has always wanted."

"No. I mean, yes, but...I want it, too. Yes, I do. You talk so much about changing society and giving women more power, but there's nothing more powerful than a duchess. Well, aside from the queen. I'll be the most powerful woman in the kingdom after Her Majesty. What can be better?"

"A husband you love?"

Helen shrugged. "As long as he isn't despicable, I'm happy."

"You don't sound happy."

Helen hesitated before speaking. "Let's say that once I'm married, Mother will stop forcing me to play the piano and study languages. That would make me happy."

Isabella slid off the bed. "Well, Your Grace, I wish you all the happiness you deserve." She kissed her sister's cheek. "As for me, I want to take a walk and explore the grounds. Do you want to come with me?"

Helen scrunched up her face. "I'd rather listen to Father and his friends talk about cricket. I have no intention of soiling my boots with mud or getting too much sun. I don't want to sweat, and there are too many insects out there. And Lawson should be here soon to help me get dressed."

"Well, I'm going. I need to stretch out my legs."

"Don't get lost and don't be late for dinner. You need to get ready, too."

"I won't be late. I'll take just a quick walk."

"Don't do anything odd."

"Fine!" She rolled her eyes. "Oh, Helen?" She paused at the door.

"Yes?"

"If you marry the duke, I won't need to meet the queen, will I?"

Helen laughed.

three

All the years spent fencing, boxing, and marching at Sandhurst had made Anthony restless when he was inactive. The day at Dockerly Castle was too clear and unseasonably warm for him to remain indoors.

After working for several hours with his secretary and reviewing the ridiculous amount of documents he had to read and sign, he opted for a walk before dinner. He hadn't seen his guests yet, but they would be busy refreshing themselves, and to be honest, he wasn't eager to talk to Helen.

He remembered her to be pretty, quiet, and sweet. Not much else. End of story.

In a plain but robust tweed suit, he started to trek uphill.

The crisp air was thick with the scent of pine resin and wet soil, a good change from his stuffy room that smelt of centuries of power, intrigues, and bloody battles. The path through the forest was steep but empty. Solitude and the sounds of the forest, exactly what he needed.

As he climbed, he wondered if Helen would be happy with him. An arranged marriage was one thing, but a miserable life was another. If he couldn't have passion, at least he wished for a friendly relationship with his future wife, companionship and who knew, perhaps something deeper. He had the last word, though, as much as he respected Grandmama. And he would like to—

"Hullo!" a feminine voice called. "Hey, you! Over here!"

He turned around. A dark-haired young woman waved to him from the trees lining the path.

"Me?" he asked.

"Yes. Would you come, please, sir? It's an emergency."

"What sort of emergency?" He strode off the path towards the woman until he understood what the emergency was.

A fawn had got itself tangled in a thicket of cleavers and other vines. Its large eyes were filled with terror. The more the young deer struggled, the worse it got tangled.

"I've been trying to rip these stems for ten minutes," the young woman said, "but they're too thick. Do you have a blade?"

He knelt. "Yes. Keep the vines lifted so I won't hurt the fawn."

He used his Scottish dirk to make short work of cutting the stems. The fawn let out long bleats while trying to kick its long legs.

"Calm down," she said. "Your mother must be close, right?"

"Likely. It's better not to touch it. The mother won't like our scents."

He ripped the last vine, and the fawn sprang out of the bush, bleating louder. It vanished into the forest with quick leaps. At least it wasn't hurt.

The young woman exhaled. "Thank you. I didn't know what to do."

He put his blade in the sheath, wincing as a few bristles stung his hands. "Bloody thorns."

"Let me. I'm an expert in removing thorns. I deal with thorns on a daily basis. I'm fairly quick, too."

Before he could utter a word, she grasped his hand and used her half-moon-shaped fingernails to extract the thorns with deft moves.

He got lost in the sensation of her soft hand on his and her focused expression as she pulled out the biting spines.

"And the last one, I think." She removed another thorn and then stroked his hand with gentle fingers. "I don't feel any more of them. Do you?"

"No, I don't." He withdrew his hand, annoyed by a flutter in his chest.

"I'm Isabella. I'm from London, but my family have been invited to the castle. Do you work there? Goodness, there are so many servants it's like a small village, and I've already forgotten their names." She laughed. "I mean, we have servants in our house in London and our manor in Devon, but here there is a small army of people, and the castle is huge! What's your name?"

He was tempted to lie, just to listen to her chatter for longer, but since she had to be Helen's sister, she would learn soon enough who he was. "I'm Anthony Beaufort, Duke of Gloucester."

Her rosy cheeks turned crimson before paling. "I'm so sorry, Your Grace." She shot up to her feet and brushed leaves from her skirt. "I had no idea. I mistook you for a servant, sir."

"Do not worry." He rose as well. "And you can call me Anthony."

"I can't. It wouldn't be appropriate. Your grandmother won't be pleased."

"You must be Lady Isabella."

"I am she." She bobbed a curtsy. "Your Grace, please don't mention this meeting with anyone."

"Because it might be considered compromising?"

"Oh, no. I wish it were only that. I mean, I don't." She rubbed her brow. "Helen warned me not to do anything odd."

"You saved a poor, scared fawn. That's not odd."

"I should return to the castle before Mother realises I went out. I wasn't supposed to leave my room. I wasn't supposed to meet you here...informally. It's all wrong."

Somehow, he disagreed. "I'll escort you."

She pressed her lips together. "We shouldn't be seen together."

"We won't. I'll show you the safest and most secluded way to enter the castle unseen."

Her obsidian eyes flared wide, glowing. "A secret passage? That's a treat. I bet the castle holds many secret passages and nooks."

"When I was ten, I got lost in the eastern wing. They found me the next day."

"How exciting!"

He laughed and wondered when the last time he'd laughed so heartily had been.

"My lady." He offered her his arm.

She slid her arm through his, seemingly not at all intimidated by his build or his title. "Your grandmother told us you went to Sandhurst. Did you enjoy it?"

"In a way, yes. I like order, discipline, and rules. I like being busy." The busier he was, the lesser he thought.

She twitched her nose. "Heavens. That's what my sister would say about being a proper lady. She's so clever. You two are going to get along just fine." She clamped a hand over her mouth. "Apologies. That was too bold."

"No, say what you think. I'm surrounded by people who say only what they think I want to hear."

"Not the Dowager." She scrunched up her face. "Too bold again."

"Not at all. That was accurate."

He led her to the rear of the castle and opened a narrow wrought-iron gate half hidden by the English ivy.

She tilted her head back to stare at the turrets. Her sable curls fell back, stroking her cheeks. "I've never stayed in a castle so ancient, so big, and with so much history."

"We had another estate close by, Maiden Hill, connected to Dockerly Castle through an underground tunnel."

"I would love to see it."

"The tunnel is closed now. Maiden Hill had belonged to my family since the eleventh century, but we lost it." He held the gate open for her.

She brushed past him, and he caught a whiff of her rose scent. "How did you lose it?"

"My father spent the summer in Maiden Hill." He made an effort to control his voice. "He met my mother in the forest where we've been. She was dancing and singing and he was struck by her voice...I'm digressing."

"It sounds like a beautiful story."

No, not so beautiful. "When my father died, my grandfather came to hate the house so deeply he broke the entail through a long and complicated process, angering Grandmother. He sold Maiden Hill to a foreign buyer, unaware of his identity. My grandfather was furious when he learnt an Austrian count, von Gruner, had bought Maiden Hill."

"Why?"

"Von Gruner had a dispute with my father years ago. He bought Maiden Hill out of spite. I want Maiden Hill back. It belongs to my family. It's our soul."

He had no idea why he was blathering about his family to a young woman he'd just met, although his family's tragedy was no secret.

But there was something in the way Isabella listened and paid attention to him that calmed the constant turmoil within him. Maybe because she treated him like a normal person and seemed genuinely interested in knowing him.

She paused. "Why did your grandfather hate the house?"

"My father died in it. He spent his last days there after my mother's death."

"I'm sorry." She seemed about to say something else but pressed her lips together.

"What did you want to say?"

"I've already been too bold."

"I insist."

She trapped her bottom lip between her teeth. "How did your parents die?"

"My mother contracted typhoid fever while volunteering at a children's home. She died in a matter of days. My father never recovered from the loss. Grief became his disease. It ate him from the inside out. There was nothing we could do to help him." Not even his love.

She touched his arm gently, her eyes shining with compassion. She didn't say anything, and he was grateful for that because he felt oddly vulnerable, and a word from her might hurt him too much.

"I'm sorry to have made you sad," he said.

"I asked." She removed her hand. "And when you share sorrow, it weighs a little less."

They walked side by side in silence until they arrived at the end of the path.

He opened another gate, revealing a dark passageway. "We're almost there."

She peeked into it. "That's one frightening tunnel." She glanced at him. "Please, don't tell my mama we were alone in a tunnel."

He smiled. "This conversation never happened."

The passageway was so narrow his arm brushed against hers, and he had to squeeze his shoulders.

Her steps became hesitant when they walked along the constricting hallway. "The walls must be thick."

"Five feet, give or take. Dockerly Castle was mainly a fortress. My ancestors lived in Maiden Hill but would find refuge here from the many Viking raids, fleeing to the castle through the underground tunnel."

"Five feet. We could scream at the top of our lungs, and no one would hear us. I don't hear any noise coming from the other side of the wall." She paused and tilted her head. "Nothing."

"I've never noticed that."

"That would be the perfect place for me to practise singing."

"Do you sing?"

"Not well. Do you want to hear me?"

"By all means, go ahead."

She cleared her throat and made a few gurgling noises. "Just so you know, I don't speak French. I'll make up the words."

He shrugged. "Fine."

Then she drew a deep breath before starting an aria from *Carmen*. She wasn't terrible. A few passages were too high-pitched. Very high-pitched. And off-key. She fared better with the low notes.

In retrospect, he should have told her not to do it. Likely, his eardrums had been permanently damaged. Having nowhere to go, the sound of her loud singing bounced off the walls, getting amplified and punching everything in its path.

They both laughed when she finished. When he burst out laughing, his throat burned, so unused it was to laughter.

They resumed walking down the tunnel.

"Blimey." He touched his ears. "That was powerful."

"And only you heard me." She had barely spoken before voices came from the other side of the tunnel.

"Did you hear that?" a man said.

"A woman was screaming."

"It sounded like she was being murdered."

"We must check the grounds. Find the gamekeeper. Tell him to bring the rifle."

Isabella clamped a hand over her mouth. "And now what?"

He wanted to stay serious, but another laugh burst out of him.

"This way." He took a lateral passage and guided her up a flight of stairs.

As they went to the upper floors, the voices of the servants came muffled until they died down.

She was breathing hard when they arrived at an arcade. "Silly idea."

"No. I think I was mistaken about the width of the walls. Anyway, now we know the walls don't block the sound."

"Mother would kill me if she knew."

"I promised you no one would see us, and I always keep my promises."

He stopped in a dark nook when footsteps thundered from around the corner. She pressed herself against him, and he didn't mind. He liked it.

He glanced at her flushed face and the excitement radiating from her. She was brimming with life and happiness with her curious attitude, and her energy was contagious. For the first time in years, he'd laughed and been excited. He'd forgotten how excitement felt. The rush of blood through his veins was foreign to him.

"I think they've gone," she whispered.

He cleared his throat. "Yes."

"I feel like a spy."

He shuddered when she held his hand in a casual gesture. He had no explanation for the flutter in his chest or the sense of dizziness taking him.

Through yet another door, they arrived at an anteroom behind one of the cloakrooms, far from the drama unfolding on the other side. She released his hand, and he nearly snatched her hand again as a moment of nonsensical panic hit him. His chest heaved with a breath.

"Are you all right?" she asked. "Are you worried?"

"No." Yes, but not in the way she meant. He was worried he would never be as happy as he'd been with her.

"I hope I didn't cause you trouble. Well, aside from..." She waved in the opposite direction. "...the fact your servants now believe a woman has been murdered in your castle."

He chuckled, and the oppressive feeling left him. "I'll manage. Through that door, you'll get to the corridor where your room is. If you're careful, no one will see you, and anyway, at this time, the servants should be downstairs in the kitchen and the dining room, getting ready for dinner."

"Thank you, Your Grace." She smiled. "The afternoon has been most exciting."

And he found himself smiling, too. "Be careful."

"Don't worry about me." A mischievous twinkle sparkled in her eyes. "I'll be as quiet as a mouse."

Somehow, he doubted that.

four

Isabella kept going back and forth on her choice.

Should she tell Helen she'd met the duke? Or should she remain silent?

Running into the duke had been a chance meeting, a pleasant one, but she wasn't sure Helen would be happy to know her sister and her probable betrothed had wandered through the castle alone, laughing and frolicking like two children. She did most of those two, but still, he'd followed her.

She shifted on the stuffed stool in front of the vanity, getting ready for dinner.

"Please, stay still," Lawson said, fixing one of Isabella's wayward curls. "What's got into you? You're more skittish than usual."

"I went out for a walk earlier—"

"Alone?"

"—and I met the duke." There. She said it.

Lawson's mouth dropped open. "You met the duke informally whilst you were around on your own while you should have been in your room?"

"There was this beautiful fawn who was stuck in a thicket of thorns, and I didn't have a blade, but Anthony...the duke had one, and we freed the poor creature, and we walked to the castle together, without the fawn, of course," she said in one breath. "Nothing happened, and it was all very innocent. We laughed together. He isn't as gloomy as I thought. But I don't know if I should talk to Helen."

"Lady Isabella," Lawson said, staring at her in the mirror. "The Dukedom of Gloucester is one of the most powerful in the kingdom. This family isn't normal. They breathe aristocracy. They have so much money and power they would crush your family in a moment without regrets. Do you think an earl is powerful? Not nearly powerful enough."

She let out a shaky chuckle that lacked confidence. "You're so dramatic."

Lawson put down the comb. "What I'm saying is that your sister has the chance to be part of this ancient family, something she and your parents want desperately. The dowager duchess chose her among the aristocratic girls, not just in the kingdom, but among the European courts. Don't do anything that might compromise your sister's chances. Please."

Isabella nodded, swallowing past the sickening lump in her throat. But then again, she hadn't done anything that could compromise Helen's future, had she? "Did the Dowager consider European aristocrats as well?"

"Of course she did. The duke is a desirable match for many European families. I heard even some wealthy American girls wouldn't mind tying the knot with His Grace. So you see, your sister won a fierce competition."

The last word upset Isabella. Anthony might be a great match, but he wasn't a prize to be won. He was kind and, while his attitude was rather stern, he was also funny.

"Don't mention anything to anyone." Lawson finished braiding Isabella's hair. "Smile, be polite, and keep quiet, please."

"As usual."

She didn't say a word as she joined Father, Mother, and Helen in the corridor waiting to go to the dining room together. For some reason, the conversation with Lawson bothered her, which didn't make sense because she was often told to stay quiet and be polite.

"Let me take a look at you." Mother inspected Helen's chignon, earrings, gown, and necklace. "Good. At the table, keep your back straight and your elbows tight. The same rules apply to you, Isabella."

Keep smiling, be polite, and be quiet. Isabella nodded.

Helen touched her necklace, a thick, princess length, gold chain. "Actually, I was thinking of wearing the velvet cameo choker, the one Grandmother gave me for—"

"Nonsense." Mother waved a dismissive hand. "Gold is perfect."

"But I love it and it matches—"

"Helen, are you listening to me? I don't want to hear another word."

Helen flushed to the roots of her hair, muttering an apology. Isabella had to think about the seedlings in her conservatory in order not to protest against Mother's harshness.

"Benjamin." Mother turned her scowl to Father. "No politics."

He frowned back. "I meet the duke in Parliament regularly."

"Exactly. Keep the political discussions there."

"If the duke is going to marry my daughter, I would like to know his opinion on certain delicate matters."

"Not here. Not now." Mother pointed a finger at him. "You become easily incensed when talking about politics. Just for tonight, talk about something else."

He huffed, working his jaw.

Tension thickened the air as she went down the stairs with her family. Helen hadn't married the duke yet, but her family had already changed.

The hairs on the back of her neck stood on end like before a thunderstorm, and her stomach seemed filled with ice.

"Why don't you argue with Mother and defend your choices?" she whispered to Helen after her parents were a few feet away.

Helen kept her stare on the floor. "She has my best interest at heart."

"She's obsessed with dukes."

"It's understandable."

"For someone who dislikes politics, you would make an excellent politician."

Mother paused before entering the sitting room to take a deep breath. "Girls, make me proud."

"Yes, Mother." Helen sounded unemotional.

Isabella was terrified. "Yes, Mother."

"I'm already proud of my girls," Father muttered grudgingly under his breath.

A footman opened the double doors and bowed, announcing them.

Isabella squinted for a moment at the brightness of the room. Heavy furniture and thick carpets took up half the space. The other half was occupied by the largest chandeliers Isabella had ever seen. She had to fight the impulse to look up and just stare at the magnificent crystals.

She suppressed a little gasp upon seeing Anthony. In his tailored dark suit, he looked as imposing and intimidating as the duke he was. His auburn curls enhanced his green eyes, the same as his grandmother's, but even though he was smiling, a forlorn aura radiated from him.

The Dowager stood regal and elegant, making Isabella feel inadequate just by existing. Instead, Lord Patrick, Anthony's brother, was a ray of sunlight, literally. With his golden hair and sparkling blue eyes, he stood out like Apollo next to Hades.

"Lady Helen, I'm pleased to see you again." Anthony bowed

over Helen's gloved hand. When he turned to Isabella, she had to control her smile, lest she smile too much.

"Your Grace." Helen dipped in a curtsy. The moment of sadness from before seemed to never have happened. She looked perfectly happy and serene.

After a round of greetings, curtsies, and bows, drinks were served, but Isabella was distracted by a large frame hanging on the wall and filled with dried, pressed flowers.

She had conflicted feelings about the dried flowers; they were pretty but too similar to mummies.

When the butler announced dinner was ready, she was about to walk to the dining room, but a glare from Mother stopped her. Rules and etiquette. The duke led the way with Helen and Mother, then the Dowager with Father, which left Isabella with Lord Patrick.

"Eerie, aren't they?" Lord Patrick whispered, taking her arm.

"What?"

"The dead flowers."

"Goodness." She was impressed he guessed what she'd been thinking.

She sat on a chair next to Lord Patrick and smiled again, determined not to say a word unless she had to. She would keep her elbows locked to her waist throughout the dinner, her attitude would be demure, and she would be quiet. Easier than dealing with the firethorn.

Anthony sat at the head of the table, and her composure cracked a little when he gave her a quick smile. A smile that held an entire conversation. There was companionship, understanding, and a hint of mischief. She returned the smile and lowered her gaze to her plate while Mother and the dowager duchess talked about the challenges of managing an estate as big as Dockerly Castle.

Helen sat in the position of honour, at the duke's right, a clear sign of a future courtship.

"...of course, it's all nonsense," the Dowager said from the other end of the table, raising an eyebrow. "The servants say they heard a woman's scream coming from the west wing. They checked the whole area, and no one was found."

Anthony glanced at her. Her cheeks warmed.

"It must be a ghost," Lord Patrick said, "as Cook suggested. The ghost of a lady who was murdered here, she said." His cheeky tone made her chuckle.

"Tosh." The Dowager shook her head. "This castle has never been haunted."

"Maybe it is now." Lord Patrick sounded thrilled.

"I think the appearance of a ghost here would be interesting. What do you think, Lady Isabella?" Anthony asked.

Oh, the scoundrel. She dabbed her mouth with her napkin, feeling Mother and Helen's stares on her. They had to wonder why on earth the duke asked for her opinion.

"Well, a ghost would attract tourists."

The Dowager raised both eyebrows. "Tourists? We don't need tourists here."

"I heard that some lords open their castles to tourists for an extra income," she said.

The look the Dowager shot her was so frosty the tip of her nose hurt as if frostbitten. "I assure you, Isabella, that the Beauforts don't need *extra income*."

Tarnation. How had a simple conversation gone so wrong, so quickly?

Helen lowered her gaze as if she were the one the Dowager scolded. Mother remained still. Father seemed about to say something but then remained silent.

What was she supposed to do? Say something else to repair the damage or remain quiet? Feign a headache and leave, perhaps? Faint?

Anthony became serious. "Grandmama, I'm sure Lady Isabella didn't mean to offend with her comment."

"I didn't," she said, "and I apologise if I did. It's that I know a lady who takes advantage of the tourist attraction in her mansion in Halifax."

Anthony nodded. "The Married Women's Property Act enabled wives to buy, own, and sell property and to keep their own earnings now."

She gave him a grateful glance.

Helen listened with interest, but Mother averted her gaze. Father watched the duke closely as if waiting for him to say something he disapproved of.

The Dowager didn't soften. Quite the opposite. "Isabella, are you one of those women who...how do they call themselves? Suffragettes?"

Isabella paused eating. Lying sounded like a betrayal to her principles, but, call it a hunch, the Dowager wouldn't appreciate the truth. "No, I'm not, madam."

Father coughed in his fist. "But you said Mrs. Pankhurst—"

"Benjamin," Mother whispered a warning.

Though Isabella itched to reply, the Dowager had started the conversation, and lying was the only solution to end it.

The Dowager dabbed the corner of her mouth. "I heard of that woman, of course. Apparently, she thinks women don't have any power in our kingdom, despite the fact we're led by a strong queen, undoubtedly the most powerful woman in the world."

Isabella wasn't going to say anything as promised, but the Dowager was like a bloodhound.

"Tell me, Isabella, do I look like a woman without power?"

Silence dropped. She could hear a flea coughing.

"Er, no, madam," she said in a low tone.

"Speak up." The Dowager prompted. "Tell me what you really think."

Anthony gave her another encouraging nod.

"Well." She tilted her chin up. The Dowager had asked a direct question, and it seemed that, whatever she did, she did wrong. "Of course, you're a powerful woman, madam. But Mrs. Pankhurst's point is the average woman in the kingdom has no say in the matters discussed in Parliament."

"The average woman, or man, doesn't need to have a say because they don't understand what governing an empire means," the Dowager said. "Not all men can vote, as it should be. I don't need to march in the streets, shouting silly slogans to get things done, and certainly, I don't want a bunch of uneducated women to give me their unwanted opinions on matters they don't understand. I hope you won't discuss this further."

But Isabella had barely said anything!

"Oh no," Lord Patrick said. "Please do go on. This is most entertaining."

Father was flustered. "Then perhaps we should take care of these uneducated women and make sure they receive the education they need to be active members of the country. Your Grace."

"And wasting money and resources to turn a seamstress into an expert in politics?" the Dowager asked. "For what possible reason? We don't need everyone's opinion to govern the country. This isn't a democracy. Do you want to vote, Helen?"

Helen took a sip of water before answering. "Heavens, no. Why would I?"

The Dowager raised her brow at Isabella. "See?"

"That's fair," she said. "If Helen doesn't want to vote, it's all right, as long as it's her choice. It's also fair that a woman who wishes to vote has the right to do it." *Drat*. She'd just admitted to support women's suffrage.

Father ignored Mother's glances. "Exactly."

"And I believe—" Isabella continued.

Mother angled towards her. "Enough, darling." She turned towards Father. "Please."

The Dowager shot Isabella a glacial stare. "A piece of advice, Isabella. Power works well only when it's exclusive. When everyone, even the undeserving ones, has the same power, chaos ensues, and chaos in a kingdom means riots, and riots mean dead people. Those who hold the power must protect people."

Isabella bowed her head. She'd talked too much.

Anthony cleared his throat. "I agree with Lady Isabella and Montrose."

The Dowager didn't show any mercy for her grandson. "Do you now?"

He put down his fork even though he'd barely touched his duck *à l'orange*. "I met Mrs. Pankhurst, and she's a clever, well-educated woman who has strong arguments in favour of women's suffrage. I promised her to support her petition in Parliament."

Isabella's heart leapt as she wished she could hug him, but one look from the Dowager crushed all her enthusiasm. Only the Dowager had the uncanny power of making her feel small and wrong with one glance.

Father beamed, but Mother paled, and Helen seemed to have drunk vinegar. The Dowager would likely give her grandson a piece of her mind in private.

Lord Patrick broke the frosty silence by raising his glass in a toast. "Ladies and gentlemen, I propose a toast to ghosts and extra income, both things I'm absolutely interested in."

Anthony raised his glass too, smiling at her. "And to well-educated women."

FOR THE REST of the dinner, Isabella kept quiet and stiff. She couldn't enjoy the food, despite the fact the duck was delicious. The fruit sorbet was smooth and sweet, but she could have eaten old parchment for all the pleasure it gave her. She didn't follow the conversation either, focused on not saying or doing anything wrong. If she were the wife of the duke, she would go mad under the constant pressure to be perfect.

It was with relief she rose from her chair once the dinner was over.

In the drawing room, Anthony sat next to Helen on the silk sofa, a little detached from the rest of the group, to chat with her in private.

Isabella desperately needed something to do before she got trapped in a conversation with the Dowager. But what could she do? After the disastrous dinner, she didn't feel confident enough to play the piano. She was too agitated for that.

If Helen married Anthony, Isabella feared those dinners and holidays shared with the duke and his grandmother would be a nightmare.

"Lady Isabella." Patrick gestured at a small table on the other side of the room. "Care to join me for a chess game?"

"Oh gosh, yes. I mean, I'd be delighted."

He offered her his arm. "Don't be afraid of Grandmama," he whispered. "She's sweeter than she seems."

"She must have a terrible opinion of me."

Patrick held the chair for her. "Yes, but it's not personal. She has a terrible opinion of everyone."

The tension riding her neck eased a little as they faced each other across the chessboard.

He flashed a wicked grin. "I must warn you. I'm an extraordinary player. I reckon I'll win in ten minutes and leave you in tears, begging for mercy."

"Challenge accepted."

Twenty minutes later, Anthony and Helen were still deep in conversation about something; Mother, Father, and the Dowager were chatting as well, and Isabella was winning at chess!

"...and my bishop goes here," Patrick said.

"That's your queen."

"Really? These pieces look all bloody the same. Apologies. All right. So..." He took the queen back but placed it in the wrong square while knocking the knight off the chessboard.

"Careful." She grabbed the knight before it fell off the table.

He reached out for it at the same time, and his hand closed around hers.

"Sorry," they said together, laughing.

Finally, she was enjoying herself.

Patrick scoffed and huffed, ruffling his hair. "I have something to confess."

"I have a hunch."

"I'm a terrible chess player."

She laughed again. "I'm not good either. It's the first time I've almost won."

"I've made a mess." He held the knight, studying the chessboard. "Where was the knight?"

"I don't remember."

"Sod it, pardon my French. Shall we start over?"

"But I was winning." She feigned outrage.

He scratched his chin. "Then you win. This match is yours. Obviously. I wanted to impress you." He clicked his tongue. "I guess I failed."

"No, I was impressed by how you couldn't tell apart your queen from your king or the rook."

"Ha-ha, funny."

They collected the pieces among glances and quick smiles.

"Are we going to be related?" he whispered, nodding towards the sofa where Anthony and Helen were chatting.

"I don't know, but my sister is well-spoken and beautiful. Your brother might be easily charmed by her."

Patrick grinned. "Anthony? Easily charmed? Since he started at the military academy, he'd turned into a boring, grumpy man. But I agree. Your sister is as lovely as you are."

"Thank you." Her face flamed again.

"You're blushing. Have I made you uncomfortable?"

"I don't receive many compliments."

"That's a shame, and I shall make sure you receive all the compliments you deserve."

"Shush."

"Lady Isabella, you aren't simply lovely but clever, witty, and pleasant to spend time with."

"Stop."

"And I immediately love anyone who openly disagrees with Grandmama. I had no opinion on women's suffrage, but by Jove, now I support it."

She laughed, maybe too loudly because she felt the Dowager's glacial stare on her like when snowflakes slid under the collar of her coat.

She stopped laughing and raised her gaze. Yes, the Dowager was staring at her, and there was no need for words. That stare held not merely an entire conversation, but a complete course in manners, too.

She composed herself and focused on the chessboard. "So, shall we start?"

five

Anthony couldn't stop thinking of Isabella even during his conversation with Helen. Maybe because he could hear Isabella's open and free laughter as she played chess with Patrick. When she laughed, she reclined her head and showed her pearly teeth with abandon. He liked that. He liked how calm and happy her laughter made him feel. Not that Helen wasn't pretty, intelligent, or sensible, but she lacked any spark or opinion.

"What do you like to do in the summer?" Helen asked, distracting him from watching Isabella imitating the knight's steps for some reason.

"I prefer spending the summer in the country," he said. "London can be too warm and humid."

"I agree. The country is so beautiful. I love nature."

He waited for her to say something more specific, but she didn't add anything. "I love taking long walks up the hills, being in contact with nature."

"I love that too."

Again he waited. But nothing.

"Sometimes I enjoy climbing rocky cliffs in the Peak District."

He showed her his hands covered in calluses from gripping the limestone rocks. "The emotion of being on the top of a cliff after an arduous climb is intoxicating."

Her perfect smile faltered, and her left eyebrow twitched. "I love that." She lacked enthusiasm and confidence. It was like talking with an automaton.

He worked his jaw.

Helen had done nothing but agree with everything he'd said. Apparently, she loved everything he did, found everything he said fascinating, and approved of his every choice. Whilst they might share the same tastes, her voice sounded disingenuous and pretentious. Or perhaps he expected too much from a future wife, and she was simply nervous and overwhelmed.

Managing a dukedom as ancient and powerful as that of his family was a burden. He wished to find a wife who wasn't only someone he admired and liked, but who could also share that encumbrance with him and help him by proposing different ideas and points of view.

He didn't mind an argument or disagreement. Sometimes, the best ideas and solutions came from disagreements. But Helen was offering him only polite smiles and hollow answers. Unlike Isabella.

The brief conversation he'd shared with her had been enjoyable and down-to-earth. Above all, she'd been herself as she was now with Patrick, and she hadn't let Grandmama intimidate her too much.

She was someone he could trust because deceit didn't come easily to her. Helen, on the other hand, kept pretending to be someone she wasn't. And last but not least, Isabella made him smile, and happiness was the most powerful feeling after love.

Isabella and Patrick walked over to them, laughing and chatting. He'd like that too. Having a wife who was also his companion, friend, and lover. Probably he had too-high expectations, but dammit if she didn't meet them. And to think he hadn't cared about finding the perfect wife.

"After the most disastrous chess game of my life, I'd like a nice cup of tea," Patrick said. "What about you?"

Helen didn't answer but angled towards Anthony, waiting for his answer. He wanted to tell her not to wait for him.

"I'll take the queen's favourite drink," he said. "A claret with whisky."

Helen hesitated. He could bet she'd meant to ask for whatever he wanted, but she didn't want a claret with whisky.

She fluttered her eyelashes. "Perhaps I shall have the same."

Isabella leant closer to her sister. "Excuse me. You drinking claret with whisky? Since when?"

"I do now and then." Helen blinked quickly.

"What about you, Isabella?" Patrick asked.

"I'll have a...coffee," she whispered the last word. "Mother detests it. We never drink it at home. She doesn't even want to hear its name. She's convinced that drinking coffee makes people rebellious like the Americans. She doesn't want anything from the Americas in our home. She had a fit when Uncle Thomas decided to move to Boston."

"Isabella." Helen arched her eyebrows in a cautionary manner.

"Potatoes are from the Americas," he said. "Your mother ate roasted potatoes tonight."

"Shush." Isabella waved him off. "Oh, please, do not tell her. She'll take them off the menu, and I love them."

"Isabella, you're talking with the duke." Helen clenched her fists.

"Let's find Rogers," Patrick said. "So you can drink your coffee even though Grandmama detests it, too."

After the drinks were served, Anthony sat between Helen and Isabella at a table far from Lady and Lord Montrose and Grandmama.

Helen scrunched up her nose as she drank the claret with whisky. She suppressed a gag and swallowed. Her eyes welled up.

No, he didn't find the situation funny in the least.

He dipped his head to meet her gaze. "If you don't like it, you should leave it."

She blinked teary eyes. "It's delicious."

Bloody hell.

Isabella, instead, drank her coffee with her eyes closed, savouring every sip. She'd added a generous dose of cream, milk, tonnes of sugar, and a few spices. He seriously doubted the drink still tasted like coffee, but he couldn't help enjoying her enthusiasm and appreciation. She gulped down the drink, emptying the cup with one final tilt of her head, and when she finished, a white puff of cream sat on the tip of her nose.

Patrick burst out laughing. Helen flushed crimson.

Anthony smiled, pointing at her nose. "You have a dollop of cream."

She laughed, wiping the cream. "Apologies. The coffee was so good."

"What coffee?" Patrick asked. "There was barely any speck of it."

"That's how I like it. Sweet but strong, rich but gentle."

"Like men?" Patrick arched his brow. "Because, you know, that description fits—"

"Patrick." Anthony gave him a pointed look, but he didn't need to worry.

Isabella didn't seem embarrassed or annoyed. "I like men who make me laugh."

Helen gave up drinking the claret and kept her gaze down, embarrassed by he had no idea what.

When Anthony said his goodnight to the ladies, he lingered in front of Isabella.

"Thank you," he said before he could think, not sure what he was thanking her for.

Her honesty, perhaps, or her contagious laughter.

He was grateful for the ray of sunlight she so easily brought into his life, but that was a concept difficult to explain in one sentence.

"You're welcome, Your Grace. What for?" Her large black eyes regarded him with curiosity and trust.

He was about to say more when Grandmama called him.

"Anthony. A word?"

"Good night, Isabella." He bowed to her, her mother, and Helen, who replied with an icy and stiff nod of the head.

He had no idea whether he'd offended Helen or if her mood change depended on something else. Isabella gave him a little wave of her hand before starting up the stairs. A wave only for him. It was a tiny, innocent gesture, but it showed their secret under-standing of each other and that she wasn't intimidated by his status. For some reason, the gesture meant so much to him, more than the entire conversation he'd shared with Helen.

"Anthony." Grandmama waited for him.

He shut the door behind him when he entered the drawing room.

"Well? What do you think about Helen?" She was as enthusi-astic as a débutante.

"Helen is very pretty."

"And?"

"Early days. I want to know her better."

"So this is it? That's all you have to say about her?" She pressed her lips in a displeased line. "Helen is such a refined young lady, unlike her sister. I'm afraid that, if you marry Helen, we'll never get rid of that wild, romping young woman. Heaven, when she laughed, Cook could have heard her from the kitchen."

"Don't be so harsh. Isabella is just as lovely as Helen. She's more spontaneous and honest than her sister."

Grandmama waved. "Tosh. Who needs spontaneity? But never mind. Patrick seems to be interested in her."

He wasn't sure how he felt about that. No, he was sure he didn't like it. "Would you approve?"

"Well, since we won't get rid of the woman if you marry her sister, then she might be a good match for Patrick." She paused, touching her chin. "On second thought, no. Unless we send them to the estate in the deep north in the Highlands. The horrible weather and desolate landscape will do wonders for their rumbustious characters."

"Grandmama, please."

"Also." Her voice lowered to a dangerous tone. "Since when do you approve of that nonsense about women's suffrage?"

"Since I researched the subject and learnt more about it. Women are organising themselves across the world. From the Americas to the Colonies, they're asking for the same rights."

"That doesn't mean we ought to listen to them."

"We can't ignore their demands, especially since they're reasonable. We can't govern anymore as we did decades ago. The world is changing, Grandmama. We must change with it."

"You're giving me a headache." She touched her temples. "Promise me you'll spend more time with Helen."

"I don't think it'll help."

"Anthony. Helen came here to know you better. Don't be rude to her. Besides, you said it's early days."

"I will talk to her again."

"Good." She put a hand on his arm. "How are you faring?"

"I'm all right."

"I hoped meeting Helen would lift your spirits."

Meeting Isabella accomplished that. "Stop worrying about me." He slipped his arm out of her touch.

"How can I?" Her voice cracked. "I lost my son to the same malady afflicting you."

"Nothing afflicts me." He opened the door. "Good night."

"Anthony."

"I have nothing else to say on the matter."

The more she insisted on talking about his mood, the more difficult it was for him to talk. Although since he'd laughed so easily with Isabella, he wondered if he was more troubled than he thought.

six

Anthony walked up the stairs towards his room, bothered by something else Grandmama had said. Patrick liked all the girls, and they liked him.

But he liked many girls at the same time, and he didn't care whether they were married, engaged, widowed, or débutantes searching for a husband. The only honourable thing about his dissolute behaviour was that he always informed his paramours of his intentions, which meant no marriage and no romantic entanglements.

At least the ladies knew what to expect.

Isabella would be disappointed if she believed Patrick had serious intentions. But Anthony might be mistaken. Perhaps Patrick meant to court her properly. He hoped not.

"Anthony," a voice whispered from a dark corner of the corridor.

"Isabella?"

"Lower your voice. Come here. Quick." She gave him orders now.

He shouldn't find that so enticing.

She waved at him from a nook in the wall, half hidden by the darkness.

"You're lost," he said.

"No, thank you. I could walk through this castle with a blindfold at night and find my bedroom without a moment of hesitation."

He laughed; it was becoming a habit when she was around. "I would love to see that. I don't know all the crannies and passages of the castle myself. What do you need?"

She became serious. "I just wanted to apologise."

"I don't remember you offending me."

She worried at her lower lip. "My behaviour isn't a reflection of my family. Do you know what I mean?"

"Absolutely not."

"Helen would never embarrass you in front of other people." Her tone changed into a low, grave one. "She's well-mannered and sensible. She would never laugh too loudly or cover her face with cream."

"You don't embarrass anyone, Isabella, much less me. Don't be ashamed of who you are."

"I'm not ashamed. But I'm not like Helen, and if it were just me, I wouldn't care, but I don't want to hurt her or my family. I don't want to be the cause of Helen's unhappiness."

He put a hand on his chest. "I promise you whatever you do, I won't be embarrassed and my opinion of Helen won't change."

Her shoulders sagged. "Thank you. I can sleep now. I was so anxious."

"If anything, I should apologise for having asked you about the ghost. I meant it as a jest, but Grandmama took the opportunity to scold you."

She lifted a shoulder. "It doesn't matter. It's Helen I'm worried about."

"Nothing has been decided yet." He wanted her to know that.

At least officially nothing had been decided yet.

"That's why I'm worried. I don't want you to reject her because you would be ashamed of having me as your sister."

On impulse, he held her hand. "I would never be ashamed of you."

Her lips parted as she looked at his hand over hers. He released her, not without noticing how soft and silky her skin was.

"You should return to your bedroom," he said in a more severe tone than he meant.

"I should. Thank you for talking to me."

He inclined his head. "Good night then."

"Good night." She didn't leave the nook but gazed around.

He took a few steps. "Good night."

She showed a forced smile. "Nighty-night." She didn't move.

"You are indeed lost."

"Botheration!" She shot her gaze skywards. "I asked Patrick where your room was. Don't worry. He didn't believe we were having an assignation. I was very subtle with my inquiry."

Somehow, he doubted that.

"Finding your room was easy, but all these corridors look the same! I don't know where to go from here. I got distracted looking at a suit of armour, and now I don't remember if my room is on the left or the right."

He folded his arms over his chest. "So you won't find your room blindfolded at night."

"I often exaggerate for a dramatic effect."

He laughed and offered her his arm. "Let me escort you."

"What if someone sees us?"

"No one will. I can move through the castle unseen when I want."

A little thrill went through him when she took his arm.

He entered one of the many libraries of the castle. This one had five floor-to-ceiling windows that let the moonlight in. The view of the gentle hills covered in silver light gave him peace as Isabella did.

"Beautiful." She gazed around.

"Father was a collector of rare books. And he loved libraries."

"Who doesn't?"

"But don't be too impressed. Half of these books are treatises on economy and politics."

"Not surprising. You must spend a lot of time in the House of Lords."

He sighed. "I do. The House of Lords is not different from a battlefield. And we're on the brink of causing a riot. New factories are sprouting throughout the country, and we don't have the laws to regulate their extremely fast growth. Employees are working endless hours for small wages, exploited by the owners, and some managers dare to hire children..." He glanced at her. "Apologies. That must bore you."

"Not at all. And I agree about the riots. Unless the government intervenes, angry mobs will flood our streets. Starving people don't have anything to lose. We should protect our workers, give them higher wages, and above all, send children to school."

"Thank you for your assessment." He meant it.

"Being informed of what's happening in our country is a right and a duty."

"I agree."

"Do you really support women's right of suffrage?"

"Absolutely. Although I'm worried about whom Grandmama would choose to vote for if she could."

She burst out laughing before clamping a hand over her mouth. "Sorry. That was awful of me."

He laughed too. "No, it wasn't."

He opened a narrow door at the end of the room. The passage was so tight their shoulders and arms touched.

"I love these hidden corridors and passages." She leant on him, seemingly uncaring about their closeness.

"It would take a week to explore them all." He opened another door to enter a lateral hallway. "Patrick and I spent the summers exploring the castle. We drew a map with all its secrets."

"I need it, so I won't—" She skidded to a stop in front of a flight of stairs leading up. "Look at that. Isn't that perfect?"

"The stairs? I believe there are plenty."

"Yes, but these are special. The bannister is large, flat, and straight." She released his arm and shifted her weight from one foot to the other. "I really have to do it."

"What?" He knit his eyebrows. "You have the same expression as this morning before screaming bloody murder, and I'm worried."

"You meant it when you said you wouldn't be embarrassed by me, didn't you?"

He was lost. "Yes, I did."

"Then allow me to do this. Please."

"By all means. But what is *this*? Another scream? Please no. My eardrums have barely recovered."

"No, no, no. No screaming. I'll be quiet."

"I'm curious. A little worried but curious."

She darted up the stairs. Her skirt fluttered up, exposing her slender ankles and calves, and he shouldn't look, but he did.

She stopped at the top of the stairs and faced him.

"Isabella?"

There was a swish of fabric. Then she mounted the bannister backwards and rushed down. A whoop of delight echoed off the walls as she flew down like a bullet. She was going to hurt herself if she didn't slow down. The bloody floor was hard stone. No carpet. She might break a bone.

"Isabella—" He barely had time to shoot forwards before grabbing her.

Grabbing was the wrong term. She smashed her rear against his chest, and caught by the momentum, he fell over backwards with her in his arms. As her chignon came undone, her hair ended up in his mouth while her skirt and petticoats twisted themselves around him like the tentacles of an octopus.

"What the hell!" He tried to free himself from the entanglement of her hair and gown.

She trembled in his arms.

"Are you hurt?" he asked.

"No, no." She laughed. "It was fantastic."

She shifted and writhed to stand up. Her elbows sank into his stomach, and her knee hit his groin.

"Ouch!" He groaned.

"Sorry. The floor is slippery." She scrambled up to her feet, towering over him still on the floor on his back.

Her hair was flowing down past her waist, and with her gown in disarray, she looked like a warrior goddess.

"I'm so sorry." She helped him up, grabbing his arm.

He winced.

"Where did I hit you?" She brushed his jacket.

"Let's put it this way." He ignored his throbbing crotch. "I'm not sure I'll ever be able to produce an heir."

"I think you have a flair for the dramatic, too."

"I'm astonished that you're making fun of my pain." He feigned being offended.

"I truly am sorry, Your Grace. But the straight flight of stairs was too much of a temptation."

"At least one of us had fun." He took deep breaths, his groin on fire. "I'm curious. What would you have done if I'd died?"

She burst out laughing his favourite laugh. "Hide your body under one of the tapestries and just leave you there. I reckon no one would have found you for a long time. And the castle is haunted, apparently."

"Lady Isabella, you're wicked."

She curtsied. "Thank you." She took his arm again. "Are you sore?"

"I'll live." Physically, yes. But emotionally...he hadn't experienced anything so powerful and deep in a long time. And it was great.

Isabella shook his senses awake. He finally felt something that wasn't apathy, pain, or disappointment. Her arm on his was a sweet weight he easily became used to.

"Has your opinion of me changed?" she asked.

"Of course it has." He rubbed his sore shoulder because he'd hit the floor with it as well. "It's the first time a lady has barrelled into me, wrestled me to the floor, and threatened to end my lineage."

She laughed again but muffled the sound by hiding her face in his chest. The riot of emotions bursting through him was like a fresh summer rain after weeks of stifling heat.

Only more devastating.

Another lady would have cowered in front of him. But then again, another lady wouldn't have rushed down the bannister of a flight of stairs at night and hit him.

"I can't apologise enough. I miscalculated my speed and the steepness of the stairs."

"Thank you," he said.

She gazed up at him in surprise. "For having hurt you?"

"For the laughter. It's something more precious than people think."

"You must lead a hard, serious life if you don't laugh often."

"I can't complain. I have everything I need."

"Obviously, you don't if you're unhappy."

"Good point."

"May I ask you something personal?"

"After you tried to kill me? Of course."

"Your cheeks are a bit hollow. You don't seem to enjoy yourself at all, and you don't laugh often." She tilted her head, and a dark curl, a survivor of the chignon disaster, gave up and tumbled down her shoulder. "Is it because of the military academy? I heard you went to war."

"I did, but I didn't."

"Is it a riddle?"

"I was deployed, sailed on a ship, and arrived on the battlefield, but I never engaged in combat. My fellow soldiers and I were deployed to multiple locations without discharging a firearm. For one reason or another—incorrect intelligence, tardiness, or just chance—we never met the enemy. The fear and anxiety of being about to die had been there, but then nothing happened. I returned home without having been in battle."

"But something troubles you."

"It does." He clenched his teeth. "We saw plenty of battlefields after the battle was over. I'll spare you the details, but the carnage remained impressed in my memories. And then my parents died. My Father never had the chance to be the duke. My grandfather died after him, and then I inherited the title. I feel guilty as if I robbed my father of his rights. And I wasn't ready to be the duke. I'm not ready now. I don't want to be the duke."

"I understand now. Only laughter will keep the darkness away." She touched his hand briefly, and once again, her compassion and spontaneity surprised him.

A knot of emotion lodged in his throat. "You give me hope."

If it was something inappropriate to say because he'd known her for too short a time to say it, he didn't give a damn.

"I wish you didn't feel so alone because you aren't. Your brother and grandmother care about you and need you." She touched his hand again.

He didn't know what to say, but she didn't prompt him for an answer, which he appreciated because the turmoil within him didn't make sense.

They resumed walking down the corridor lit only by the moonlight, but with her at his side, it was like walking in the sunshine. No one had ever subverted his mood so quickly and deeply as Isabella. She was like a storm that had come without warning, only to sweep him off his feet and shake the very core of his being. She made his physician look like an amateur.

He slowed down once at the end of the corridor. "That door over there opens to your room."

She put a hand on the narrow door. "Are you sure? My door is a lot wider."

He pushed the door open. "This is a secondary door concealed under the wallpaper."

She entered her bedroom and examined the door. "Crikey."

He was careful to remain out of her bedroom. He had already gone too far with her. Not that he regretted the time they'd spent together, but he didn't want to worry her.

"Well, good night, Anthony." She was about to shut the door.

"Wait. May I ask you something?" Again, he'd acted on impulse.

"Of course."

He hesitated, worried she might say no. "Would you come with me to Maiden Hill?"

She squeezed his hand. "Of course."

"I'll see you tomorrow morning then, on the top of the hill."

She nodded. "I had a lovely time, and thank you for your kindness, Anthony."

No, he should thank her.

She had no idea what a great present she'd given him.

seven

Isabella shut the concealed door and leant against it after Anthony had left.

What had happened? She wasn't sure. Well, she'd hit and attacked a duke, disregarded etiquette, and asked him personal questions. Questions he'd answered, though. The truth was she hadn't expected him to be so vulnerable and in need of a laugh underneath his stony composure. She felt sorry for him, and wasn't that absurd?

He was a blasted duke, one of the most powerful men in the kingdom. He had everything he wanted. Choosing a wife was a chore for him because noblewomen from half the world wanted to marry him.

Yet he carried a sadness so heavy she'd sensed it on her shoulders like a heavy cloak. She couldn't have refused when he'd asked her to visit Maiden Hill, but the visit posed a huge problem. Another secret meeting with the duke.

The sharp knock on the main door jolted her. "Isabella. Are you back?"

That was Helen.

She opened the door. "Yes?"

Helen and Mother slid inside, casting curious glances at her.

"What happened to your hair?" Mother asked at the same time as Helen asked, "Why did you stay behind?"

She braided her hair quickly. "I just needed a walk before going to bed, so I went to the library. Are you angry with me? Did I do something wrong?"

What if Anthony had told Mother about the stairs? No, he wouldn't say anything. She trusted him.

Mother exhaled. "You could avoid laughing loudly or making comments on the duke's income. Or giggling—"

Another knock interrupted her.

"What a busy night." She opened the door and smiled at her father.

"I knew it." He hugged her and kissed her cheek as if he hadn't seen her in a long time. "Your mother and your sister are here to scold you, aren't they?"

"Why wouldn't I?" Mother put her hands on her hips. "And I want to scold you as well. I specifically asked you both not to talk about politics."

"It was my fault," she said. "Father has nothing to do with that."

Father huffed. "The Dowager asked you a question. You couldn't refuse to answer."

"You don't realise how important this arrangement with the duke is." Mother paced.

"The duke agreed with Isabella and me," Father said. "I don't believe we caused any damage."

"Father is right. Don't be so harsh, Mother." Helen sat on the bed. "And I didn't come here to scold Isabella. The Dowager trapped her in a complicated conversation. I want to know about you and Lord Patrick."

At hearing Patrick's name, her parents faced her.

She fixed her chignon again. "He's charming and funny. I enjoy spending time with him."

"Is he bothered by your wild manners?" Mother asked.

"Olivia." Father exhaled.

"Patrick didn't say anything about my manners. He told me he enjoyed my company, too."

"Wouldn't it be wonderful if Isabella married Patrick?" Helen's joy sounded genuine. "I would feel less alone."

Isabella didn't have time to inquire about what Helen meant by that.

Mother didn't share her enthusiasm. "We'll see. Isabella won't become a member of the Beaufort family unless her behaviour is impeccable."

She wanted to say the duke didn't care about that, but that would lead to another argument and questions she couldn't answer. "How did it go with the duke?"

Helen lost some of her radiance. "I don't know. I did my best to please him and show him we could get along well, but he seemed annoyed by my answers for some reason. I'm not sure. I don't understand him."

"Did you behave as I'd told you?" Mother asked.

"I did. I followed your instructions to the letter." An annoyed note crept in Helen's tone. "As always."

"Perhaps stop being so agreeable and tell him what you think about everything," Father said. "He seems to appreciate honesty."

"Pish." Mother shook her head. "Don't do that, Helen. A man like the duke doesn't want to hear his wife's opinion. He desires a proper lady with refined manners, able to provide him with a strong heir. That's it, and thank goodness for that."

"That sounds atrocious," Isabella said. "Helen won't be anything more than cattle."

"Quite the opposite. It means freedom to her. The moment she gives the duke an heir and a spare, she'll be free to do as she pleases. He'll live his boring life of meetings at Parliament, and she'll flourish. The more you meddle with your husband's affairs, the more difficult the marriage will be. You'll end up arguing with him all the time."

Helen nodded, seemingly tired, but Isabella wasn't sure she agreed.

"That's not true," Father said. "I'm always more than happy to hear your opinion."

"And every time I give you my opinion on something, we end up arguing as we're doing now."

Isabella had no experience with men. She'd never had a suitor, never truly thought about a husband—not even during her Season—and never thought about her married life. But the duke didn't give her the impression of being a man who wanted a cold, detached wife who lived a separate life from his. She might be wrong though.

"Isabella." Mother took her hands. "Please think about the opportunity you and your sister have. Don't do anything reckless. Be good."

Her throat tightened. Was she such a terrible daughter? Was she really an embarrassment to her family? She was lucky Mother didn't know what happened with the duke.

"If we play our cards well," Mother said, "you two could both be married into the Beaufort family. There's nothing I want more than to see my two beautiful daughters settled, and being part of this family is such an honour. Isn't it, Benjamin?"

Father rubbed his forehead. "I only want you two to be happy. But your mother is right. The Beauforts are a powerful family, and I respect the duke. He's an honourable man. But if you think you'll be miserable next to him, I want you to tell me, and I don't want you to feel forced to marry him."

Helen nodded. "Thank you, Father." She hugged him with a desperation Isabella found exaggerated.

"Isabella?" Mother asked. "Do we understand each other?"

"I'll do my best, Mother. I promise."

AFTER AN ALMOST SLEEPLESS NIGHT, Isabella had woken up early and left the castle to meet Anthony before Lawson could come with her or send a maid in her place.

Thank goodness finding the main front door was easy. It'd taken her only a few minutes to reach the path to the hill.

The urgency in Mother's words had overwhelmed her with doubts. She wanted to be herself and laugh as much as she pleased, but she didn't want to ruin her sister's future.

If the duke didn't marry Helen because of her behaviour, she would never forgive herself. And maybe Mother was right about Patrick. He was handsome and funny. Perhaps it was time for her to think about getting married, too.

Her breath turned into mist as she trekked uphill at a fast pace.

Wheezing, she paused at the top of the hill under the shadow of an oak tree. The air was thick with the scent of wet soil and bluebells. From that point, she had an unobstructed view of the castle. It was huge, ancient, and with centuries of history like the Beauforts. Too much. Too overwhelming.

The prospect of being bound to such a powerful family started a choking sensation in her throat. Not even Father had dismissed the importance of Helen marrying the duke.

"Isabella!"

Doubts gnawed at her as Anthony arrived from the path. He wore the same plain clothes as the first time they'd met, but it seemed that a year had passed since that moment.

She shouldn't have another secret meeting with him and maybe ruin her sister's chances by saying or doing something silly. Something that was...herself.

He removed his flat hat and bowed. His auburn curls tumbled over his sharp cheeks and strong jaw. "Good morning. How are you today?"

"I'm afraid I can't do this. I'm sorry."

"What's the matter? You can't do what?"

"You."

"Me?"

"I can't spend time with you. I'm sorry." She went to move, but he took her hand gently.

"Did I do something that offended you? I'll make amends."

Her heart cracked a little. "No, you didn't do anything. It's me. I don't want to be the cause of my sister's unhappiness."

"I don't understand." He didn't release her hand. "We already discussed that. I told you I don't care about your behaviour."

"It's not just my behaviour. I'm not what you might call an accomplished lady. I don't speak foreign languages as fluently as Helen does. I don't have gracious conversation skills. My only ambition is to attend to the flowers in my conservatory. What kind of ambition is that?" She had to take a deep breath not to sob.

Anthony listened to her patiently. His eyebrows plunged in a deep V. "It's your ambition. It's who you are."

"Your family is so powerful and ancient that being part of it, even through Helen's marriage to you, is a huge responsibility, and I don't want to embarrass my family."

Anthony's gaze became so intense she stopped blabbering. There was no hiding from his emerald eyes.

He cupped her cheek with a light hand. "You aren't going to embarrass your family. I find your honesty and happiness refreshing. I wouldn't want you to change for any reason, and you shouldn't be intimidated by my family."

"The Dowager doesn't like me. She doesn't want me to have anything to do with your family." She leant into his touch.

"You're being too dramatic, and Grandmama doesn't decide my future. Stop worrying. Please."

"What about Helen? I don't want her to be penalised because of me."

He withdrew his hand, and she missed the comfort it provided. "Helen won't be penalised. I promise."

"She's so clever, you know. She studies and memorises even subjects she doesn't like. She hates the piano, but she plays it divinely. I received the same education, but with not-so-brilliant results. Not that I cared until now."

"Enough." He gave her a stern look. "As I said, Helen and your family won't be humiliated, ridiculed, or punished in any way. And I don't think you're an embarrassment. I wouldn't be here with you right now if I thought ill of you. Grandmama enjoys giving orders, but this is my life, and I decide whom I want to marry. So stop this fuss. You're worrying about nothing."

She stooped her shoulders, tension leaving her body. "Thank you."

"Do you want to get back to the castle?" He offered her his arm.

She'd made a promise, and he'd been very kind to her. "No, I want to see Maiden Hill with you."

"It's not far."

He held her hand as they went down the path, and she quite liked the gesture.

Maiden Hill came into view after a curve. The imposing three-storey manor must have had shining limestone walls in the past. Now English ivy and weeds crawled over them like a disease sprouted from the ground. A diamond window on the ground floor was broken, and moss covered the roof.

Anthony gripped her hand more tightly as they stopped in the drive where weeds competed for space.

"No one lives here." She craned her neck to see past the over-grown trees, but the upper floor was hidden by the vegetation.

"Von Gruner doesn't care about this place."

"Why did he buy it then?"

"Out of spite. He had a dispute with my father years ago. Von Gruner wished to marry my mother, but she chose my father." He led her to the front door. "Grandmama also insulted him, and he's a proud man. So he let Maiden Hill rot. In just a few years of neglect, the house has started to crumble."

The front door screeched on its hinges like a cry for help when he pushed it open. A flutter of wings welcomed them when they stepped inside. From a hole in the roof, dry leaves and dirt poured into the majestic entry hall. Birds nested in the nooks on the walls.

"Von Gruner ordered the demolition of the house, but he changed his mind after the work had started. And that's the result." Anthony's body tensed, and his eyes glowed with turmoil.

A shiver crawled down her neck as eerie noises echoed in the hall.

"My bedroom is upstairs." His voice cracked, and pain slipped through. "We were happy here. We were a proper family. What is the point of being powerful if I can't save the house my parents loved the most? My father proposed to my mother here. He died here. I was born here and spent the most wonderful years with my parents. My father believed parents should spend as much time as possible with their children. We had a nanny and a governess, but he cared a lot about feeding us when we were children and sharing our meals. Mother loved singing. Her sweet voice echoed through the house." He took a deep breath. "I've talked too much."

"I'm so sorry." She closed her hands around his. "It's cruel to deprive you of this place and treat it like that."

He shuddered. "What hurts the most is that I failed my parents."

"No. You didn't sell Maiden Hill."

"But I can't get it back. Von Gruner doesn't even want to talk to me."

"Can I help?"

He averted his gaze from the sweeping stairs to focus on her. A slow smile transformed his face from desperate to peaceful. "Thank you."

"I'm pretty useless, as you know—"

"No, I don't."

"But if you need help, I'm here."

"You've already helped me a lot just by being here."

They remained in silence for a few moments, listening to the birds' song. Not as eerie as she'd thought.

She nudged him with her elbow. "Do you know what I'm thinking?"

"Something about climbing over the roof to jump through the hole?"

She laughed, and he focused on her as if he were hearing the most enchanting sound. "I'd love to see this house restored to its former beauty. Imagine rushing down those sweeping stairs."

He burst out laughing, scaring a group of collared doves. "Please never change, Isabella."

"You're the first one to ever tell me that. Aside from my papa."

He offered her his arm. "We should return to the castle."

"Yes, and I promise I won't do anything silly."

"That's a shame. I enjoy your silly things."

"I almost killed you last night. When I thought about that this morning, I felt so ashamed of myself." And Mother's speech had made her think.

"You can be yourself with me. As for my grandmama, I'd suggest you avoid knocking her off her feet."

"Heavens. She would ask the queen to expel me from the country."

He laughed again.

As they walked the same path as the previous day, her muscles loosened, releasing the tension that had tormented her for the whole night.

"So you want to be a gardener." He sounded genuinely curious.

"I love growing plants. When I'm home, I spend most of the time in the conservatory. My dream is to have a glasshouse where there are always blossoming flowers of every colour, and plants from distant places. It would be like holding the whole world under the same roof. Imagine, plants from the cold Scandinavia to the warm Amazon, all in one place. It's silly, I know."

He frowned, holding the gate to the castle for her. "You should stop referring to yourself as silly."

"Well, if anything, it's good that Helen is your possible choice of a wife. She'll fill the role of the duchess perfectly." She must have said something he didn't like because his frown deepened. Perhaps she shouldn't talk about his choices since nothing had been decided yet.

Once inside the castle, they took a route new to her that ran along a set of arched windows.

"This way is more spectacular." She stopped to admire the view of the forest.

"It's less safe than the one we took yesterday. Sometimes servants use this passage to go to the tower—"

"The tower!" She faced him.

His harsh lines softened. "Right here. Come."

Large stone steps formed a steep spiral staircase. As they went up, the sound of their footfalls filled the silence.

She gasped when they arrived at the top.

A round room was lined with large windows from which the whole of England was visible. Gentle hills rose in the distance through a veil of fog. A river shone like a silver ribbon across a green expanse, and the forest looked like a dormant giant.

"Beautiful." She leant over a window. The trees below seemed like toys.

"Careful." He pulled her back gently by taking her waist. "These stones are ancient. You never know."

The contact started a flutter in her belly, and he stared at her with the usual awe that made her feel special.

"Thank you for this gift," she said.

He lowered his gaze as if worried she might see the emotions in his eyes. How she wished he would let her see them. She wanted to see him lose his stony composure and fully enjoy himself for once, without the burden of his sadness returning to weigh down on him.

"We should go back." Something had changed in him because his tone had nothing of the warmth from before. His constant sadness punished him every time he was happy.

Or perhaps she'd been too loud or too annoying. "Of course."

They walked the rest of the way in silence. Their hands brushed against each other a few times, and she could swear he tried to lace his fingers through hers.

He stopped in the same spot as the other day. "Thank you for your company. It means a lot."

He sounded so formal she didn't know how to respond.

"Thank you for your understanding."

They stared at each other in the dimly lit room that had to be centuries old and must have seen generations of dukes and duchesses exercising their power. But at that moment, as she stared into his sad green eyes, she saw only a man who carried a heavy burden. A burden she wasn't sure he would let her share with him.

eight

After the walk with Isabella, Anthony found it difficult to focus on reading his correspondence.

Isabella's sense of unworthiness troubled him, but her happiness and desire to live hurt him as well, like when a wound was cauterised.

Before talking to her, he'd had no idea she perceived his family as so overwhelming and intimidating. If he were to propose to her instead of Helen, she would be crushed. Unless he reassured her he would support her.

His family needed a duchess like her, a woman who stood next to him, proud and strong. Hell, he needed a woman like her, as selfish as it sounded. She made him want to be alive and laugh again. She saw things he didn't. Her light would balance his darkness.

His last entries in his diary were all about Isabella and the joy she brought to his life. He felt like a thief, stealing her merriment and laughter.

He wasn't sure what to do about his supposed betrothal to Helen, and reading the report from his steward didn't improve his mood.

The steward had quietly inspected Maiden Hill, and the result had been abysmal although not surprising. The roof was unstable. A side of the house had collapsed as the result of having meddled with the underground tunnel. Maiden Hill would need months of work to be rebuilt. The grounds would require an army of workers to be cleared.

The more Maiden Hill rotted, the more guilty he felt. His parents were buried in the family's crypt in London, but their souls rested in that manor.

Von Gruner didn't care about Maiden Hill and what it meant to the Beauforts. Or rather, he knew exactly what it meant and tortured them on purpose.

He folded the report and pushed his anger down.

"*Bonjour.*" Patrick entered the study, chomping on an apple. "Want some?" He offered him the apple. "It comes from our orchard. It's so delicious you'll write about it in that gloomy diary of yours."

He leant back in his chair, not at all amused.

Patrick had the decency to stop smiling. "Apologies. I didn't mean to make fun of your condition."

Condition. The word made everything sound more serious.

"Never mind. Sit."

Patrick pulled a face. "Oh no. What is it now? Can't you ask your secretary? He's more prepared than I am on whatever you're about to ask me to do."

"I know he is. I want to talk about Isabella."

"All right." Smirking, Patrick eased back on the chair. "Do you want to have a tumble with her before marrying her sister? I approve and understand. That's interesting."

"That's shameful. Stop thinking with your bollocks for a moment."

"Sure." He lobbed the apple core into the hearth. "Tell me everything. Did she cause trouble? I hope she did. She's one wild lady. I'm sure she's just as wild in the bedsheets."

"Dammit!" He thumped the desk, causing the ink bottle to rattle. "Stop talking about her in these terms, or I swear I'll cut all your expenses and you'll have to work."

Patrick held up his hands. "Fair enough. I had no idea you cared about her so much. What about Isabella?"

"Do you have any intentions of courting her?"

The smirk disappeared from Patrick's face. "Courting her? I like her, but why are we talking about marriage after I play one chess game with her?"

"I just want to make sure you don't hurt her in any way."

"I won't. I promise. She's going to be part of this family, and I'm not stupid enough to bother her."

"So you aren't interested in her."

Patrick shook his head. "No, I'm not."

"Good."

"May I go now?" Patrick half-stood up.

"I haven't finished yet."

Patrick huffed, sitting down again. "Yes."

"From now on, I want you to work close to my secretary when I'm busy."

"Anthony!"

"Brooks can work unsupervised, but you can't. You'll follow his work closely and learn what he does."

"Why?"

"Because you're part of this family and you'll share the responsibilities."

"I'm the spare."

"What if something happens to me?"

"I am an optimistic chap."

"Patrick!" He raised his voice.

Patrick rested his forehead on his head in a dramatic pose. "I'll die out of boredom working next to Brooks. I need entertainment or I'll go mad."

"It's incredible how you set very low personal goals and then fail to achieve them consistently."

Patrick rolled his eyes. "I'm not made for a life of duty. I wouldn't have been born as the spare otherwise."

"Thank you for your enthusiastic cooperation. I'm impressed."

"Joke if you want. May I go now?"

He gave him a sharp nod.

As Patrick left, scoffing, Anthony couldn't stop a smile of relief. He was free to pursue Isabella.

NOT A DROP of ink had been spared for Helen in Anthony's personal diary, which made him feel guilty.

As he promenaded next to her along the path in the garden, he cast glances at her. She was composed, serious, and elegant while Isabella was loud and vivacious. She was talking with Patrick about the latest types of dances, waving her arms about and improvising the music and steps. She and Patrick had nothing in common.

Patrick was a rake who enjoyed spending his days playing cricket, ravishing ladies, and cheating at cards. She was an innocent, vibrant young woman who just wanted to be free. Yet they talked and talked as if they'd known each other for years.

"Your sister seems to enjoy herself," he said just to break the silence.

"I apologise for her behaviour."

He stiffened. That was the wrong thing to say. "I don't understand why you feel the need to apologise on her behalf."

"She's boisterous and loud. I understand you're used to more sombre people."

"I'm used to honesty."

"Oh, she lies sometimes, too."

He exhaled through his teeth. The situation had to be his fault. Everything he said came out twisted. "You can express your opinion about anything you want when you're with me. I would prefer it."

Her smile didn't reach her eyes.

"You don't have to agree with me all the time." There. He had to be blunt.

Another smile.

"What do you like to do in your spare time?"

Her eyebrow twitched. "I like playing the piano. Would you like me to play the piano for you?"

So Helen lied sometimes, too.

"Later, perhaps."

"Of course."

Isabella hooked her arm through Patrick's, and they improvised a gallop in the middle of the path. She smiled so brightly her whole face transformed. Patrick laughed, too. Grandmama, sitting on a bench with Lady Montrose, frowned. All normal.

"That's what I mean, Anthony," Helen whispered. "Mother asked Isabella to behave, but she didn't listen."

"They aren't doing anything inappropriate, and Patrick is as boisterous as Isabella."

Her cheeks reddened. "Naturally. You're right. There's nothing wrong. I actually admire her spontaneity."

Bloody hell. Did Helen have an opinion that was her own? Although the last statement seemed her first genuine one.

There was a quick exchange of glances between Isabella and her mother, and the moment after, Isabella stopped dancing. Her merriment vanished, and her cheeks paled as she talked in hushed tones with Patrick.

Anger flared up in his chest. Anything she did was criticised and doused by her family. She already doubted herself without the added worry of being perfect all the time.

The more he thought about her, the more he believed she would be his perfect duchess. And the more he thought of her as his duchess, the more a fluttery feeling in his chest started. He liked her. He liked himself when he was with her. Her light and happiness were becoming an addiction for him.

The only question was if he had the right to take her into a family where her light and fire would be challenged further.

THE CRUSHING feeling on Anthony's chest was utterly unjustified as he bade farewell to Isabella the next day. The speed with which her infectious personality had affected him was ridiculous, but he was going to see her soon.

Her family's luggage was gathered in the courtyard, taken care of by the footmen. Lord and Lady Montrose were talking with Grandmama. Helen was exchanging a few polite words with Patrick, which left Isabella only for him.

"Thank you for your company," he said, fighting the urge to take her hand.

"I'm sorry to have attacked you," she whispered. "And thank you for not mentioning the incident to anyone."

"I would never, but I doubt anyone would believe me."

Once the carriages were ready, he helped her get in. He wished he could pull her close and ask her to stay with him. When she sat down, he reluctantly left her hand.

"Have a pleasant journey back."

The others talked and bade farewell, but he kept his attention on Isabella's bright face. The moment the footman shut the carriage door, darkness claimed his thoughts. Now that he'd experienced her joy, he was afraid of returning to his solitude.

"Why are you so forlorn?" Grandmama asked. "You're going to see her soon."

By '*her*' she meant Helen, but he didn't correct her assumption. He didn't want to tell her Helen was never going to be his wife.

He wanted to keep his secret for a little longer and cherish Isabella's presence in his heart.

nine

Isabella left Dockerly Castle with a riot of emotions in her chest, and she had no idea how to deal with them. Patrick was charming, witty, and had the wildest ideas. Anthony was kind, kinder than she'd expected a duke to be. But being close to the Beauforts, and especially the Dowager, made her feel more inadequate than she ever did. She'd never cared about being adequate until she'd met the Beauforts.

No, that wasn't true. Anthony and Patrick didn't make her feel inadequate. Quite the opposite. The two brothers were very different, but both appreciated her for who she was. Patrick had her same recklessness, and she couldn't deny she enjoyed his sense of humour and outrageous behaviour. Anthony was sweet and funny but sad. He carried an aura of sadness that worried her. Was every duke as burdened as he was?

The gentle rocking of the carriage didn't cover the endless chatter of Mother and Helen. Father looked out of the window, his expression tense.

"The Dowager is on our side," Mother said. "She assured me the marriage would happen. She likes you, which means you're going to be a duchess, darling. She's the one who makes all the decisions."

Isabella shook her head. "I don't think so."

Mother pressed her lips. "Oh, what do you know about it?"

Officially, nothing. Her encounters with the duke had never happened.

Helen nodded. "It's a dream. I'm looking forward to becoming a duchess. I hope I can get married as soon as possible. I'll be free..." As if realising she'd said too much, she cleared her throat. "The Dowager is right. Duchesses have power."

"But do you like the duke?" she asked. "If you marry him, you're going to spend the rest of your life with him. Castle or not, your life might be miserable if you don't enjoy his company at least a little."

"Listen to your sister," Father said.

"Don't listen to your sister." Mother waved dismissively. "Of course, Helen likes the duke."

"Do you?" Isabella nudged her sister with an elbow.

Helen shrugged. "I don't know him well. Certainly, I don't share his tastes in hobbies and drinks, and he often asks my opinion on matters I know nothing about. He was quite insistent."

"Opinions like what?" she said.

"Like fair wages, child labour, and other matters. I didn't want to say something that offended or bothered him."

"Why not? How can you have an honest conversation with your future husband if you don't take the risk of offending him with *your* opinions?"

"I don't know anything about fair wages." Helen lifted a shoulder.

"I often discuss these topics at home, darling," Father said. "Surely, you remember a thing or two I said."

"Please, Benjamin." Mother exhaled. "Your talking about politics isn't charming. And Helen's situation is not that simple. The duke won't ask for his wife's opinion on matters regarding politics or the social situation. Why would he? Whatever Helen thinks of those affairs, he won't care anyway. I believe his questions were a test to understand if Helen was one of those women who meddled in her husband's affairs. I'm sure she passed the test with flying colours."

Well, Isabella hadn't spent a great deal of time with Anthony, but he hadn't struck her as someone who wouldn't care about his wife's opinion, and if she were his wife, she'd give him her opinion anyway.

"No one listens to me," Father muttered under his breath, folding his arms over his chest.

"The duke is quite gloomy, though," Helen said. "He's a sad man."

"He's a duke. What do you expect?" Mother said.

Isabella was tempted to tell everything she knew about Anthony just to make them understand how vulnerable he was and to make them stop talking about him like that. But she wouldn't betray his trust. "Patrick is more cheerful."

Mother glowed. "I'm so happy for you. Patrick is a handsome gentleman."

"He is, but we haven't talked about anything serious."

"No matter. We're going to see the duke and his brother soon. The Dowager is going to organise a ball in two weeks," Mother said, excited again. "She assured me Anthony will make his decision then."

"Heavens." Helen brought a hand to her mouth. "I can't wait. We should start ordering a proper wedding gown from the modiste."

"Absolutely, darling."

Father rubbed his forehead, seemingly tired.

Isabella leant against the wall, not wanting to ruin Helen's moment of happiness. It was too soon to order a gown, in her opinion. Anthony hadn't seemed eager to make a decision. But then again, what did she know about dukes?

It took Isabella two days, between the carriage and the train, to arrive home, and the more she heard talking about wedding preparations, the more she wanted to scream.

In the two days of the journey, Mother and Helen had planned the engagement party, the wedding reception, the honeymoon, and the birthday party of Helen and Anthony's first-born. Had it been another day of travelling, they would have even planned the heir's graduation ceremony.

As she entered her house and removed her hat, she wondered why she was so bitter. Helen was happy. Mother was happy. Father was sort of happy. Isabella should share their happiness. Instead, her mood was as gloomy as London's sky.

"My lady." The maid took her coat. "While you were away, the parcel from Guatemala arrived and—"

"The orchids!" She didn't wait for the maid to finish and raced down the corridor to the conservatory.

The fatigue of the last days was gone by the time she barged into the glasshouse.

"Where are they?" She gazed around.

The gardener should have planted them. She beamed when she found the series of pots with the small plants in them.

"Are they—"

Her heart took a dip to her stomach. The seedlings were wilted. A couple were etiolated—yellow and drawn out—but the others didn't fare better. She touched the tender leaves with a fingertip. It was so easy to kill the seedlings. They were full of energy and life, but if they lacked sunlight or received too much water, they became limp and withered.

Instead, all they needed was space to grow and a gentle hand.

Two things that seemed difficult to come by.

ten

The cold, judgemental stare of Grandmama never failed to make Anthony feel guilty even when he had no reason to.

The preparations for tonight's ball had gone smoothly. The guests had been invited ahead of time, and the ballroom was decorated in an elegant but not too excessive fashion as Grandmama wanted. Still, she always found something to complain about.

The chandeliers were too low. The music was too loud. The champagne was too warm.

He suspected the fact Helen and Isabella were present had something to do with Grandmama's ill humour. He was nervous, too. He was supposed to make a choice tonight and decide whom he wanted to court. Grandmama had invited other possible candidates although Helen was her absolute favourite.

Pity she wasn't Anthony's.

Grandmama surveyed the ballroom, slowly fanning herself.

"What is it, Grandmama?" he asked, watching the dancing couples.

"Fashion." She tilted her chin up, half-hiding her face behind the fan. "This new type of skirt hem is a complete disaster. I wonder who thought reducing the length of the skirt was a good idea."

"I don't understand why it's a disaster."

"The skirt goes up when the ladies jump or twirl too quickly. Goodness, all those ankles! It's outrageous."

He lowered his gaze. Yes, the ladies' ankles were exposed during the gallop but only for a second or two.

Grandmama huffed. "I can't look."

"I can."

"Now, now, Anthony." She pointed her fan towards the orchestra. "I'm going to send Rogers to the maestro and ask not to play gallops, polkas, and mazurkas. And no waltz either."

"That leaves only the minuet."

She narrowed her eyes, looking exactly like his late father. "I want everyone to believe this is a respectable house and that you're a respectable duke."

"I don't think anyone has doubts."

"Speaking of doubts." She cast a scorching glare at a gentleman who was laughing too loudly. Once the fellow realised she was watching him, he almost choked on air in his hurry to stop laughing. She returned her attention to Anthony. "I was saying, this story has been going on for too long."

"What story?"

She touched his arm with her fan. "I want you to make a decision about Helen and talk to her father tonight."

Oh, he'd made a decision. Those two weeks without Isabella's laughter had been awful. If she agreed to marry him, he would do everything to make her happy.

"Perhaps I would give the announcement of your engagement after supper," she said. "Helen looks lovely tonight, doesn't she?"

She did, but he couldn't take his eyes off Isabella in her delicate pink gown and extraordinary smile. Isabella was the one he wanted to marry. End of story. Her laughter was intoxicating. She'd carved her way to his heart, and he didn't mind.

She took a stroll around the room with Patrick, and he reminded himself that Patrick had told him he wasn't interested in pursuing Isabella.

"Well," Grandmama said. "I need to talk to Rogers. The maestro better do as I say." She headed to the butler on the other side of the room.

Anthony's heart gave a kick when Isabella walked over to him alone. She made him feel like a normal man and not only a duke, but above all, happy as his spiking pulse reminded him.

"Isabella, you look lovely tonight."

She bowed her head. "Your Grace. This ballroom is huge. How many guests did you invite?"

"It'll be quicker to tell you whom I didn't. Grandmama wanted a memorable event."

"She succeeded." Her cheeks were flushed from the dance, exalting her large black eyes. He'd never seen eyes that dark, shiny and glossy.

"What's your favourite dance?" Anthony asked.

"The waltz." She fanned herself. "I'm looking forward to dancing. The orchestra hasn't played it yet. I guess the maestro is reserving it as the supper dance."

Damn. "Of course. I would consider myself honoured if you would agree to dance the waltz with me."

Her smile became a little strained. "I believe Helen would like to dance the waltz with you. She's over there, talking with a friend. I'll fetch her for you."

"I wish to dance with you."

Something flickered in her gaze. "In that case, I accept. A lady never refuses a duke."

"You can, if you want. I don't want you to feel forced, but I don't want to dance the waltz with Helen. I trust you to tell me what you think every time."

Her expression softened, and the warmth in her eyes reached his heart. "I would love to dance with you, Anthony."

He loved the intimacy of his name on her lips. "Excellent. If you'll excuse me a moment, I need a word with the maestro."

He weaved through the throng of guests, almost bumping into his grandmother going the opposite way.

"What are you doing?" Grandmama looked alarmed. "What's the hurry?"

"The maestro must play the supper waltz."

She wiggled a finger to say no. "Out of the question. He's already received the order to play only slow contredanses."

"Sorry, Grandmama, but I'm going to dance the waltz with Isabella," he said in a tone that hopefully would discourage further arguments.

Her countenance cracked for a split second. "You must be joking. You haven't danced with Lady Coulter-Smith yet. She's the highest-ranking lady guest present."

"I promised the waltz to Isabella. I won't change my mind."

She craned her neck in the direction of Isabella who was talking with Patrick. "Oh no. Don't tell me..." She beckoned him to follow her with her fan.

He guessed he ought to inform her of his decision. He smiled and bowed at his guests, catching a glimpse of Lady Montrose and Helen. He wouldn't enjoy disappointing Helen, but surely, she would agree with him that they weren't compatible in the least. Likely, she'd been trapped by her mother and Grandmama into an arranged marriage with a duke and didn't know how to get out of it. He would give her a way out.

Grandmama slipped into a parlour and locked them in. "What's happening?"

"I don't want to marry Helen. I want Isabella."

The moment of shocked silence lowered the room temperature.

"Why not Helen? She's perfect."

"She doesn't have an opinion of her own. I spent days with her without learning anything about her. She agrees to everything I say."

Grandmama opened her arms. "And what is the problem with that?"

"You didn't agree with everything Grandpapa said, did you?"

She pressed her lips in a hard line, her eyes narrowing to slits. "We aren't talking about me. If you don't like Helen, you can find someone else. Someone who will be a better wife than Isabella. She's too..." She waved a hand. "Did you see her gown? That pink is too strong, and she's far too happy to be a duchess. She doesn't speak French and isn't accomplished in anything."

"Isabella is very clever and always expresses her opinions without being intimidated by me. That's why I like her." And because she was the essence of life itself, wrapped in pink silk. "And I'm going to dance the supper waltz with her." Which meant he would escort her to supper and sit next to her at the dinner table.

"She has too many opinions," Grandmama said.

"Thank goodness for that."

She huffed. "Don't be such a child. The next Duchess of Gloucester can't be a suffragette who thinks we need to open our castle to tourists. Helen is the perfect wife for you."

He clasped his hands behind his back. "I love you, Grandmama, and I always respect your opinion. But I want Isabella. Or no one."

She pressed two fingers to her temples. "You present me with a *fait accompli.*"

"We usually agree on every strategy. Not this time. I mean to court Isabella, and if she agrees, I'll marry her."

They stared at each other. The moment reminded him of a boxing session against an adversary, and Grandmama was an extraordinary adversary.

He was tempted to argue further, but it would be a mistake. With Grandmama, short, decisive speeches were more effective.

"I hope you won't regret your choice," she said, conceding the victory to him.

"You won't regret it, either."

eleven

The darned ballroom was too brightly lit for Isabella. Not that she minded the light, but she couldn't find a quiet dark place where she could remove her slippers and rub her sore feet. Her shoes were a menace and not made for human anatomy. One had to have the toes of a cat not to suffer in those shoes.

Anthony and Patrick had disappeared, and she took advantage of their absence to cross the ballroom and find a spot where she could rest. If she had to dance the waltz with the duke, she wanted to wiggle her toes first and let the blood circulate again, lest they fall off.

She sighed when she sat on a settee in a quiet nook. She would be quick and return to the ballroom in a moment. Relief swept through her when she removed her shoes. Sheer heaven. The cool marble floor was a blessing for her overheated, cramped toes.

"Isabella."

"Gah!"

Upon hearing the Dowager's authoritarian voice, Isabella jolted. The woman had to possess some uncanny power and be able to sense whenever someone did something inappropriate.

"I'm sorry, Your Grace." She hurried to stuff her feet into the shoes, ignoring the sting of pain in her toes. "My toes are incredibly warm and a little sweaty." She shot up.

The Dowager's eyebrows drew together. She and Anthony shared the same terrifying authority. But while Anthony had a kind heart, the Dowager was all harshness.

"Good gracious, girl. You don't need to inform me of every little change in your body. There are things better kept to oneself."

"Yes, of course. I was simply explaining why...never mind. I'll return to the ballroom, Your Grace." She dropped a curtsy, bobbing on her feet.

"I gather Anthony invited you to dance the supper waltz with him." The Dowager raked a glance over at Isabella, likely not impressed by the bobbing curtsy.

"He did, and I accepted the invitation."

"Tell me about yourself, Isabella. What do you enjoy doing in your free time aside from subverting the order in our country?"

The question shocked her. "Ah, gardening."

The Dowager stopped fanning herself. "Gardening."

"I love flowers and plants, and I'm studying the ancient art of flower arrangement. It's fascinating, complicated, and requires a lot of patience and creativity."

"It's still gardening."

"In a way, yes." Where was her mother? That was a good moment to be taken away by a relative, friend, or natural disaster.

"What else aside from gardening?" the Dowager said.

"I love long walks, especially uphill. My father has an estate in the Lake District, and we spend the summer hiking up and down the hills."

She fell silent at the horrified face of the Dowager. If Isabella had said she enjoyed eating dirt, the matron wouldn't look about to faint as she looked now.

"Hiking. Why would anyone sweat to climb a hill?"

"The view," she said. "Gorgeous."

The Dowager exhaled, resuming fanning herself. "Heavens. Modern times. It could be worse, I guess."

"You don't approve, madam? My grandmother loved taking long walks in nature."

"You're perfectly free to enjoy yourself in whichever fashion you consider suitable, and, under normal circumstances, I wouldn't care about how you spend your free time. But these aren't normal circumstances. I suspect my grandson has a keen interest in you. Very keen. He wishes to court you."

Patrick. Isabella perked up. Where was her mother when a possible courtship was discussed? She had no idea how to navigate a marriage discussion. She had no idea if she wanted to, either.

"I believe Patrick enjoys hiking as well."

"Patrick? I'm talking about the duke." The Dowager frowned with the implacability of a warrior. "We wouldn't have this conversation otherwise."

For a moment, the music, the chatter, and the sound of glass and china stopped. A moment of perfect silence enveloped her. She didn't hear that right. Anthony wanted to court *her*? Why hadn't she understood his intentions?

So the waltz was the first step before announcing their engagement. No, he would ask her first, wouldn't he? He wouldn't give the announcement in front of everyone... goodness, Helen, Mother.

She shook her head. "It can't be. Anthony is supposed to marry Helen."

"And Napoleon was supposed to stay in exile. Yet he escaped and invaded Europe again." The Dowager fanned herself slowly. "He likes you against my better judgement."

Isabella's legs threatened to give up. Her breathing sped up. Anthony wanted to propose. First, she'd never thought about marriage seriously, and second, Helen would be distraught. Isabella had doubted Anthony wanted to marry Helen, but she hadn't guessed he wanted to marry *her*.

Well, she'd felt a connection with him, but his wish to marry her came as a surprise.

The whole affair was her fault. She shouldn't have talked to him in secret. Blast it all, Mother had been right. She should have stayed silent like a freshly caught criminal.

"It's all wrong. I can't be his duchess. I simply can't."

"I agree. Being a duchess requires some qualities an inexperienced woman like you doesn't have."

"I agree, too. I shouldn't be a duchess. I'm not prepared for that."

"Good. At least you know your place." The Dowager gave her another assessing glance. "You have a...bubbly personality and are very pretty. I'm sure you'll find a suitable match. Are you going to refuse my grandson's proposal then?"

"Ah..." Her first instinct was to say yes, but, again, just like a criminal who asked for a solicitor before talking, she should have a word with her mother. She didn't want to cause Helen or her family any more trouble, and a sharp refusal would likely do that.

Besides, she would soon have the chance to talk with Anthony alone. She wanted to discuss the matter with him first before making any decisions.

"I see." The Dowager surveyed the ballroom. "I guess a ducal match is a ducal match."

"No, it's..." Silence. She ought to be silent.

"For goodness' sake, girl, straighten your back," the Dowager said. "Chin out. In the remote possibility you might be a duchess, you must learn to behave like one."

"Yes, madam." Isabella did as told.

"Come with me." It was an order.

She reluctantly followed the Dowager to the edge of the ballroom. The music and chatter grated on her nerves now.

"Just in case Anthony persisted in courting you and you agreed to become a member of my prestigious family..." The Dowager knew how to lighten the atmosphere. "I want you to look at everyone as if you were judging them, because you actually are." She surveyed the crowded room.

Isabella fiddled with her hands, wondering why she hadn't stayed home to re-pot the crocuses.

"Open your fan," the Dowager said. "So you'll stop fidgeting like a five years old."

Isabella opened her fan, but it nearly slipped out of her fingers. She snatched it before it hit the floor with a clumsy move. "Sorry," she mumbled.

"You know, cats use their tails to express their opinions. We use our fans. And cats and duchesses have a lot in common." The Dowager snapped it open with a dry, precise gesture that reminded Isabella of a sword master. "Look at the girl over there, the one in the blue gown."

She followed the Dowager's stare. A young woman was laughing out loud while talking with a gentleman.

"She laughs so loudly she'll crack the glass. Unacceptable." The Dowager moved her fan very little while staring at the girl.

As if summoned by the stare, the girl turned towards the Dowager, and their gazes locked. The girl's smile vanished as she stopped laughing, her cheek reddening.

"Done." The Dowager nodded.

"Goodness," Isabella said. "You didn't need to go to the girl or use your voice."

"It's the power of a duchess. When you're powerful, people will feel your stare."

"Like magic."

"It's better than magic." The Dowager tilted her chin towards another corner. "It's a matter of will. That gentleman over there next to the window."

Isabella ran a glance over at the man without finding any flaws in his behaviour. He didn't speak too loudly, his glass was perfectly held between his fingers, and his smile was polite but not too flashy.

"I don't see what the problem is."

"The first button on his waistcoat. It's almost undone, dangling on a thread. Once he starts dancing, the button will fall on the floor and open his waistcoat. Inappropriate."

"Maybe he doesn't realise his waistcoat has come loose."

"That's even worse. What sort of gentleman isn't aware of his clothes getting undone?" The Dowager pinned her duchess glare on him, her fan twitching with small movements.

And surely enough, the man glanced around until he met the Dowager's unforgiving stare. He was flustered and started checking himself until he touched his waistcoat. Next, he excused himself and left the group, a hand on the loose button.

"Crikey," Isabella whispered.

"Don't use that expression," the Dowager said. "It's a duchess's duty to make sure everything is right and proper in the room."

"It's impressive." Terrifying, but impressive.

"You try." The Dowager tilted her fan towards a dancing couple. "Look at those two. She's practically sagging against him as if she were fainting. He enjoys the physical contact obviously, judging by his daft smile. Open your fan and stare at them from over the rim while thinking about scolding them for their absolute inappropriateness."

Inappropriateness. Isabella couldn't even think about that word without her brain tripping.

She flipped the fan open, trying to imitate the Dowager's expertise, only to hit her bottom lip hard with the sharp edge. Her lip throbbed.

She winced. "Ouch! Absolute agony! I think I cut my lip. I can taste blood."

The Dowager pinched the bridge of her nose. "Dear, dear, dear."

"I think I'm bleeding."

"Duchesses are like soldiers. Blood doesn't affect them. So stop whining. Duchesses don't complain, nor do they get discouraged. They take action."

She rolled her bottom lip between her teeth. "Yes, I'm bleeding. I think I might faint."

"For heaven's sake, pull yourself together." The Dowager gestured for her to come. "Follow me. And don't let the blood stain your gown."

She swallowed blood, and her stomach churned.

As the Dowager strode along the corridor, the servants hurried to make room for her, bowing at her passage. She barely glanced at them.

"In you go." The Dowager ushered Isabella into a lady's room.

She sat on the stuffed stool in front of a mirror. Her lip was swelling. "I'm sorry."

"Don't apologise to me. You should apologise to yourself." The Dowager opened an elegant cabinet and took out a white cloth and a glass jar. "We need to work together if we want this arrangement to work."

Possible but unlikely arrangement.

The Dowager sat in front of her. "Let me see."

She released her bottom lip, forcing herself not to wince again.

"It's just a tiny cut." The Dowager applied a clear salve smelling of mint on Isabella's injured lip. She was surprisingly gentle. "The cream shouldn't sting, and it'll stop the bleeding immediately. The swelling will diminish, too."

"Thank you."

The Dowager exhaled, giving her another assessing glance. "I want you to think carefully about your answer when Anthony asks you to marry him." She took Isabella's chin gently. "Our choices are rarely easy. A duchess's choices are always hard. That's your first choice to make." She rose in a swish of satin and lace. She paused at the door. "I don't hate you, Isabella. I'm just sorry for you."

She closed the door behind her, leaving Isabella confused and smelling of mint.

twelve

Where the hell was Isabella?

After Anthony had instructed the maestro to play the waltz and stopped to chat with a few of his guests, he'd lost sight of her. He couldn't find Patrick, either.

"Anthony."

He came to a halt at hearing Grandmama's voice. "It's done. The waltz is next."

"I know." There was a sadness about her that worried him. "Isabella is in the ladies' room at the end of the corridor. She had a little accident."

"What accident? Did you tell her anything?"

Her green eyes flashed. "Don't use that tone with me. I didn't do anything. She cut her lip on her own. Now go and find her. I'll tell her parents you wish to talk to them in private."

"Please no. I need to talk to Isabella first."

"All right."

He kissed her cheek. "Thank you, Grandmama." He started to dash towards the corridor, but she stopped him.

"I hope you know what you're doing. For her sake."

So did he.

"She's younger than you are, inexperienced and very naïve."

"I know."

She snapped her fan open and closed it again. "Just go."

He found Isabella in the middle of the corridor patting her curls and looking around. Grandmama was wrong. The pink gown suited Isabella perfectly; it exalted her rosy cheeks and pink lips. She fiddled with her hands when she saw him.

"What happened?" he asked. "Grandmama said you cut your lip."

"I did. With my fan." She pointed to her bottom lip where a thin slash marred her skin. "Not my proudest moment. But Her Grace was of great help. She was very kind."

She lowered her gaze, and he doubted his grandmother had been completely kind.

For a split moment, he wished he could kiss her lips and soothe the pain. Or simply hold her.

He offered her his hand. "May I have the honour? The waltz is about to begin."

"Of course." She took his arm hesitantly.

Anthony sucked in a breath when she slid her gloved hand over his arm. "Thank you for accepting my invitation."

She smiled, and he forgot what the hell he was doing for a moment.

"I didn't have the time to talk to my mother," she said as they walked towards the ballroom.

"We're just dancing a waltz for now. I won't make any formal announcement."

"Yes, but everyone will spread rumours about us."

He stopped before entering the ballroom. "If you don't want to dance, I won't insist."

She gripped his arm more tightly, and his heart stuttered as he feared she might say she didn't want to have anything to do with him.

"I don't mean to be cruel to your sister, but I'm sure she realises we aren't a good match," he said.

The other dancers formed a circle around the ballroom among mutters and whispers since the music didn't start. The maestro was waiting for Anthony.

"You don't mean to propose to Helen, do you?" Isabella whispered.

"No."

"Why?"

"She's beautiful and graceful. My grandmother adores her. But I find her lack of honesty disappointing."

Isabella's delicate eyebrows drew together. "Lack of honesty?"

"She never says what she thinks. She only says what she thinks will please me. I'm surrounded by people like her. I need a wife who shares her true thoughts and feelings with me." And whose happy energy was contagious.

"Becoming a duchess is everything for her." She gripped his arm.

"Exactly."

"So do you wish to propose to..."

"You."

She stumbled. "Anthony, I'll break Helen's heart."

"Her dream is to become a duchess, not to marry *me*. She doesn't care about me. I doubt she likes me."

"But we...we don't really know each other, either."

"We'll spend time together to know each other. I won't force a decision on you. I won't talk to your father unless you want me to. I want you to be completely free to make a decision. All I'm asking is to give me the chance and the honour of courting you. You'll have plenty of time to think. I won't rush you." He dipped his head. "For now, will you dance with me?"

The other couples got ready to begin the dance, craning their necks at the maestro.

"I need a wife who understands me when I talk about the

parliamentary bills, the constant disagreements between the Tories and the Social Democratic Federation, a wife who can help me in my decisions."

"I'm not an expert."

"I'm not asking you to be one. I don't want you to be one. I'm surrounded by experts in politics. I only need your honest opinion."

"Do you think I can be of help?"

"You're more clever than you think."

A few sweet notes came from the orchestra as the dancers grew impatient. He coiled his arm around her waist, pulling her closer. Her rose scent covered that of the other ladies' perfumes.

He wasn't being completely honest because, while he needed all those things in a wife, he also liked her because she made him laugh and because she was kind and compassionate. When they were together, the world was less dark, and a little flame of life sparked in his heart.

He leant closer to her and whispered, "Dance with me. Please."

"With pleasure."

Relief overwhelmed him. He led her to the middle of the ball-room, ignoring the glances. He nodded at the maestro.

The music started. He took the first box steps, and she followed him with hesitant movements. He had to slow down to guide her through the next sequence.

"Is everything all right?" He made her twirl.

"My shoes are a tad tight, and my toes are crushed and sweaty."

He chuckled. "See? I like your honesty. Another lady wouldn't have said that."

"I love dancing, but the wrong shoes turn it into a challenge. And just so you know, I love gardening, too."

"My mother loved flowers and plants. I'm afraid that since her passing, our conservatory has been neglected. But if you wish to take care of it, I'll be more than happy."

"If I agree to be your duchess?"

"Even if you don't."

She gave him her first bright smile since the beginning of the ball.

On the sweet notes of *The Blue Danube*, he let her twirl around the ballroom. She laughed when she turned under his arm and during the quick chassés. He silently thanked the Duke of Kent for having introduced many waltz steps decades ago. The two-hands-across step brought him so close to Isabella that he could see the golden specks in her irises, and when they clasped hands, the world became perfect.

If her parents were watching, he couldn't tell. His focus was only on her.

When the waltz ended and the couples clapped at the maestro, she was radiant. And he basked in her radiance like someone who saw the sun after a long time in the dark.

"Wonderful." She brushed a curl from her cheek.

"I couldn't agree more."

He escorted her to the dining room, looking forward to sharing dinner with her. Grandmama followed him with her keen gaze that promised a long conversation afterwards. From a corner, Helen glared at them as well, her face flushed.

Isabella drew in a breath. "Helen must be furious with me."

"We can talk to her together if you wish. I'll tell her it was only a waltz."

"But it wasn't."

He was about to tell her that Helen would forget him easily when Rogers stopped next to him and leant closer.

"Your Grace, there's an urgent matter that requires your immediate intervention."

He hoped it wasn't another scandalous fashion emergency. "If you'll excuse me, Isabella."

Isabella bowed her head.

"I'm sorry to leave you in a moment like this. I'll be back as soon as possible."

"Do not worry." She touched his arm briefly, but his heart stuttered.

Anthony followed the butler out of the dining room and along the corridor towards the library.

"What's the matter?" he asked.

He didn't need an answer; the angry voice of Lord McFall echoed in the hallway.

"How dare you?" McFall roared.

"It's a misunderstanding." That was Patrick.

Anthony strode into the library, skidding to a stop at the threshold.

Lady McFall trembled in a corner next to the window, covering herself with a curtain; she was visible only from the neck up. Patrick's shirt was open, and his waistcoat and jacket were on the carpet. The scene didn't bode well at all.

"What is the meaning of this?" he demanded.

Patrick rubbed his chin. "Lord McFall is under the impression that something untoward must have happened here between his wife and me."

The lady in question shivered, her eyes widening.

"Gloucester." Lord McFall's neck was so tense a tendon stood out. "Your brother was seducing my wife here on that table, and he has the audacity to negate the truth. I saw them with my own eyes."

"Nothing happened. McFall is overreacting. That's all," Patrick said with nonchalance.

Had Anthony been alone with his brother, he would have told him not to insult his intelligence. He didn't know what was worse—Patrick having seduced a married lady or Patrick's flippant attitude. No, the worst thing was poor Lady McFall's reputation.

He turned to his butler. "Rogers, fetch Mrs. Stamell to assist Lady McFall and take her to the ladies' room."

"Sir." Rogers hurried away.

"McFall," he said. "Perhaps we should let the lady go and collect herself while we discuss the matter."

McFall closed a fist. "My wife isn't going anywhere until I hear the truth from Lord Patrick."

Good luck with that.

They could spend the whole week in the library. What Patrick lacked in common sense, he made up for with his stubbornness in always deflecting responsibilities.

"As I said, nothing serious happened. We were simply joking around." Patrick buttoned his shirt and had the decency to offer his jacket to the lady since her clothes were nowhere to be seen. "Then McFall barged into the room and started shouting."

"I'm not stupid, Lord Patrick," McFall said. "You don't expect me to believe your cock-and-bull story, do you? My wife is half naked."

Patrick shrugged. "Yes, but as I said, nothing happened."

"Because I intervened." McFall thumped the desk.

Dammit. "Patrick." Anthony kept his tone calm. "At least you could clear the lady's name and take responsibility for whatever happened here."

Patrick held up his hands. "Of course. Everything that has never happened here is my sole responsibility."

"McFall, be reasonable. We should avoid a scene." Anthony glanced at the lady. "Let your wife compose herself."

McFall straightened. "Gloucester, you're right. We should end the conversation here."

Anthony glanced at the still half-hidden lady when the housekeeper arrived. "My lady, you should leave. My housekeeper, Mrs. Stamell, will take good care of you."

Mrs. Stamell curtsied from the door. "Your Grace."

Lady McFall walked out of the room, clutching the front of Patrick's jacket. Layers of fabric fell in disarray over her legs. Her stockings were bunched at the ankles.

Anthony shot a burning glare at his brother before turning

towards the woman. "My lady, wait." He followed her to the dimly lit hallway and lowered his voice. "Are you afraid of going home with your husband? Perhaps you should go to a relative or a friend's house tonight. Mrs. Stamell will have a carriage ready for you to take you wherever you want." He didn't believe McFall to be violent towards his wife, but better to be cautious.

Lady McFall curtsied. "Thank you. I'll go to my sister's."

"Good." After a nod to Mrs. Stamell, Anthony inhaled deeply before entering the library again where the tension was oppressive. "McFall, I'm sure Patrick will apologise for his behaviour."

Patrick arched his brow but didn't say a word. Good for him.

"I have a better idea." McFall straightened in front of Patrick and slapped him with a glove. "Lord Patrick, I'll see you at dawn. Battersea Park. Pistols. Don't be late."

Bloody hell. Anthony rubbed his forehead.

Patrick flourished a hand and bowed. "As you wish."

"What?" Anthony roared. "Patrick, apologise this instant."

"McFall challenged me. I want to accept the challenge."

"This challenge is ridiculous," Anthony said.

McFall's cold demeanour was more disturbing than his hot anger. "Your brother accepted the challenge. There's nothing else to discuss." He went to leave the library.

Anthony stepped in front of him. "You know this is a mistake."

"The only one who made a mistake is Lord Patrick. He insulted me and humiliated me. I'll see you tomorrow, Gloucester." McFall strode out of the library, his heels clicking against the marble floor.

Anthony grabbed Patrick by the shoulders. "Why the hell did you accept the challenge? Are you barking mad? McFall was the best shooter in the Scots Guards, and he's now in the Coldstream Guards. And your idea is to agree to duel with him?"

Patrick shrugged himself free. "He's a bloody buffoon."

"He's a scorned husband with excellent aim and more than

fifteen years of impeccable service in the army while you've never fired a shot without hurting yourself. You'll be dead in a minute."

"Thanks for the vote of confidence. But I'm cleverer than you think. Duels are illegal. I'll go to Battersea Fields with the entire constabulary of London, and while McFall will be in trouble, I'll be free." Patrick winked. "Genius."

The shock silenced Anthony for a moment. "Honestly, you're depriving a village somewhere of an idiot. This duel will be considered valid and fair, because a well-respected military officer is involved. The entire constabulary will turn their backs and leave you alone. Do you have any idea of how many soldiers McFall saved? He risked his neck to retrieve wounded men from the battlefield, and just so you know, half of the police officers in London are former soldiers who worship him. No one will stop McFall, and if he asked one of the peelers to shoot you, they would bloody do it."

Finally, Patrick lost his cocksure attitude. "But McFall won't kill me, will he?"

"If you want to take the chance, be my guest." Anthony ran out of the library, chasing McFall down the corridor. He ought to stop this nonsense. "McFall! You must listen to me."

Working his jaw, McFall stopped, his nostrils flaring. "Gloucester."

"I'm sure we can settle the matter in some other way."

McFall lifted his chin, fists clenched at his sides. "I respect you, and I don't have any quarrels with you. But your brother's behaviour was utterly disgraceful."

"I agree," Anthony said, "but a duel is an extreme solution."

"More than fair, Gloucester."

"You're a renowned shooter. My brother has never hit anything and has no military training. It's not fair."

"That's not my problem," McFall said. "Tomorrow. At dawn. Or I swear I'll come here and shoot him in cold blood. And this is the last time we discuss the matter." He bowed and walked away. The sound of his angry footsteps thundered.

Anthony returned to the library, half-wishing to strangle his brother. "What the hell were you thinking?"

Pale and shivering, Patrick flinched at the tone. "He over-reacted."

"You were ravishing his wife."

"I'm not her only lover. Lady McFall has a string of lovers and so many affairs—"

"How does that make your situation better? Bloody hell!" He rubbed his aching forehead. "Go to your room. We'd better get ready for tomorrow. We need a strategy and to practise."

"You're overreacting, too. He won't kill me. He's angry now. Tomorrow morning, he'll understand a duel is madness, and I'll be fine."

"I'll have those words engraved on your tombstone."

thirteen

Isabella shifted her position on the seat in the carriage.

The atmosphere was so thick that she could cut it with a butter knife. After Anthony had left the ballroom, she hadn't seen him throughout the dinner. The butler had given her Anthony's apologies for not being able to join her. The Dowager had seemed preoccupied, and Patrick had vanished as well. She hadn't had time to discuss with Mother and Helen what had happened with the duke. She wasn't sure she should. Certainly, she wasn't going to mention his proposal.

Helen sat slumped in her seat as if distraught, and Mother kept fidgeting. Father seemed oblivious to the tension.

"Lovely evening," he said. "Did you enjoy yourselves, girls?"

"Lovely evening my foot." Mother ignored him. "What happened tonight, Isabella?"

"Why did the duke dance the supper waltz with you?" Helen asked.

"He asked me, and I said yes."

Isabella had been lucky that something urgent had happened and Anthony hadn't been able to sit with her at dinner, or she wouldn't be forced to tell everything.

Her silence would be short-lived though, but she needed a moment to think about her options, and after all, Anthony had asked her to think about it. She meant to think about his proposal seriously because she liked him. She wasn't in love, and surely, neither was he. When he'd listed the reasons why he wanted to marry her, he'd sounded like an employer looking for the ideal clerk. But she couldn't deny they had fun together.

Still, right now, there wasn't any need to inform Mother and Helen of anything. Their opinions and arguments would meddle her thoughts and cause more confusion. And Helen would be upset.

Father drew his eyebrows together. "He must have told you something when he invited you."

"Very little. Then he vanished."

If even Father started asking questions, she would never see the end of the conversation. She didn't want to be pushed to do anything. She simply wanted a few days of peace and quiet to think on her own.

"What did he exactly tell you?" Mother insisted. "I was certain the duke would have danced with Helen before supper. The Dowager told me that. And I thought there wouldn't be any waltz."

"I don't know about the waltz. As I said, the duke asked me to dance, and I said yes."

Helen's expression didn't soften. "Why didn't you refuse?"

"Refuse?" Isabella steeled her voice. "I couldn't reject the duke's invitation, and he asked me personally."

Mother nodded. "Isabella is right. Refusing to dance would have been a grave offence."

"But the question remains," Helen said. "Don't be offended, Isabella, but why invite you? I told everyone the duke was going to dance with me after the Dowager reassured me of that. Imagine my humiliation when he had you at his arm. And you didn't tell me anything. You could have warned me."

"I'm sorry you felt humiliated. It wasn't my intention, but as I said, I was in a difficult position and couldn't say no."

Father didn't say anything, which was worse than him talking. Likely, he guessed she wasn't being completely honest.

Mother patted Helen's hand. "Don't worry. I'll talk with the Dowager and clear up this misunderstanding. There must be a reason for the invitation."

Yes, there was.

"And the fact the duke and Lord Patrick disappeared," Mother said, "makes me think that something happened and changed the plans. The Dowager looked particularly tense after the butler talked to her. She vanished for a while as well."

"Anyway." Helen sighed. "What did you and the duke talk about during the waltz?"

"The current unrest in Parliament about the workers' rights."

That shut up Helen and Mother.

She just hoped that whatever emergency had happened to Anthony would keep him busy for a little longer.

A LIGHT MIST lingered over Battersea Fields the next morning as Anthony waited for the duel to begin. Dew glistened on the grass blades, and patches of frost covered the ground. Not the best conditions for a duel, especially for an inexperienced shooter.

Patrick shifted his weight from one foot to another, blowing warm air on his hands. "Bloody freezing."

"Dawn is the coldest hour. If you had ever risen before eleven, you would know."

"I don't need your attitude." Patrick shook his head. "A bloody idiot wants to shoot me. Thank you very much."

Anthony kept a comment to himself. Reminding Patrick the situation was his entire fault wouldn't help him survive the day. If he couldn't keep his instincts under control, then at least he should learn to be more discreet with his paramours.

They'd spent the night shooting at targets, but Patrick was utterly hopeless with a firearm. His arm was unsteady, and his aim was terrible. He had more chances to hit McFall if he aimed at a tree.

Speaking of the devil. McFall strode towards them in his shiny captain uniform. A Victoria Cross hung from his chest—a further reminder of McFall's excellent fighting skills.

A few rigid nods were exchanged.

"McFall," Anthony said, "would you accept my brother's apology and renounce the duel?"

"I'm sorry for what happened." Patrick bowed his head.

McFall shot a glacial glare at him. "We're ready to start. Twenty paces, then turn."

"Would you accept me as your opponent instead of Patrick?" Anthony asked.

"Anthony!" Patrick said at the same time as McFall said, "No."

"Your sacrifice is honourable. Unfortunately, your brother isn't. Shall we?"

Anthony and McFall's second inspected the guns and made sure only one bullet was in the chamber.

When McFall crossed the field to go to his position, Anthony grabbed Patrick's shoulder. Worry gnawed at him from the inside out. He'd lost his parents. He couldn't lose even his little brother for a damn duel. He was supposed to protect Patrick, yet here they were, risking Patrick's life for no reason.

He swallowed hard. "Focus on your shot and nothing else. Don't think. Don't breathe. Don't blink. Keep your arm steady, and remember to stay balanced between your feet."

Patrick nodded. No jokes and no comebacks, a testament to his worry. He should be worried.

Anthony stood at the edge of the duelling field, wondering if he should knock Patrick unconscious, take him home, and face McFall's wrath.

The duellists stood back to back before starting to pace in opposite directions. Anthony's heart stuttered as he wiped his clammy hands on his jacket.

While McFall held the pistol in the correct position, Patrick was visibly shaking. He stumbled, and the pistol nearly slipped out of his grip.

"Bloody hell, Patrick," Anthony muttered. "Come on."

McFall finished the twentieth step and turned around with one smooth move in a flutter of coattails. Patrick staggered again, and by Jove, was holding the pistol back to front.

McFall raised his arm, his gaze as cold and unforgiving as the morning air. Instead, Patrick had turned into a bumbling ass.

His little brother was going to get killed right in front of him. Visions of the battlefields covered with dead soldiers flashed through his mind. All those young men gone. And Patrick would join them.

McFall closed one eye to take aim. Patrick wheezed in panic, paling by the minute, and cast a terrified glance at Anthony.

"Patrick!" Anthony shouted.

Patrick stood petrified. He couldn't be an easier target.

Anthony's legs moved before he could think. He sprinted forwards, eager to drag a frozen Patrick away. A shot rang out. Anthony pounced on his brother, and a searing, excruciating pain lanced through his face. Warm blood soaked his cheeks and lips, and white light filled his vision. The agony was so intense he couldn't shout.

"Anthony!" Patrick's voice seemed to come from a distance and through water.

"...damn fool..." That sounded like McFall.

Boots surrounded him as he lay on the frosted grass. The world spun. Voices called his name. Someone touched his face, shooting pain through his body. Hell, he wanted to throw up.

Anthony's head became light, and the sounds receded.

He closed his eyes and when he opened them again, he was lying on a carriage seat. His head rested on Patrick's lap, and only his right eye worked. The left one was swollen shut or maybe it was missing. He couldn't tell.

Patrick pressed a cloth against Anthony's face. A face that was burning and throbbing without mercy.

"What the hell is happening?" Patrick asked someone. "Why aren't we moving?"

"A riot, my lord," the footman said from somewhere. "The protesters and the police are blocking the street."

"Go around them. Find another way."

Anthony groaned. His throat and mouth tasted of copper and seemed filled with glass shards.

"Anthony, can you hear me?" Patrick's worried face filled Anthony's field of vision. "I'm taking you to the hospital."

"The bullet?" he slurred.

"I'm not sure what happened. There's too much blood, and the flesh is all torn." Patrick's voice shook with fear.

"My eye?"

"I don't know." Patrick was shaking so hard his teeth chattered.

Anthony wanted to reassure him, but talking required too much effort.

The carriage rolled onwards for a while before stopping with a jolt. Loud voices sounded. People thumped the carriage, yelling slogans against the government. Hundreds of feet thundered. Anthony tried to sit up.

"Don't." Patrick pushed him down.

"Let me." He wasn't sure he could sit up without feeling sick, but he needed to do something other than lie helplessly.

Patrick helped him, still pressing the cloth against the burning cheek. "You jumped in front of me to protect me. You shouldn't have."

What was he supposed to do? Watch his brother get killed?

He swallowed the bitter taste in his mouth and replaced Patrick's hand with his. The world tilted again, but if he rested his head on the wall, he could sit without feeling sick although the protestants rocked the carriage right and left on the spot. The horses snorted.

"Take us out of here!" Patrick yelled to the coachman.

"I'm trying, my lord."

The cloth was soaked, and the pain was agonising, but Anthony's mind was clear. He took deep breaths, glancing out of the window. Men waving the flag of the Social Democratic Federation were clashing against another group he couldn't identify, and his carriage stood in the middle of the riot.

"What's this?" Each word was like a stab to his face.

"Socialists against protectionists. It's a huge riot. Every bloody street seems blocked." Patrick let out a sob. "I'm sorry, Anthony. It's my fault."

He didn't have the strength to reply. Lying down seemed like a bloody good idea.

The last thing he heard before closing his only working eye was Patrick apologising again.

Isabella sat beside her mother and Helen on the sofa in Gloucester House.

The ticking of the grandfather clock was the only sound. In front of her on a low table lay the latest issue of *The Times*.

The newspapers hadn't dedicated much space to the news of a shooting incident in Battersea Park, involving the duke a few weeks ago. She guessed the Beauforts were powerful enough to silence the press when they wanted to. Surely, a shooting wasn't the type of news the Dowager would want her family involved with.

The aftermaths of the disastrous West End Riots were still the main topic. Windows had been smashed, stores on Oxford Street had been destroyed and ransacked, and the Police Commissioner had resigned amid accusations of incompetence after the destruction the rioters had left behind throughout London. There had been many wounded as well.

Guilt gnawed at her for Anthony's condition. When she'd wished for something to keep him busy after his unexpected proposal, she hadn't meant a shooting incident that had almost killed him.

There was a lingering, mourning feeling in the air, like during a vigil, and she hoped the duke wasn't on his deathbed as some people rumoured. If the newspapers had been quiet about the duke's condition, the Dowager and Patrick had been vague. They'd answered politely to Mother and Father's messages, but that was it. No explanation.

After a few more exchanges of curt messages, the Dowager had quite coldly invited them to Gloucester House, but Isabella doubted the invitation was sincere.

"Perhaps we should leave," she whispered. "I feel like we're intruding into their difficult moment."

"We won't stay long," Mother said in a low voice. "We'll enquire about His Grace's health and leave. If he can receive visitors, Helen will go. The duke will be happy to see you."

Helen nodded.

"For goodness' sake, Helen," Mother continued, "why did you wear those awful shoes? I should have checked you before leaving the house."

Helen swallowed a couple of times. Either she forced herself not to say anything or she felt humiliated. "Sorry, Mother."

"Well, I doubt the duke will notice them anyway." Mother sighed. "Sometimes I think neither of you two listen to me."

Isabella wondered if her mother cared about Anthony at all. "Mother. The poor man is wounded. We've been waiting here for twenty minutes. We aren't welcome."

"I won't tire him," Helen said. "But he must know I'll be by his side, no matter what."

They sat bolt upright when the door inched inwards.

Patrick entered the sitting room and offered a bow, his face pale and strained. "Lady Montrose, Isabella, Helen. Thank you for coming. I apologise for having made you wait."

"Do not worry. How is His Grace?" Mother put her cup of tea down on the low table.

His paleness and red-rimmed eyes spoke of a lot of worry and little sleep. "His injury is serious but slowly improving although the infection is barely under control. He needs rest, and his recovery will take time."

"What happened to him?" she asked.

Patrick fidgeted with his hands. "Anthony was in the wrong place at the wrong time. A shooting was happening, and he took a bullet."

Mother gasped despite the fact he hadn't said anything new. "Good Lord."

Isabella had heaps of questions.

He hung his head. "The shot wasn't the only problem. Unfortunately, the delay in taking him to the hospital caused by the West End Riots worsened the severity of his injury. Had the surgeon operated on him sooner, my brother would feel better."

"Does he accept visitors?" Helen asked.

"The physician has been very strict, but if one of you wants to see him for no more than a few minutes, a visitor might cheer him up."

Helen rose before anyone could say anything. If Isabella had to be honest, she wished to see Anthony. But she couldn't justify her need to see him without telling the whole truth.

Patrick opened the door for Helen. "Very well. Rogers will show you to Anthony's room."

"Thank you." Helen walked out of the room, following the butler.

"We're sorry," Isabella said. "Anthony must be in great pain."

"He is."

Maybe it was Isabella's imagination, but the way Patrick avoided her gaze and hunched his shoulders made him look guilty.

"Do you need anything, my lord?" Mother said. "Company or a walk in the park? A bit of fresh air would do you good. Forgive me if I say you look rather pale and tired."

"The past weeks have been difficult for us." He rubbed his face.

"We can take a walk tomorrow if you want," Isabella said. "Just an hour if you can spare it."

He didn't smile. "Tomorrow, then. Thank you."

"How's the Dowager?" she asked.

"Preoccupied. But you know my grandmama. She's a strong woman."

"Thank you, Patrick."

The Dowager walked in, dressed in one of her impeccable, high-necked gowns. Her hair was styled in the usual old-fashioned chignon, but her green eyes were clouded, and her hollow cheeks showed the same suffering as her grandson's.

"Your Grace." Isabella said. "We're deeply sorry about the incident."

The Dowager remained unfathomable. The only sign of her distress was the down-turned curve of her mouth. "As a family, we've been through many troubles. We overcame those. We'll overcome this one. Just something for you to think about." She patted Isabella's cheek lightly before excusing herself and heading out.

A little quiver ran down Isabella's neck. The Dowager's words sounded like a warning.

Mother cast her a puzzled look, but if she searched for answers, Isabella wouldn't know what to say.

Helen returned to the drawing room with red cheeks and lips pressed together. Her shoulders were shaking. She hadn't gone for more than three minutes, but her composure had changed.

"How's His Grace?" Mother asked.

"Recovering." Helen bowed her head to Patrick without looking at him. "We should leave and let the duke rest."

Rogers entered the room and cleared his throat, addressing Patrick. "My lord, Lord McFall is here."

"Again?" Patrick's voice rose, but he composed himself. "Apologies, ladies."

After a quick round of polite goodbyes, Isabella left the room confused.

Lord McFall stood in a corner of the entry hall as pale and shaken as Patrick. The tension between him and Patrick was palpable. She couldn't hear their conversation as the footman escorted them out.

"What happened with the duke?" she asked once in the carriage with Helen and Mother.

"It was awful. I shouldn't have disturbed him." Helen dabbed her forehead with a handkerchief. "His face is completely bandaged, he can barely talk, and he's weak. I fear he might die."

Isabella's chest clenched for Anthony. The pain must be unbearable.

"Why is his face bandaged? Where was he shot?"

"Somewhere in the face." Helen twisted the handkerchief. "The infection is the main problem, and I didn't understand if it's completely under control now. Our marriage is unsure. Oh, Mother. All our plans. And if he was shot in the face, he'll look grotesque."

"Helen!" Isabella used a commanding tone she didn't know she could produce. "How can you be so selfish? The duke nearly died, and he must be suffering a great deal, but you worry about your wedding plans and how he would look."

Helen lowered her gaze, her cheeks reddening. "I care about him. I do, but I was looking forward to announcing my wedding, to starting my new life with him. And then the incident happened. And yes, I'm worried about his looks. There's nothing wrong with that. You know how cruel people can be. He'll be ridiculed by everyone. Gossip will spread. Life with him will be brutal."

"You shouldn't worry about his looks. For heaven's sake, he might die."

Anger flamed red in Helen's cheeks. "You don't have to remind me of that. I'm just saying that his face might be ruined forever."

"Girls," Mother said. "Enough. Nothing is certain yet, and nothing has been decided. For now, we must show our support and loyalty to the duke. Helen, you ought to remember we're talking about one of the most powerful families in the kingdom.

The Dowager is a personal friend of the queen. No matter what disfigurement the duke will endure, if any, his position won't be questioned, and rumours come and go. There's little we can do about them."

"You're right, Mother," Helen said. "Although I'm afraid he's going to be shunned by everyone. It won't matter how close to the queen his family is."

"You'll be by his side," Mother insisted, "as a devout wife would do. No one will take away his power and money."

Isabella had to trap her bottom lip between her teeth not to speak again. She wasn't as eager as Helen was to marry a duke, but reducing Anthony only to his money and power was cruel. He was kind and so very lonely she was worried the incident would demoralise him further.

Not to mention the small detail that Anthony didn't want to marry Helen.

～

ANTHONY HAD to force himself not to scratch his face raw.

The constant itching was only a fraction of the general discomfort he'd experienced in the past weeks. The pain came and went in merciless waves with a fever that left him shaking and sweating. When he didn't feel pain and the fever didn't plague him, he was confused and nauseous thanks to the laudanum.

His personal journal pages had been empty for weeks on end, so weak he'd been unable to write. He was alive, but he wasn't sure if that was a blessing or a curse. He'd barely found a moment of joy in his life before it was snatched from him.

Patrick entered the bedroom silently after Helen had left. The beam of light hurt his working eye. Seeing Isabella would have been better, but on second thought, Anthony preferred not to be seen like that by her.

"Lord McFall is here. Do you want to see him?" Patrick asked.

Since after the incident, Patrick insisted on fussing around Anthony.

"Hell, yes. I can't keep sending him away." His voice sounded raspy to his own ears.

McFall's confident stride faltered when he saw Anthony. Not that there was much to see. His face was almost entirely covered by the bandages.

Patrick lowered his gaze when McFall entered.

"Gloucester." McFall bowed his head. "I came here to apologise."

He flexed open his fingers not to touch his face. "The incident wasn't your fault, but I did ask you many times to renounce the duel. I told you a duel was ridiculous." The words came out slowly, but the physician had told him to speak anyway to keep his facial muscles active. Or what was left of them.

"I haven't forgiven your brother," McFall said, "but I'll make amends to you."

"Just promise me you won't hurt Patrick, and we're even."

McFall took a long pause. "I promise."

Anthony stretched out an arm from the armchair to shake the captain's hand.

"There's more." McFall stared at him straight into his eye. "I happen to know about your dispute with an Austrian count, von Gruner. I would like to offer my help."

"Yes?"

"Von Gruner and I aren't close friends, but I saved his son's life years ago, and he's always told me he's indebted to me. I took the liberty to enquire with him about Maiden Hill, and under my solicitation, he agreed to start a negotiation with you. He will no longer ignore your letters."

Anthony would grin if he could. "That means a lot to my family and me."

McFall bowed his head. "You should receive a letter from von Gruner soon, but I can already tell you von Gruner will invite you to Vienna for a meeting. He won't travel here due to health problems."

Well, Anthony had health problems, too.

"Also, if I may," McFall continued, "his daughter, Sophia, has a great influence on him. She might be a more sympathetic ear to your predicament. I reckon if she agrees to return Maiden Hill to you, her father will follow suit."

"Thank you, McFall." Patrick offered his hand to the captain.

McFall shook Patrick's hand without enthusiasm.

Anthony exhaled when McFall left. "Good news." Although it didn't feel as such.

"McFall did us a great service."

"He did." He exhaled and closed his uncovered eye for a moment. "Did Isabella come?"

"She was with Helen and her mother," Patrick said. "Helen volunteered to see you, but if you want to see Isabella, I'll let her see you next time. I didn't know you wanted to see Isabella."

"I don't. It doesn't matter." He had to be careful to move his lips as little as possible when he talked, because, while his facial muscles needed exercise, they would burn with pain, and the stitches would bleed again if stimulated too much.

"Listen." Patrick took a step closer. He seemed aged ten years in the past weeks. "Lady Montrose invited me for a walk tomorrow. I won't be gone for more than an hour. But if you don't want me to go, I'll stay here."

"Go. I don't want you to stay here for me." He reclined his head on the back of the armchair.

"You took a bullet for me."

"You would do the same for me. Stop feeling guilty. Jumping on you was my choice."

"But I'm the reason you got shot." Patrick sucked in a deep breath. "It's my fault."

"Shut it. Your staying here instead of taking a walk isn't going to change anything. And I'm not alone anyway."

"I promise I'll change." Patrick nodded. "I'll do my best to be better."

"Take a walk. Leave this room for a while. And stop worrying about me."

Patrick scrubbed the back of his neck.

Anthony hated snapping at him, but for crying out loud, Patrick didn't need to keep apologising. "What do you want?"

"Do you mean to marry Helen?"

Right now, Anthony didn't want to marry anyone. Helen's horrified face and palpable disgust at his condition had subdued his nuptial enthusiasm, and the pain left him with only a few moments of lucid thoughts.

"No," he said, thinking of Isabella. "Sod the marriage."

And he meant it.

fifteen

The sense of guilt never really left Isabella after the visit to Anthony, but promenading in the park with Patrick lightened her chest and chased away the darkness.

Patrick's impeccable dark coat enhanced the brightness of his golden hair and his straight shoulders but also his pallor. Compared to his brother, he was slender and elegant although his gaunt cheeks worried her.

Mother and Helen walked next to her, but Helen hadn't stopped looking worried since yesterday. The visit to Anthony had shaken her deeply. Likely, she was thinking about her future as a shunned duchess next to a probably disfigured husband. Not quite the fairy tale she'd dreamt of.

"The rioters of the West End Riots damaged Hyde Park as well," Patrick said, pointing at a broken wooden bench. "How shameful. They destroyed the city, and for what? The Tories want to tax importations and facilitate exportation. The socialists think this practice will ruin the country and cause the rise of unemployment."

"And who's right in your opinion?" Isabella asked.

He flashed a crooked smile. "You're asking the wrong brother.

It's enough that I know this much about politics. I swear nothing is more boring than laws and bills. Thank goodness, my brother has to deal with that."

"But you help your brother with his work, don't you?" Isabella asked. "Especially now."

"Of course. Anthony needs me. It's usually the other way around." His tone became serious. "He's my elder brother. He's always protected me. When I was a boy, I used to play cricket in the big dining room in winter. Mother hated that I played inside. More than once, she forbade me to do it. I didn't listen. So one day, I broke her favourite mirror. Anthony took the blame."

"Why?"

"I'd received many warnings, and destroying the mirror would have been the last straw. Mother would have punished me severely had she known I was to blame. He had never done anything to anger my parents, so he took the responsibility for the damage." He drew his eyebrows together. "I should have told the truth."

"How does His Grace feel?" Helen asked. "I mean, is he in good spirits despite everything, or is he distraught?"

Patrick took his time to answer. "He's strong. He isn't complaining or showing us how much he's suffering. But he's changed his mind about a few projects he wanted to undertake in the future."

By the manner in which he lowered his voice and slanted a glance at them, Isabella suspected the projects he mentioned were of the bridal nature.

"When is the duke ready to resume his normal life?" Helen asked.

Patrick hesitated before answering again. He'd always been chatty and quick to talk. His hesitation was likely due to the fact he wasn't at liberty to answer freely.

"I don't know. But it'll take weeks, perhaps months, before he'll resume his normal life."

Only sorrow for Anthony overwhelmed Isabella. He didn't

strike her as a cheerful man who enjoyed people's company as Patrick did, and the incident must have demoralised him further.

"I'll be happy to visit him if he likes some company," she said.

"Absolutely," Helen chimed in. "We'll be delighted."

Patrick's smile held only sadness. "When he's ready, I'm sure he'll want to see you."

Mother was flustered. "I hope we have the chance to see His Grace soon. My husband and I are leaving for Boston, heaven help me."

"Boston? Are you really?" he asked.

Mother looked resigned. "My husband's brother lives in Boston, and they do business together. If I think of all the coffee I'll have to smell...We'll be away for nearly a year."

Patrick's face remained deadpan. "I'm sure Anthony will be fully recovered by the time you return."

ANTHONY FORCED himself not to grimace when the physician removed the bandages from around his head.

Eight weeks had passed since the incident. Weeks he'd spent at home, never setting foot outside. Weeks of medications, high fever, nausea, and few visits.

While he looked forward to getting rid of the bandages, he couldn't deny being worried about his looks. He'd never cared much about his face, but if the pain he'd experienced matched the degree of damage, he would look like a monster.

"We're almost done, Your Grace." The physician gently peeled the last layer of gauze and bandage.

The air on his face was nothing new. The physician had changed the bandages regularly, and many times, Anthony had been half unconscious. But it was the first time the bandages wouldn't be applied again.

"Your left eye might hurt for a while," the physician said.

Anthony doubted he would notice any difference. Pain had been his faithful companion for weeks on end.

He blinked. The physician had drawn the curtains shut and lit only a few candles to give Anthony's left eye the time to adjust. For a moment, he couldn't see anything from his left eye aside from a blurred black halo. The bad left sight affected even his right side. Slowly, he made out the shape of his bed, armoire, and the concerned face of the physician.

"How do you feel, Your Grace?"

Odd. Sore. Angry. And as if his face were bloated by the stings of a thousand wasps.

"I can see."

"Excellent. I'll pull the curtains a little."

The spring sunlight cut through the darkness, catching his bad eye. He lowered his gaze as a headache started to pound. The physician opened the curtains another inch until they were fully open.

"Is it bearable?"

"Yes." He stood up and walked towards the wall mirror, but the doctor stopped him.

"Your Grace," he warned.

Anthony cleared his throat. "I want to look at myself in a mirror."

The physician collected the bandages, focusing on his leather bag. "I have to discourage you from doing that, sir. Let a few days pass. The flesh will be less swollen and red, and you'll have a clearer idea of the...the..."

"Damage? Bad news doesn't improve by ignoring it."

"Of course, sir." The physician kept arranging his bottles and tools.

Anthony couldn't deny the rising anxiety in his chest as he approached the mirror. There was a reason why he'd asked Patrick and Grandmama to leave him alone with the doctor that day. He wanted to be the first to see his face after the physician.

Once he stood in front of the mirror, he raised his gaze. He suppressed a gasp. He should have asked to be alone. Although there was no escaping the horror in front of him.

His right side was normal, a bit pale, if anything. His left eye was whole, which was good, he guessed. But the flesh around it was bumped and torn, forming a sort of grotesque, blossoming flower across his cheek.

The point where the bullet had shredded his face was the centre of the flower with the petals stretching in every direction towards his nose, chin, and temple. The bullet hadn't gone through his face, but the infection had done most of the damage, starting the tissue inflammation and causing further scarring.

"It'll get better, Your Grace," the physician said. "The swelling will settle, and…well, the scars will stay, of course, but they won't be so evident once the flesh returns to normal."

He nodded, not trusting himself to speak. Besides, he didn't believe a word the physician had said.

The doctor put a hand on the doorknob. "Would you like to see your brother and grandmother?"

Another nod.

The physician slid out of the room quietly. The moment he shut the door, Anthony released a long breath.

Bloody hell. He looked like a monster who had been mauled by another monster. He tentatively touched the mangled flesh. It wasn't as sore as he expected, but it felt rough and uneven to the touch and odd as if it didn't belong to him.

The door inched inwards, and Grandmama and Patrick entered.

"How are you, darling?" Grandmama fell silent when he turned around. Tears welled up in her eyes as she clamped a trembling hand over her mouth. "Heavens," she said among sobs.

Patrick stood frozen, his expression horrified. "Hell."

"It is what it is," Anthony said. "There's little I can do."

He barely finished the sentence before Grandmama hugged him. She was as tall as he was and managed to make him feel small and little. The hug broke something in his chest, and he swallowed past the lump in his throat.

Patrick joined them, hugging them both.

He took deep breaths, suddenly tired of feeling pain and being worried, of pretending he didn't care about his face.

"Dear, dear boy." Grandmama cupped Anthony's good cheek. "We'll go through this together as we always do. The Beauforts of Gloucester have never cowered in front of a challenge. We won't start now."

"You'll grow a beard," Patrick said. "And your hair as well. A long beard and long hair."

Anthony smiled, but Grandmama glared at Patrick.

"How dare you make a joke?" she said.

Patrick shrugged. "I'm not joking."

"Well, I disagree with the beard." Grandmama tilted her chin up. "Anthony shouldn't be ashamed. If anyone dares make a joke about you or disparage you, they'll have to deal with me. You have nothing to hide."

"Yes, we do," Patrick said. "We didn't reveal the real reason why Anthony was shot. Our silence coupled with that scar will have us drowned in rumours. People will make up their own stories about how Anthony got that scar. I'm ready to take the blame, as it should be."

Grandmama stroked Anthony's hair and took Patrick's hand. "No one will hurt my dear grandchildren. Let the people talk. I don't care what they say. Once Anthony is married and with an heir, the gossip will stop. Showing everyone that a lady married him is better than growing a beard."

Anthony stepped back from her touch. Marriage. Just the thought of showing Isabella his face made him queasy. He had to accept his new face first before showing it to anyone else, and Isabella wasn't the first one.

"I don't want to think about marrying anyone now. I can

barely tolerate staring at my own reflection. I can't expect a bride to be happy to see my face every day."

"That's nonsense." Grandmama regained her stern tone. "Your bride will be sensible enough to understand who you are without judging you for your scar. You've spent too much time cooped up in this room. Your spirits are low. Once you start going out again, everything will be better."

"When I stare at myself without grimacing, I'll be ready for a bride. Or for going out." He was in no hurry. "I want Patrick to go to von Gruner's meeting," he said in the spur of the moment.

Grandmama and Patrick showed matching shocked faces.

"Me?" Patrick pointed a finger at himself.

"Anthony, you must go." Grandmama didn't show mercy.

"Von Gruner invited me to his house in Cabo Verde. Needless to say, I'm not able to undertake such a long journey. At the same time, if I refuse the meeting and ask for more time, he won't send a second invitation, no matter how many times I tell him I have health problems. We have this one opportunity, and I can't go."

He expected Patrick to complain. Instead, Patrick nodded.

"If you trust me, I'll go."

"Brooks and my solicitor will come with you and instruct you on what to say. You have a few weeks before leaving."

"And on what not to say." Scepticism crept into Grandmama's voice. "Patrick isn't ready."

"I'm not ready either. The infection might start again if I travel to Cabo Verde."

She wasn't finished. "Then you must show yourself to the House of Lords."

"No."

"It's your duty. You've been away for weeks, and you don't have any physical impediments to prevent you from going."

"I would say a face like mine is a physical impediment."

Grandmama opened her mouth, but Patrick cut her off.

"Grandmama," Patrick said. "Have some mercy."

"Mercy?" Her voice sounded like steel. "Our enemies will be at our throats the moment they believe the duke isn't fit to do his duty. Anthony, you must go."

"No."

"You must leave the house! I understand a trip to Cabo Verde is too much, but you can't stay in your room forever."

"I will not show my face to the House of Lords until I'm ready."

"Anthony—"

"No. I want to be alone. Out!" It was the first time he'd raised his voice with Grandmama.

The shock froze her, and she was about to say something, but Patrick led her out of the room.

Breathing hard, he turned his back to the mirror.

For once, he didn't want to do his duty. For once, he wished the darkness would take him again.

sixteen

Weeks had passed since Isabella's visit to Gloucester House, and she hadn't seen Anthony once.

Everyone said he had recovered well, but for some reason, he didn't receive anyone or go out. Between his work and family matters, he had to be busy. After her first visit with Mother and Helen, she'd tried to see him a few times with no success, and while she didn't expect special treatment from him, she couldn't deny her disappointment at the constant rejections of her visits or lack of answers to her letters. Helen had tried to meet him as well and failed.

The infection was gone, he wasn't risking his life, and yet she had no idea what he was doing and why he didn't want to see her.

Instead, she had spent a lot of time with Patrick. Long promenades and rides in the park had become their routine. Not a word about a possible marriage had ever been mentioned, and she had no clue as to what Anthony was thinking. Also, because Patrick never, ever answered any questions regarding his brother.

In the hallway in her home, she tied the bonnet under her chin, ready to meet Patrick for an afternoon tea.

Lawson helped her don her capelet. "Another meeting with Lord Patrick."

"It means nothing. He needs a distraction from his family's trouble, and we're good friends." Although she enjoyed the easy harmony between them and his humour.

Patrick was an uncomplicated, charming gentleman. A bit flippant, but his company didn't carry the burden of being with a powerful duke.

"Are you going to see Patrick?" Helen asked, going down the stairs.

"We'll have tea together in his house. Lawson will come with me. Do you need her?"

"No. I'm going with Mother to Lady Violet's house. She's going to introduce me to the Earl of Westbury." Helen pinched her cheeks in front of the mirror until they were rosy.

Isabella stopped adjusting her hat. "You're searching for a new suitor."

Oddly enough, a tiny flare of relief warmed her chest. Helen was moving forwards. She wasn't interested in the duke anymore. And in Helen's defence, Anthony had vanished from their social life without a word.

Oh, well. He had his reason, but he didn't want to marry Helen. Right now, he likely didn't want to marry anyone.

"Mother insists," Helen said. "The duke has become a recluse. Mother and Father are going to leave for Boston, and she can't negotiate my marriage with the duke unless he comes out of his house and decides to talk to me again."

"Let's go, darling." Mother hurried to the entry hall in her best coat. "We can't stay for too long. I want you to have an extra piano lesson this week."

Helen's facial muscles tightened, and for a moment, Isabella believed her sister was going to talk back. "Another lesson, Mother? I spent more time at the piano than ever."

Mother pointed a finger at her. "You played awfully the other day at Lady Theodora's house. Everyone noticed that."

Helen pressed her lips together. "I told you I didn't feel well, but you insisted on making me play."

"You must learn to play well even when you're sick. I'll see you later, Isabella," Mother said as the footman opened the door for Mother. "The earl is such a handsome gentleman. Let's hope you don't ruin everything as you did..."

The rest of Mother's words was cut off when the footman shut the door.

Helen had a point. Anthony didn't even reply to her letters. Not that Isabella could blame him, and Helen's urgency to get married was nothing new.

Lawson sat in front of her in the carriage. "You would prefer your mother's company, I guess."

"Tosh. Helen's meeting is the priority, and I love your company."

Lawson had been more present in her life than Mother. But Mother being with Helen meant they didn't want to invest more time in the duke. The marriage market worked as any other market from that point of view. Once a product disappeared from the shelf, the customers searched for a replacement.

There was something cynical about that, though.

Patrick beamed when he saw her, his handsome face brightening. She smiled back, taking his arm to enter the sitting room flooded with sunlight.

She inhaled. The buttery scent of the biscuits and pastries teased her senses. Lawson took a chair next to the window.

"How's Anthony?" Isabella asked. She always did, even though the answers were clipped at best, and vague at worst.

"The same." Which didn't mean much to her because she wasn't sure what ailed him now.

"Do you think I could see him?" Another usual question.

Patrick gave her an apologetic look. "I'm sorry." Another usual answer. "I tell him you wish to see him every time, but he's...it's a difficult moment."

"Don't worry. I understand." Although she didn't.

"I'll pass your greetings to him. But you know how he is."

"How?"

Patrick cleared his throat. "Very peaky when it comes to choosing company."

Was *she* the problem? Had Anthony realised she was nothing special? She swallowed the bitter taste in her mouth. He'd sounded honest when he'd told her he didn't mind her spontaneity. But the incident might have changed his perspective.

She added a few dollops of cream to her tea. "You seem preoccupied as well."

Patrick put down his cup. "I'm getting ready for a long journey."

Her heart sank a little. "Where to?"

"To visit von Gruner. The old ass has finally agreed to negotiate with us, but since he has no intention of making the process easy, he invited me to his house in Cabo Verde of all places, in the middle of the ocean. It'll take weeks of sailing to get there."

"Will you be gone for a long time?"

"Alas, months. On my way back to England, I have to stop on the Continent as well to settle other businesses for Anthony." He stared at his cup of tea as if wanting to divine his fortune. "I have to act on his behalf." He chuckled bitterly. "I'm far from ready, but I don't have a choice."

She touched his hand. "I'm going to miss you."

"So am I. That's why I have a surprise for you." He rose and held the door open for her.

She followed him as Lawson walked behind her. Along the corridor, he took Isabella's hand, and her heartbeat quickened.

Lawson cleared her throat, but Patrick didn't release Isabella's hand.

"I meant to show you earlier, but with everything that

happened, I forgot." He led her through a series of corridors to a set of glass double doors that revealed a view of luxurious green plants.

"What do you think?" He showed her to the conservatory.

"Heavens." She stepped into the glasshouse that was a riot of colours and delicious scents. There were orchids, peonies, and different varieties of lilies. Calling it a conservatory wasn't correct. It was a botanical park under a glass dome, three times bigger than her own. The plants needed more care though. Some brown leaves needed to be removed, and a few stems needed to be pruned. "It's lovely. I could spend hours here, tending to all these plants."

Lawson didn't show any enthusiasm.

Patrick kept holding her hand. "I come here only to...no, I never come here. It's wet and hot, but you're welcome to spend as much time as you want here."

She touched the red petals of a hibiscus. "Wonderful."

"Anthony comes here to read." He pointed to a Chesterfield sofa tucked in a sunny corner under a cascade of purple irises.

She sighed at the beauty of the flowers. "I couldn't picture a better spot."

"Neither could I." Anthony's deep voice came from the door.

Everyone turned towards him in a moment of silent shock. She wasn't ready for the surprise.

"Anthony." Patrick straightened like a soldier in front of his superior.

Lawson dropped a deep curtsy, keeping her gaze on the floor.

Anthony didn't step further into the glasshouse but stayed in the shadows. His auburn hair almost entirely covered the left side of his face, but a small patch of uneven skin could be seen.

"Your Grace." Isabella curtsied. "Have we taken your spot?"

"Yes." He put the book he was holding on a table.

"How are you?" she said, wishing she could hug him.

"Almost in one piece." He didn't smile, and she wasn't sure what to make of his comment.

She searched the shadows but couldn't see anything else of his face. "We were worried about you, sir."

He didn't answer, and an awkward silence dropped. The sound of the water dripping from either a fountain or an irrigation system filled the quiet conservatory.

"I'm so sorry," she said, both because she didn't bear the silence any longer and because she needed to apologise to him for her general sense of guilt.

"Don't be sorry for me," he hissed with venom. His long curls parted an inch, revealing a portion of swollen skin of his left cheek.

He turned around, but the Dowager came into view, and a new round of curtsies started.

The Dowager exchanged a harsh glance with Anthony. They stared at each other with such intensity she feared they might start shouting at each other.

"Your Grace." Isabella curtsied again.

The Dowager stopped staring at her grandson. "The situation isn't as dramatic as Anthony has let you think. We're eager to celebrate Anthony's complete recovery and Patrick's imminent departure with a ball, an extraordinary event. I hope you and your family will be able to attend. I reckon your parents are going to leave for the Americas soon."

"Yes, madam." She felt as if she were a child again and her governess had asked her to list all the kings of England.

Anthony didn't speak, but even in the dimly lit spot where he stood, she could tell he was clenching his jaw.

A little frown appeared on Lawson's forehead. Isabella could almost hear the lady's maid's thoughts. Mother wouldn't be able to refuse the invitation, but at the same time, she wouldn't be pleased. Not when Mother was already making other plans for Helen.

Isabella forced a smile. "We'll be delighted."

Anthony left without saying a word.

The Dowager followed his retreat with palpable disappointment. "It's decided then." She too left with the same long strides as her grandson.

Patrick exhaled when they were alone. "I apologise for my brother's rudeness."

"Please don't. He has every right to be grumpy, and we intruded into his quiet place."

He angled towards the spot where Anthony had been. "Quiet is the last thing my brother needs."

~

"ANTHONY!" Grandmama's voice echoed in the corridor as Anthony walked away from the conservatory.

Seeing Isabella again without warning had been a punch to his stomach. She was radiant and beautiful, full of life and laughter. Her obsidian eyes sparkled. Her porcelain skin was unblemished. He had never noticed how smooth her skin looked until now. How petty of him.

"Don't you walk away from me." Grandmama overtook him and blocked his path. She was one fast old woman; he would give her that. She pointed a finger at him. "There was no need to be rude to Isabella."

"You don't even like her."

"A further reason to be polite."

"There was no need to ambush me like that! I don't want a ball to celebrate my recovery." He gnashed his teeth, forcing his voice down.

"We'll give a ball and show everyone that the Duke of Gloucester is well and as powerful as ever. Rumours are circulating about your recovery. People are starting to question why you are hiding. We Beauforts don't hide from anyone."

"To hell with the House of Beaufort." He sidestepped her.

There was no point in giving a ball or seeing Isabella again. He couldn't ask her to be his wife. She shouldn't be tied to a circus freak of a duke. Only his title was left of him, a bloody cursed gift he'd never wanted.

"Don't you dare!" She gripped at his arm with surprising strength. "I've been patient with you. I gave you time to recover. But you've been hiding like a coward in your room, doing nothing but sulking and being horrible to us who love you. Enough!"

"I've been sick and weak in case you haven't noticed."

Her voice shook. "You must do this, Anthony. I'm not saying that because of our family's prestige. I'm saying it because I love you. And I'm ready to force you to do something you don't want to for your own sake. I lost my son. I won't lose my grandson, too." She strode past him, almost bumping her shoulder into his.

Her quick footfalls died down along the corridor behind him.

He closed his eyes and rubbed his face, touching the uneven, scarred skin.

He'd gone to war and returned home without a scratch, only to get scarred during a duel that hadn't involved him. Life didn't lack irony.

But he'd be damned if he put himself on display in a stupid ball. Besides, his body still needed to recover from the fever and the infection.

"Anthony." Quick and light footsteps came from behind him.

Isabella. He didn't dare to turn around and face her but remained still.

Her footsteps slowed down. Then a delicate hand touched his arm. "How are you?"

Her light touch sent a shot of sensations through him. His heart gave a kick, and tingles danced on his suddenly awakened skin.

"I was worried about you. You disappeared. Why?" She gently tightened her grip on his arm.

If she kept touching him, his darkness would infect her, and it was horrible of him to wish she would stay next to him now. A flare of anger heated his chest. Not at Isabella. But it was cruel he'd found her beautiful light, only to realise he could never have her.

He turned towards her, letting the sunlight show all his ugliness. "This is why."

Her lips parted, but she didn't release his arm. "Good Lord, Anthony."

He faced the corridor again, unable to endure her shock. "Leave, Isabella." He slid his arm out of her grip and walked away, but she stubbornly followed him in a disturbing repeat of the scene with Grandmama.

Isabella didn't block his path, though. "You didn't answer my letters."

"I know."

He'd tried many times to answer her letters, but the courage to send them had deserted him. Grandmama was right.

"Please." She took his hand, and again the whiplash of the emotions made him catch his breath. Her soft, silky fingers trailed over his knuckles, leaving him defenceless against her sweetness. And it wasn't a nice feeling.

He swallowed past the lump in his throat. "What?"

She seemed at a loss for words. "Promise me you'll give that ball. Promise me you'll be there."

She had no idea what she was asking of him.

"I can't. Look at me."

"I am looking at you. You haven't changed. You're the same man who helped me free a little animal in the forest and who showed me the secrets of an ancient castle."

Those memories were so happy and precious that he didn't wish to remember them and risk poisoning them with his foul mood.

"Promise me you'll give that ball," she said.

"I have changed."

Withdrawing his hand from hers caused him physical pain, but he couldn't lie and make a promise he could not keep.

seventeen

Isabella spurred her mare onwards. The warm morning and the nearly empty Hyde Park were the perfect combination for a ride with Patrick and for forgetting the pain of seeing Anthony.

After her brief but shocking encounter with him, she hadn't seen him again. But his pain had left a deep mark in her heart. She'd sent him another message to tell him that, if he needed a friend, she would be there for him. Surprisingly, he'd answered with a simple 'thank you,' which was promising. She would try again.

He was hurting, and maybe he'd changed his mind about her, but she didn't care; it hurt, but she wanted to be his friend anyway, if he let her.

Behind her, Patrick was in full pursuit, low on his stallion, but if there was one thing her mare could do, it was fly. Her mare raced along the track, lifting drops of mud with her hooves.

Morning dew glistened on the tree leaves, and a light mist lingered inches above the ground. She loved riding early because the park was almost empty and she could spur Marigold.

She reined in when she arrived at the receiving house next to the Serpentine. "First!" She raised a fist, panting heavily.

Patrick stopped next to her a few moments later. "Not fair."

"What's not fair?"

"You're lighter than I am." He wheezed. "Of course you're faster."

"Lord Patrick, you're not a good sport. Marigold and I won fair and square. If anything, your stallion tends to get distracted quite easily. He stopped to look at that other stallion across the field." She jumped off the saddle to give Marigold time to rest.

He dismounted as well. "I demand compensation."

"I don't have any money, and we didn't agree on a wager." She stepped onto the porch of the receiving house.

"Money is so vulgar."

"Only those with money say that."

He shook his head, inching closer. His golden curls framed his sapphire eyes. "What about a kiss?"

Her face flamed. Her whole body did. "A kiss?"

"For having humiliated my Triton and me without mercy. And he isn't easily distracted. Triton is the most focused—" He didn't finish the sentence as Triton gave a yank at the reins still in Patrick's hand and shoved him a few feet away.

The stallion lowered his proud head to sniff at a tuft of grass.

"Bloody hell." Patrick released the reins.

"What were you saying?"

"That I want a kiss." He stepped closer, and she caught a whiff of his fresh cologne.

She rose on her tiptoes and gave him a chaste peck on the cheek. "Done."

He scoffed. "That's not a kiss. Triton gives me kisses like that. I want something proper."

"There's nothing proper about a kiss." Her lips tingled at the thought of kissing him. "And I've already given you a kiss."

"Allow me to return it to you, then, because I'm not satisfied."

He took her hand and led her to a quiet, secluded spot from where the path wasn't visible. He cupped her face gently, rubbing her cheek with his thumb. "This is a kiss."

He kissed her with determination but gently. Every sensation other than the feeling of Patrick's soft lips on hers vanished. She no longer felt the warmth of the sun, the breeze on her skin, or the fatigue from the ride. Her own heartbeat seemed to pulse on her lips.

His tongue demanded entrance, and she parted her lips slowly. When she opened her mouth for him, he kissed her deeply, starting a warm tingling throughout her body.

Her first kiss. Her head spun with the onslaught of sensations.

"That's a kiss," he whispered against her lips. "And I shall consider myself compensated."

"Good gracious." Her knees threatened to buckle.

He stepped back from her when the sound of other riders came from the distance. "Have I shocked you?"

Yes. "No."

"May I kiss you again in the future?"

Cheeky sod. "Yes."

"Do more than kissing?" He arched his brow in a mischievous expression that had her heart racing in a moment.

Her body warmed all over again. "I'm not sure."

He gently took her face when the riders were gone although the receiving house hid them. "I won't do anything you don't want me to, but I must be honest. I like you a lot. You're charming, and I would like to kiss you again."

"Do you mean you want to court me?" She hated that her voice sounded small, but his proposal took her off guard. Two marriage proposals in a year! How odd.

He released her face and stepped back from her. "No, darling. I'm not going to marry you. If that bothers you, then we'll just be friends. Your choice."

"Oh." Was she disappointed? No.

She felt like an idiot for having been naïve enough to assume he wanted to marry her after just one kiss. But aside from that, his honesty lifted a weight off her shoulders. Another marriage proposal would have been too much since she'd had no idea what to do about the first one.

What he proposed was exciting, wrong, and heady. A secret affair with a handsome gentleman without the burden of the '*till death do us part*' commitment. A gentleman she trusted and who was her friend.

"Rest assured," he said. "I will not speak of our agreement to anyone. I swear it. Your reputation will remain unblemished. My rules are simple—no courting, no wedding, no gossip, only pleasure."

It should be a simple choice. She should say no, thank you, as Mother would want her to. But...all the wonderful sensations the kiss had triggered were still dancing along her body, and she liked them.

She liked how they made her feel—beautiful, desirable, and special. Was she in love with Patrick? No, she didn't think so because the thought of marrying him and spending the rest of her life with him concerned her. She wouldn't be happy with him as her husband. But she couldn't deny the attraction or the curiosity of exploring, feeling, and experiencing things new to her.

Other women her age were already experienced, having kissed or spent intimate hours with a gentleman, and she was curious. Those girls talked about passion and pleasure as the best things in life. Could it be true? Judging by how her body hummed after the kiss, yes, it could.

After a kiss on her cheek, he guided her out of the receiving house. She was floating on a cloud of pleasant opportunities.

"Think about it." He helped her onto her horse, staring at her with a hunger she'd never seen in the eyes of a man, and her pulse spiked. "I'll certainly think about it." He pulled down her glove and kissed her inner wrist right over the swift kick of a vein.

She gasped both at the audacity and the shot of pleasure his soft lips started.

She would think about his proposal, too.

Hours later, she had thought about it so much she was restless.

After their ride, she couldn't find peace in the glasshouse. Pruning and nurturing her plants did nothing to calm the rising emotion in her. A book was needed. A long, solitary activity to think.

Half an hour later, she was wandering the house with Machiavelli's *The Prince* in her hands. She'd chosen a book that didn't involve any romantic scenes, poetry, or love stories. Just a man obsessed with power and how to crush his enemies.

Her reading choice didn't help. Patrick's kiss and words were the only things she could think about. Why couldn't she enjoy herself? Gentlemen did it all the time, and no one cared. Why was she expected to enjoy herself only with her husband?

She almost bumped into Lawson hurrying along the corridor.

"...will fetch something for you," Lawson said over her shoulder before coming to a halt in front of her.

"Is something the matter?" She hadn't realised she was at the back entrance.

Lawson seemed about to cry. "You needn't worry."

"Whom were you talking to?" She craned her neck to see a young woman in tattered clothes standing at the back entrance.

Her breath caught. The gaunt, pale woman couldn't be Lady Mary, the daughter of the Earl of Teck.

"I'll be right back," Lawson said before heading upstairs.

Isabella walked over to the woman. "Mary. Is it you?"

The woman lowered her gaze. "I am she, my lady."

"You can call me Isabella, as always."

"It wouldn't be appropriate." Mary shook her head. "You'd better not let anyone see us together."

Isabella rubbed her forehead. "What happened to you? I

haven't seen you. You disappeared. Your parents said you'd left London."

"I had a child." Mary swallowed hard. "My parents asked me to leave their house, and I've been on my own ever since. They...don't want to see me again, and the father of my child refuses to see me as well."

"Oh." She didn't ask for further questions. Mary wasn't married. Now her absence and tattered clothes made sense. "I'm sorry."

"I'm not. About being a mother, I mean." Mary showed her the basket filled with clothes. "I work as a seamstress now. Thank goodness I learnt how to sew when I lived with my parents."

Isabella put a hand on her chest. She wasn't as brave and skilled as Mary. In her place, she would be dead in a week. "And your child?"

"Struggling. He's only a baby, and he's already learning how difficult life is. That's why I asked Lawson..." Mary cleared her throat. "I need help."

Lawson rushed back to the hallways. "Here." She handed a small pouch to Mary. "I hope it helps."

Mary accepted the pouch with a trembling hand. "Thank you," she whispered. "I'll repay you. I'm sorry to have come here. If I weren't desperate..."

"Do not worry, my lady," Lawson said.

A sickening lump crawled in Isabella's throat. "Wait. Please."

"There's no need." Mary flushed red.

"Yes, there is. Please wait."

She went upstairs and emptied her purse. Ten pounds, but she could do more. She stuffed a warm scarf, coat, and hat from her armoire in a satchel and added a gold brooch her maid hadn't put away yet.

She returned to the rear entrance, hoping not to meet Mother along the way. Mary was about to leave.

"Mary, wait. Take it."

Mary held the basket in front of her. "I can't."

"Yes, you can. And I'll give you more. I promise."

Mary didn't take the satchel. "If your parents know you helped me, they'll be displeased."

Not her father. "I take full responsibility for helping you, and if you need more, please come back."

Lawson gave Mary an encouraging nod. "We'll help you."

Mary accepted the bag, her eyes shining. "Thank you." She spun on her heels and left in a hurry.

Lawson shut the door. "You must be careful. Lady Mary isn't welcome in society, and being associated with her will cause you problems."

"Just because I helped her? I'm sure Father will agree with me." And she would prove that now.

Lady Mary had been the most popular débutante during the last Season. She'd collected a long queue of suitors, not only thanks to her beauty but also to her witty conversations. Everyone had loved her until she'd broken the rules.

She knocked on Father's study. "Father? May I?"

"Come in, darling."

She pushed the door, and Father opened his arms to welcome her.

"What is it? You seem upset." He patted her cheek. "Is it your mother again? She doesn't want you to spend too much time in the conservatory, does she?"

"No, it's about something else." She sat on the stuffed chair next to him.

He removed his glasses and set aside the papers he'd been working on. "Tell me everything."

"It's about Lady Mary, the daughter of the Earl of Teck."

Father stiffened.

"She disappeared from society. After her perfect Season and all the suitors interested in her, she just left. Well, it turned out, she was thrown out of her house."

"I know." He rubbed the bridge of his nose. "As a matter of fact, I'm aware of what happened to Mary."

She took his arm. "We can help her, can't we? She's in need, and her child is struggling."

"Darling." He exhaled. "What Mary did is unforgivable."

"Unforgivable?" She removed her hand. "She's a mother who needs help."

"Shush." He glanced at the door. "I don't want your mother to hear you. Mary wasn't careful. She thought only about her own enjoyment, and there are consequences for ladies who pursue pleasure. A child with no father, out of wedlock, when she wasn't even officially engaged."

"Does that matter in front of what she's facing?"

"It depends on the mistake." His tone was so firm and resolute her heart broke. "There's nothing we can do for her. Women like her, who give themselves before marriage, cause only trouble. She wasn't a common country girl. She was an earl's daughter and disgraced herself and her family."

"You agree with me that women should vote."

"What does the vote have to do with anything? Mary behaved like a reckless, ordinary girl. She should have known better." He put his glass back on. "Her reckless behaviour is an argument against the reliability of women and their judgement or their ability to vote."

"So one mistake, and she's shunned for life."

"Yes." The word was final, like the sound of a lid shutting on a coffin.

The pain his words caused shocked her into silence. She'd been so sure Father would have agreed with her.

She'd just learnt how truly naïve she was.

eighteen

By the time the ball to celebrate Anthony's recovery—a masquerade—arrived, Isabella had changed her mind about Patrick's proposal a dozen times.

He was charming, but the kiss in the park and his daring words had muddled her judgement. Using cold logic, she understood his proposal was madness.

Having a tumble with a gentleman just for the pleasure of it, without the prospect of a courtship, was against everything her mother had taught her. But exactly for that reason, a voice inside her head whispered, '*So what?*'

Why couldn't she have some fun?

Gentlemen waltzed their lives from one bed to another, having mistresses before and during their marriages, frequenting brothels, sometimes taking advantage of the maids and governesses, and having affairs with other married women. No one was in the least outraged by their behaviour.

Why couldn't a lady do the same?

Well, she didn't enjoy the idea of having tumbles with every man she met, but Patrick was a friend. She trusted him. He wouldn't blabber about her with his friends and ruin her.

Lady Mary's story had taught her to be more daring instead of more coy, especially after Father's cruel words. The way Mary was treated was unfair and brutal, and the more Isabella thought about her, the more she wanted to be a rebel and defy all the rules. Because if she cowered in front of the injustice, it would continue.

Besides, she had no suitors. Anthony had never mentioned his intention to pursue her ever again. The fact he'd agreed to the ball was encouraging for his health, but he wasn't interested in her anymore. Not his fault, but Patrick's proposal was too exciting. Patrick offered her the chance to be a true rebel. She needed only a bit of courage.

Armed with a new resolution, she adjusted her pink silk mask matching her gown. Helen wore a lovely blue gown with a blue mask that didn't hide her sorrow. With all the bright lights and the sparkling chandeliers, her sadness was on full display.

The ballroom in Gloucester House was like a giant diamond made of light and sweet music.

"Why are you so forlorn?" she asked Helen.

"I didn't want to come, but Mother insisted. She said I couldn't refuse. As usual."

"You should stand up for yourself more. If you don't want to do something, you ought to tell her."

Helen trapped her bottom lip between her teeth. "I don't have anything else aside from a good marriage. Nothing to look forward to. No other option."

"Poppycock. You're clever and educated. You can do whatever you want."

Helen didn't cheer up. "And to be honest, I'm upset with the duke. He didn't say a word about our engagement. He didn't send me any messages. He shut himself in his house and forgot about me. But I have to come to his house when he orders so."

"He was shot, for goodness' sake, and we were in touch with his family. His life changed completely." As his face.

Helen tilted her chin up. "I understand, but I had to move on and search for other opportunities although Mother said I failed."

Isabella was glad the mask hid her frustration. "You failed at what?"

"At marrying a duke."

"But it wasn't your fault."

Helen didn't have time to answer. The master of ceremonies beat his baton on the floor, attracting everyone's attention. The music stopped. "His Grace the Duke of Gloucester."

The chatter and laughter died down as Anthony entered, looking strong and healthy in an evening dress. His silk mask left only his lips visible, and his long auburn hair covered the sides of his face.

Not an inch of his scarred skin was in sight. If one didn't know Anthony had been shot in the face, it would be impossible to guess.

He greeted and bowed to his guests before heading to Isabella and Helen. The ladies talked behind their fans as he crossed the room.

She smiled, but her smile faltered when she thought about Patrick and their kiss, feeling vaguely guilty. If Patrick had talked to Anthony about it, she would burst into flames on the spot. Patrick had promised not to tell anyone, and she trusted him.

"Lady Helen, Lady Isabella." Anthony bowed.

"We're glad to see you well, Your Grace," Isabella said, as she and Helen both dipped into a curtsy."

"We're happy for your recovery." Helen said.

The dark mask made it hard to understand where he was looking, and his flat tone didn't offer any clue about his mood. "The past months have been very difficult. Forgive my absence."

"I told you not to apologise." She meant it as a joke, but it came out harsher than she thought. She was giving orders to a duke. "I'm sorry."

"Don't be," he said.

She had no idea if he meant what he'd said.

"Good evening, ladies." Patrick broke the moment. His mask had the shape of a cat's face and exalted his twinkling eyes. He flashed a cheeky smile and gave a pat on the shoulder to Anthony who didn't flinch. "Isabella, would you care for a dance?"

She turned towards Anthony, but his expression didn't offer anything.

"Has anyone else already invited you?" Patrick pointed at his brother.

Anthony clasped his hands behind his back. "No."

"Isabella?" Patrick asked.

"Of course." She offered her hand to Patrick, exchanging a glance with Anthony. "If you'll excuse me."

Isabella hesitated before following Patrick to the dance floor. He held her by the waist and launched enthusiastically into a fast-paced gallop, twirling her around with speed and energy. The room spun but in a good way. She laughed. The lights and the colours glimmered around her.

"You seem happy," she said.

"Very. Grandmama agreed to let us have gallops, polkas, and mazurkas tonight, and my departure for Cabo Verde has a date. Three weeks from now, I'll be sailing through the ocean. Then I'll be heading to France."

She struggled to contain her disappointment. "Did you set a return date?"

"Not yet. But if I fail, the trip will be quite short. Perhaps you can visit me when I'm in the Continent." He winked. "We have a lovely townhouse in Paris right in *Place de la Concorde*, and an estate in the Swiss Alps. You'd love it."

"Tempting."

When the gallop ended, he took her hand. "Did you promise the next dance to someone else?"

She glanced around. Anthony had vanished. Again. "No, I'm free. Do you want to dance the next one?"

He leant closer to whisper in her ear, "No. I want to slip out of the ballroom with you to show you something."

A little quiver of anticipation went through her as she nodded. He was a master at sneaking out of a crowded room, choosing a meandering path, leading her behind the Grecian columns lining the walls and through the darkest spots. She doubted anyone realised they were leaving. The Dowager stood on the other side of the ballroom. She was the only one not wearing a mask.

Isabella giggled once out of the ballroom. "Where are you taking me?"

He paused, smiling. "Interesting choice of words."

"You're a scoundrel."

"And a proud one at that." He went downstairs and along a dark corridor.

Her skin grew goosebumps in the cold air. "The conservatory?"

"Yes." He unlocked a door at the end of the hallway. "We have a new flower I want to show you."

He paused to give her a quick kiss on her lips. His warmth reached her body, and his heady scent teased her senses. When Patrick wasn't with her, she easily dismissed the heated sensations, the curiosity, and the anticipation of what might happen between them. But when he was close, his smiles and touches left her wanting more.

He led her through the aisles of the conservatory, past benches and large pots. "Look at this."

He stopped in front of large creamy white blooms.

He touched the petals. "They're called—"

"Moonflowers," she said with reverence. "They bloom at night." She edged closer to touch the spectacular flowers. "Stunning."

"Our gardeners work hard to ensure the moonflowers flourish."

"I would love to have them in my glasshouse."

"You can have some." He walked around the large plant, holding her hand. "Ask the gardener. And you can come here any time you want after I leave."

"I'm going to miss you. You're a good friend."

"And you're sweet and beautiful." His voice lowered as he removed her mask and then his.

He caressed her cheek gently, and she wilted under his touch. Before she knew it, they were kissing. Deep, desperate kisses that made her head dizzy and caused her heart to gallop. All that heat and pleasure gathered in her lower belly, driving her mad with a desire she didn't know she could produce.

She moaned when he slid his hands under her skirts and touched her. She had no idea his touch could be so good. All her body came alive with new sensations. Some of her friends had experienced tumbles and talked about the pleasure in wicked tones. Now she understood why so many people risked being ruined. And she wanted something exciting in her life.

He broke the kiss to search her face. "Do you want me to stop?"

"No."

"You know the rules."

She nodded, impatient to feel his hand rubbing her again.

"I need to hear you saying them." His fingers brushed her intimately, making her dizzy with need.

"No courting. No wedding. No gossip. Only pleasure."

"Do you agree with them?"

"Yes."

"There's no going back from this—"

"Please."

"No, listen. There are methods to make your future husband believe you're a virgin. I'll tell you about them, but you do realise you're going to lose your virginity, don't you?"

"Yes, and I don't care. It's overrated anyway."

"I agree." He kissed her, starting to rub her. "And I'll be careful, don't worry."

She wanted to touch him as well, so she unbuttoned his jacket, waistcoat, and shirt and unfastened the falls of his trousers. He groaned deep in his chest.

"One last time. Are you sure?" he asked, kissing a sensitive spot on her neck.

"Absolutely. I want this. I want you."

And she meant it.

nineteen

Escaping from his own guests wasn't part of tonight's plan, but Anthony had had enough of chatter, questions, curious looks, and smiles.

He left the ballroom without caring if someone noticed his disappearance. The dim lights of the quiet spot at the end of the corridor were an immediate cure-all for his anxiety. He stared out of the window at the garden. The moonlight turned the green leaves into shining silver, and the deep shadows gave him a sense of peace. He removed his mask and exhaled.

He'd agreed to give this damned ball only because Isabella had asked him. One light touch from her, and his body had come back to life. Her touch was like a charm overpowering him. And yet, he hadn't had the courage to invite her to dance with him.

He hadn't danced with anyone. Sod the rules.

When footsteps approached, he pinched the bridge of his nose, wishing for a moment of calm.

"Anthony." Isabella's voice changed his previous wish.

"What are you doing here?" It came out harsher than he wanted, but she didn't recoil at his tone.

"I needed the ladies' room." She was glowing, her cheeks

flushed and eyes shining. Her beauty held him captive for a moment.

She stepped closer with deliberate steps as if afraid of him. "I'm glad you decided to give this ball. I know being among all those people is difficult for you." She chuckled. "It's a bit difficult for me as well. You're very brave."

"Brave? I hid myself."

"But you're here now. That's all that matters."

Her simplicity was disarming.

"You made me change my mind. I'm sorry. I behaved beastly with you." He cleared his throat. "I meant to write back and see you, but it was so difficult that I let time pass."

She stared at him without wincing at his horrible face.

He gestured at the scar. "It took a long time for the flesh to settle. After the physician removed the bandages, the scar was ten times worse than it is now. It's hard to believe, isn't it? I couldn't let you see that monstrosity, and the fever came and went without rhyme or reason."

She touched his arm. "You don't have to justify yourself."

"I do. I should have answered your letters, but the more I postponed writing to you, the harder it became. I missed you." Shame burned the back of his throat. He owed her an explanation. "Will you ever forgive me?"

"Oh, Anthony." She hugged him, and he held her back, trying not to hold her too tightly. "Of course I forgive you. You have nothing to worry about. Just promise me we'll see each other again. Please."

"I promise."

"I'm here if you need me."

She stood next to him, watching the moonlit garden in silence, and that was the best exchange he'd had in a long time.

∼

Anthony removed his mask when the ball was over.

His ears rang in the quiet of his bedroom after the loud music and chatter of the ballroom.

Grandmama had wholeheartedly disagreed with the idea of a masquerade ball and had shown her disagreement by not wearing a mask. She didn't think he should hide his scars, but he wasn't ready to show his face to everyone. Isabella seeing his face had already been enough.

Hearing her laugh and watching her dance had been a ray of sunlight and a reminder that she brought happiness to his life. He'd ignored her when he should have thanked her for bringing him happiness once again.

He hadn't found the words to express himself further when she'd hugged him. The turmoil inside him had been too great.

Wilson, his valet, helped him out of his suit and don his night-shirt and dressing gown. Wilson didn't talk, but his gaze often drifted to Anthony's scar. He guessed he ought to get used to the glances and the silence.

He sat on the bed, touching his face. A phantom pain lingered when he pressed his fingers to the mauled flesh, but nothing else. If anything, the fear of pain was bigger.

"Anthony?" Patrick asked from the other side of the door.

He straightened and brushed his curls from his face. "Come in."

Patrick entered the room with his usual swagger, already half-undressed with his waistcoat unbuttoned and bow tie undone.

"How are you?" He made himself comfortable on the armchair in front of the bed.

"I'm not sure." Anthony scrubbed the back of his neck. "Grandmama was right. I shouldn't have worn a mask."

"Rubbish. The masquerade was a great idea." Patrick kicked off his shoes. "You didn't dance at all."

"No." Isabella had disappeared for a while, and when she'd

returned, he hadn't had the courage to dance again after their quiet exchange at the window.

He'd ordered some moonflowers for his conservatory with the idea to show them to Isabella as an apology for not having answered her messages, but at the last moment, he'd changed his mind, not convinced she would have appreciated the gesture.

"Try to organise another event," Patrick said. "The longer you wait to lead a normal life again, the harder it becomes."

He smiled. "Since when are you so wise?"

Patrick crossed his arms behind his head. "Since I'm leaving for Cabo Verde and the Continent on my first official mission for my family. I'm looking forward to going. Unless you need me here, of course, or unless you changed your mind."

"No, go. I've neglected my duties here for too long. I must work hard to recover the lost time. You have a delicate mission, and I'm happy you're ready to do it. Just make sure to use the right words with von Gruner."

"I have everything written down." He patted his jacket until he fished out a notepad. "All the suggestions you gave me are here. I'm studying them every day, learning them by heart."

"Remember to tell von Gruner we're sorry for the inconvenience several times. He likes that."

"Wait." He searched the room until he found a pencil on the escritoire. "Repeat several times..." he muttered while writing, "incon...invec...incon...hell, how do you spell inconvenience?"

"One letter at a time."

"Ha-ha. Funny."

Anthony chuckled, standing up. A certain restlessness bothered him, which was strange. He'd been idle for weeks, but now, all of a sudden, he needed to be active.

Patrick became serious. "Thank you for trusting me, especially on something so delicate."

"You love Maiden Hill as much as I do, but you aren't as short-tempered as I am. I believe you're a better negotiator than I am.

After all he has put us through, I would most likely end up punching von Gruner after two minutes. Besides, I don't want to give von Gruner any power over me." He rubbed his neck. "And I haven't fully recovered my strength yet."

"I know I'm not the best man for the job, but I appreciate your trust in me."

"Wait to thank me. If you think Grandmama is proud of being a Beaufort, the von Gruners are absolute fanatics about their prestigious family, and they strictly follow the Spanish court ceremonial. One mistake, and they'll send you back to England or shoot you."

Laughing, Patrick rose and hugged Anthony. "Nothing to worry about, then."

The hug caught him by surprise. It wasn't the first time Patrick had hugged him. His brother had always been the one who openly expressed his affection. But for some reason, the hug had a different flavour. He blinked to clear his vision.

"Thank you for always protecting me." Patrick squeezed Anthony.

He patted his brother's back. "Be careful in Cabo Verde. You can't behave like a rake with the von Gruners."

"I know. I know." Patrick ran a hand through his hair. "They'll shoot me."

"I'm serious. They won't take any bad behaviour lightly."

"I'll be a careful. I promise. Good night." Patrick left the room, humming a tune.

Anthony wished he were more like Patrick.

twenty

I sabella was still glowing after her secret encounter with Patrick two weeks after the ball. She had no doubts now she'd done the right thing. Times had changed, and women were gaining power. That was why she'd joined a march.

She raised a fist and shouted, "Deeds not words"—the slogan of the women's suffrage movement.

The street was packed with women chanting the motto and shaking their fists in the air. Some shouted louder than others, and some didn't shout at all. But it didn't matter.

The important thing was that thousands of women…not thousands, maybe a few hundred…were marching towards Parliament to make their voices heard. Mrs. Millicent Fawcett was leading the march although Isabella couldn't see her.

There was something empowering in being in the middle of a determined crowd with women who shared her sentiment. Or in gently getting rid of her chaperone. Lawson hated protest marches and had gladly agreed to spend her time in Oxford Street rather than following her charge.

"What do you think you're doing?" a man yelled from a cart.

He was trying to drive through the crowded street with little success. The horse snorted at the people around him.

"Right to vote!" Isabella waved one of the leaflets she'd helped type. "It's a protesting march."

"Get off the streets." The man shook a fist. "I must go to work, and you're blocking my way."

"We'll leave the street when we have the right to vote," the woman next to Isabella said.

The man pulled the reins and jumped off the seat. "I prefer using my own methods."

A group of half a dozen men leapt out of the cart.

"Move out of my way," the leader said.

As the men started to shove women aside none too gently, shouts rose from the protesters. Other people joined the fray, and Isabella kept moving to avoid being manhandled. Police officers arrived from somewhere, blowing their whistles. Women started fleeing the street, dropping their signs and leaflets.

When a man aimed at her with his fists closed, Isabella ran as well.

Sitting in his carriage, Anthony changed his mind about wearing a mask in the House of Lords, and not because Grandmama had told him to remove it.

His sense of shame and fear of being judged had pushed him to be rude to Isabella. But she'd seen his face and hadn't cared about it. It was time he dealt with his new reality without hiding, or he would never make amends as he'd promised her. She never failed to make him feel better and give him the strength to be the man he wanted to be, and he didn't remember anymore why he'd decided not to court her.

He was driving along Horse Guards Road when the coachman stopped.

"What is it?" he asked.

"A protest march, Your Grace."

A cold chill went down his spine. Not another bloody march.

"The Irish?" he asked.

"I don't know, Your Grace. I'll turn around."

The manoeuvre caused Anthony to shift right and left, not helping with his anxiety. When the carriage resumed driving, he exhaled and unclenched his fists. Loud voices came from somewhere, and a few people ran along the pavement. He looked out of the window, ready to bolt out in case another angry mob attacked him.

But it wasn't an angry mob.

He gripped the window when Isabella sprinted along the pavement, chased by a broad man.

"Stop!" Anthony ordered his coachman.

The moment the carriage stopped, he flung the door open and went after Isabella. She was fast while the man chasing her lagged behind. She would likely outrun her pursuer. Still, he had no intention of leaving her alone. Thankful he'd recently resumed boxing, he pushed himself onwards, until he closed a hand around the collar of the man's jacket.

"What are you doing?" Anthony tugged at the jacket, forcing the man to stop.

The man clenched a fist and turned around. "What the devil do you want?" His expression froze as he stared at Anthony's unmasked face. "What are you?" He trembled in genuine horror.

Anthony let him go. "Why are you chasing that lady?"

Isabella, a few yards away, glanced over her shoulder and stopped upon seeing him.

"Anthony!" She ran towards him, a broad smile on her lips. "This man wanted to manhandle me."

"What?" he prompted when the man remained silent.

"She was blocking the road," the man said but without verve.

"I was protesting with other women. Of course we were blocking the road."

"I have to go to work." The man stepped closer to her, but Anthony blocked him.

"If you have to go to work, then go. No one is holding you here." Anthony towered over the man a good foot.

The man removed his hat and stepped back from Anthony. "Fine. I'm leaving. Don't touch me." Muttering something, the man left.

"Phew!" Isabella bent over, her hands on her knees. "Thank you."

"Are you hurt?" He took her chin and tilted her head right and left to search for bruises.

"No, I'm all right." Her cheeks were flushed from the chase. "I was getting tired."

"You were leaving him behind though." He didn't withdraw his hand for a moment too long. "Let me take you home."

Her long eyelashes fluttered down. "Thank you, but I need to meet Lawson in Oxford Street."

He held her hand as they walked back to his carriage. He wasn't going to take any chances, and she didn't slip her hand out of his.

"Oxford Street," he said to the coachman before helping her into the carriage. "What were you protesting about?"

"Women's right to vote. It wasn't a big march, but we made ourselves heard." She showed him a leaflet. "And you? Where were you going?"

"The House of Lords." He fiddled with the mask next to him, wondering again if he should wear it. He almost jolted when she put her hand on his, stopping the fidgeting.

"At first, people will talk, but then they'll forget and gossip about something else. But if you wear that mask, the gossip will only be more cruel and hurtful."

"It's unbelievable how transparent I am to you."

"No, there are things I don't understand about you."

The carriage rocked gently, and a sable curl swayed back and forth over her cheek.

"Like what?"

"Like why did you want to marry me? When I asked you the first time, you made a list of strictly practical qualities, and I wondered if that was all."

He cradled his chin. "Who said I don't want to marry you even now?"

She laughed, and the sound was like silver coins bouncing off marble steps. "Well, why?"

He stared at her beautiful face, shining obsidian eyes, and rosy cheek, acknowledging the sense of calm and peace her smile brought to his heart. "You're right. I wasn't completely honest with you. The true reason I want to marry you is because you make me happy. I like your laughter, spirits, and mind. I like how you see life, and I like myself when I'm with you. There are marriages based on less than that."

She became solemn. "You might get tired of my laughter, spirits, and mind."

"The day I get tired of your laughter, spirits, and mind will be the day I get tired of life." He hadn't meant to say something so serious, but he wouldn't take his words back.

She stopped smiling though, which was unfortunate.

He cleared his throat. "I didn't mean to sound so..."

"Charming?"

He raised an eyebrow. "Charming. Now that's a term people never associate with me."

"Good. I like being unique and being the only one who notices that of you." She smoothed a fold on her skirt. "I found your reasons for wanting to marry me charming."

He had no idea how the conversation had turned so thoughtful in such a short time, but he didn't mind.

When the carriage stopped in Oxford Street, he got out and

offered her his hand. She jumped out of the carriage, holding his hand tightly, and he wished he could hold her a little longer.

"Please be careful when you take part in these marches," he said. "You never know how the people might react."

She bowed her head. "The day I stop being careful will be the day I…" Her eyebrows knit together. "I have no idea because I've never been particularly careful."

He laughed. Yes, he still wanted to marry her.

ISABELLA HEARD the words Dr. Eileen Norris had said, but try as she might, she couldn't understand them.

The consulting room at the New Hospital for Women in Mayfair seemed to turn darker. The hospital had been founded by a fellow suffragette, Dr. Elizabeth Garrett Anderson, and Isabella had always wished to visit it.

She'd changed her mind.

"Excuse me, doctor," she said in a small voice, "would you say that again?"

"You're with child, Lady Isabella. Four weeks is my guess."

The guess was more than correct because exactly four weeks ago, she'd given her virginity to Patrick in a dimly lit conservatory of all places.

With child. She was carrying Patrick's child.

The aftermath of her rendezvous with Patrick had been wonderful. She'd glowed for the whole night, for the whole month! Her body had been deliciously sensitive, reminding her of the pleasure Patrick had given her. He'd been kind and generous although it'd taken her almost half an hour to clean herself afterwards.

Her petticoats had been stained. Her hair had been a disaster. Thank goodness the mask had covered her blushes. But aside from that, she'd experienced a level of pleasure she had no idea existed.

She'd wanted to do it all again, but he'd told her to wait in case she became sore. But she hadn't experienced any soreness. Only blissful excitement.

All that pleasure wasn't worth the absolute dread of her present moment.

When her monthly bleeding hadn't come, she'd thought nothing of it, but Lawson had insisted she visit the women's hospital. So here she was, utterly terrified and feeling like an idiot.

"Lady Isabella." Dr. Norris tilted her head to catch her gaze. "I understand this is a shock."

She stammered, "But he was careful. He...he used a sheath."

"Yes, but unfortunately, the practice isn't infallible. Sometimes, a small hole in the sheath is enough."

Suddenly, there wasn't enough air in the room. "I'm not...I don't even have an intended. My family will be ruined. How can I explain this to my father? The man isn't my betrothed."

The doctor's calm voice did nothing to soothe her. "The first thing you should do is talk with the gentleman who was with you. Ideally, he would propose marriage. If he refuses, you can choose to talk to your family. Or, as many women in your situation do, you may leave London and retire to the country for a few months, give birth, and then the local parish will take care of the baby."

How could she do that without telling her parents? Did she want to give the baby away? Did she want to marry Patrick?

A sickening choking sensation crawled up her throat. A child, her parents' anger, and Patrick leaving in a matter of days. Too many things to consider with no preparation.

"It's overwhelming," Dr. Norris said. "But you aren't the first woman in this situation, and you have options. Talk to the gentleman."

She gripped the armrests as the room tilted and the sunlight darkened.

"Lady Isabella, take deep breaths."

She did as told. When the oppressive sensation on her chest eased, she licked her dry lips. "What do you recommend?"

Dr. Norris took her hand. "It's for you to decide. But the best option for you and the child is a wedding. A quick one. Not necessarily with the father."

Yes, because finding someone who wanted to marry a pregnant woman was easy.

twenty-one

Isabella couldn't stop shivering as she walked to Gloucester House with Lawson.

Patrick was a gentleman. He would marry her even though they weren't in love. They'd spent a lot of time together, and he was leaving for a long journey. Their sudden marriage wouldn't surprise anyone. She might go with him to Europe and visit Paris as he'd said. The situation might turn into a great opportunity and a new beginning.

Lawson touched her arm. "You must be strong."

"Everything is a bit too much." Her voice sounded different as if it didn't belong to her.

Lawson shook her head. "What were you—" She fell silent, exhaling. "There's no point in scolding you now. It is what it is."

"Trust me, I perfectly understand my situation."

Lady Mary had impressed on her clearly what her future would be if she didn't get married.

Lawson knocked on the door of Gloucester House, trembling as well.

"Gloucester House," Rogers said, opening the door. "Lady

Isabella. I didn't know you were expected today." He held the door open for her.

"This is an unplanned visit." As many other unplanned things. "Is Lord Patrick at home? I need to talk to him."

The butler frowned. "I'm afraid that's not possible. Lord Patrick left for Southampton last night. He had to bring up his departure due to a problem with the railway. He's likely already on board the ship bound for Cabo Verde. He should have sent you a message, I believe."

The floor quaked under Isabella's feet.

"I didn't get any messages."

"I'm sorry, my lady. Lord Patrick's departure was quite abrupt. He might have forgotten."

She shifted her weight from one foot to another. Her legs threatened to give out. "Thank you."

"Rogers, I need to send for my secretary—" Anthony came out of a door and stopped upon seeing her.

Her first impulse was to flee the house. He would be disappointed if he knew what she'd done.

Lawson hid a gasp behind her closed fist.

He didn't wear any mask, his hair didn't cover his face, and the bright sunlight hit his scar. It was a huge scar. It had the shape of a lily with the petals stretching out under his left eye, towards his temple, and down his cheek, as if someone had tried to open his face by pulling the flesh apart.

She understood Lawson's reaction but gave her a warning glance. "Your Grace."

"Lady Isabella was looking for Lord Patrick, Your Grace," Rogers said. "I told her he left earlier than planned."

Anthony ignored Lawson and smiled at Isabella. "Please stay for a cup of tea or coffee, Isabella."

She needed a cup, and his company would do her good. She took a seat at a round table in the sunroom, glad to sit down. Lawson sat on a chair in a corner, tense and pale.

"I believe Patrick sent you a message," Anthony said as the butler served the drinks.

"I must have missed it."

"Or he forgot. I wouldn't be surprised. Anything urgent?"

"Nothing of importance."

They stirred their drinks in silence. The sound of the teaspoons against the porcelain thundered.

"We haven't spent some time together in a while." Anthony smiled but stopped immediately as if regretting having tried. The ruined skin on his left side twitched, making the scar more evident. "I've been awfully busy catching up with my work."

A bitter taste filled her mouth when she sipped the coffee despite the sugar, cream, and cinnamon. "I understand."

He cleared his throat. "You look upset. Something happened."

Was it that obvious?

"Is it me?" he asked. "I understand if—"

"Good gracious, no!" Her voice strengthened. "I'm not upset with you."

His green eyes brightened. "So what troubles you?"

"Please do not worry."

The answer saddened him if the way he lowered his eyebrows was any indication. "I can be of help. Or maybe Patrick's departure upset you."

"Oh, no. I mean, I'll miss him, but I'm just tired." She rubbed her forehead. In truth, she did feel peculiar, and the coffee smelt horribly.

"You're pale."

"I walked here. Perhaps it's that." The room tilted, and she closed her eyes for a moment.

When she opened them, a dark halo appeared at the edge of her field of vision. She stood up, but her head became light, and her knees buckled.

∾

Anthony grabbed Isabella before she collapsed. "Isabella!"

"My lady." The maid hurried to help.

He gathered Isabella in his arms and laid her on the sofa. "Is she sick?"

"No, Your Grace." Her voice cracked, though. "Lady Isabella didn't have lunch today, and we walked all morning. Just that. A moment of fatigue."

"I'll send for my physician."

"Not necessary, Your Grace."

"Lady Isabella needs help."

Lawson paled. "It's nothing. Please, trust me, Your Grace."

Isabella blinked her eyes open. Her cheeks remained pale. She tried to sit up, but he stopped her.

"Lie down. You fainted."

She exhaled. "I'm sorry to cause you trouble."

"Not at all. Lawson, ask Rogers to bring a repast. Something to help Lady Isabella feel better."

"Immediately." The maid exchanged a glance with Isabella before leaving the room.

He held Isabella's hand, checking her pulse. "I'll have a carriage ready to escort you home."

"I can hail a cab."

"No."

She gripped his hand with surprising strength. "Anthony."

He stroked her trembling fingers. "What is it?"

Lawson returned with a tray of oat biscuits. "My lady, have one."

"I'm not hungry."

Lawson insisted. "Only one. You'll feel better."

Anthony sat on the chair, waiting for Isabella to finish eating. If he didn't know better, he would say she was scared. He wasn't surprised she didn't confide in him. He'd shunned her for weeks. The relationship they'd built had barely started again.

She chewed the biscuit slowly. "I'm already better. Thank you."

"You're still pale, and your pulse is slow."

"It was a moment of weakness."

He didn't know what to think. Something had happened to her before coming here, but he wouldn't insist.

"Your Grace," Rogers said, "the carriage is ready."

"Good." He helped Isabella up. "I'll accompany you."

"You don't have to."

"I know. Rogers, I'll be back in half an hour."

Rogers's mouth dropped open. "Of course, Your Grace."

Going out was a shock for Anthony as well. He'd managed to go to the House of Lords a couple of times, but aside from that, he didn't leave the house.

He'd meant to invite Isabella for a walk after their last encounter at the march, but work had truly overwhelmed him.

She leant against him as he walked her out. He hesitated outside the door. The usual grey London weather had been swapped with an unseasonably bright day that had no mercy on him. The sunlight was determined to expose all his ugliness. But he had no intention of leaving Isabella alone. He could ask a footman to escort her, and Lawson was present, but he wanted to do it himself. He ran a hand through his hair to let the curls fall over his scar.

He lowered the curtain of the window once in the carriage, blocking the ruthless sun.

"It's not as scary as you think," she whispered.

He smiled ruefully. "You'll forgive me if I don't believe you."

"I truly mean it. It doesn't bother me."

Aside from Grandmama and Patrick, she was the first person to tell him that. Many people were scared of making any comments about his face. Others showed their disgust in their stares. But she was the first one who gave him her opinion without fear. Her honesty and consideration were some of the best things that had happened to him since the incident. No, since ever.

He helped her out of the carriage when they arrived. She slid her hand into his, and he gripped her fingers for a moment too long.

"I hope to see you soon," he said. "Have tea with me tomorrow."

Isabella looked down. "I will."

He watched her enter the house. Once again, she'd addressed his fears and told him to pull himself together with the simplicity that belonged to her only.

And once again, he was utterly charmed.

twenty-two

The worst part of Isabella's predicament was that she had no one to talk about it with, aside from Lawson.

Even worse, she had to control herself all the time, lest her mother or sister understand what was happening. Hiding the fact she kept casting up her accounts and eating very little was difficult. Time was ticking away. Each day that passed was closer to the moment when she wouldn't be able to hide the truth, and she didn't have a plan.

She could send a message to Patrick, but an unexpected child wasn't something that could be discussed via a letter. Besides, it would take weeks for the letter to reach Patrick, and more weeks for his reply to reach her. Meanwhile, she would be showing, and by the time they found an agreement, the baby would be born, and she would be living on the streets.

She lay in her bed, even though it was afternoon, but constant worries and nausea were an exhausting combination.

Helen entered the room, looking as fresh as a peach and absolutely pretty. "How are you? You're spending a lot of time in bed as of late."

"You're spending a lot of time at tea parties."

"They're better than balls to find a husband, in my opinion. More talking in a shorter time. It's easier to understand if the gentleman is a good match. And the more tea parties, the less time to take more lessons on being a lady." Helen rubbed her forehead. "I feel ungrateful when I say that."

"You shouldn't. There's nothing wrong in having your personal interests, and Mother can be tiring."

Helen seemed aged a few years in a moment. "She can."

"Are you going to marry that earl?"

"I don't know." Helen sat on the bed. "Mother keeps saying a duke would be better. The duke took you home the other day."

"He was very kind."

"Do you think he'll answer my letters now?"

"I don't know. I'll ask him."

Helen toyed with a ribbon on her skirt. "Mother says I should—"

"Helen, please, stop doing everything Mother orders you to do." She regretted her tone. But honestly, if she heard '*Mother keeps saying*' one more time, she would yell at the top of her voice.

"It's easy for you say that." Helen sat up. "You're strong-willed, and Mother doesn't bother you as much as she bothers me."

"Just tell her what you want or don't want to do. Grow a spine, for Pete's sake. It's that simple." Again, her frustration and worry crept into her voice, but she hadn't meant to be so bitter. But everything was too much right now.

Helen flinched, her mouth opening.

Isabella sat up. "I didn't mean to be so harsh."

"Helen?" Mother called from the corridor. "We need to plan your week. Come quickly."

Helen stooped her shoulders. "Plan my life is more correct." She left before Isabella could say anything else.

"I'm sorry," she said, but her sister was already gone. She lay back with a huff. Everything she did ended up a mess.

Lawson brought her mint tea. Tea was the only thing Isabella could drink without feeling sick.

"You should talk to your mother." Lawson set aside a dirty cup and a book to make room for the tray.

"Mother will be horrified. She'll demand to know who the father is, and it'll be a disaster. Father will preach to me about having broken the rules, and I'll be on the street before the week ends."

"You have no choice. If you want to move to the country for the next few months, your mother must know."

She sat upright. "Dozens of girls enjoy themselves constantly with no consequences. I have fun one single time, with all the precautions, and this happens."

"There's no point in ruminating about what happened. Focus on finding a solution. You should go to the estate in the Lake District to give birth," Lawson said. "Far from London."

"It's not that easy. I can't simply leave for the Lake District without an explanation, and I would need to tell Mother." She massaged her temples.

Every solution brought bigger problems.

Lawson lowered her voice. "Please don't think about seeing a midwife to end your problem. You have no idea how many women die at the hands of these so-called experts. They often use dirty tools that start lethal infections, and too many times the parsley apiol causes the woman to bleed to death."

Her head was about to burst with all the bad news. "I don't want to see a midwife for that."

"Then there's only one solution. Marriage."

"Patrick won't be back in months."

"I'm talking about his brother." Lawson sat on the chair, her expression grave. "I've seen how the duke looks at you."

"Concerned. That's how."

"He's attracted to you. And you know that, too."

"Even if he wants to marry me, he wouldn't want a hasty wedding."

"I think he would. The duke isn't a man who likes frills. If he decides to marry you, he'll be happy to have a quick wedding."

She put a hand on her belly. "I don't want to lie to him."

"The child is his nephew. He has only to believe the child is his son."

"I can't deceive him like that."

Lawson took her shoulders. "What's the alternative? If you tell him the truth, he won't marry you. If you wait too long, your belly will show. And then what? Your parents will disown you or send you away. You saw what happened to Lady Mary. Or do you want to see the midwife and bleed to death on a dirty table?"

A sob remained trapped in her chest. "There must be another solution."

"I'm sorry to be blunt, but aside from the duke, you don't have any other suitors. The timing is perfect. You and the duke are getting close again. He wanted to propose. He can do it now. And to be honest, I doubt Lord Patrick will marry you. He'll ask you to take the apiol."

"We don't know that."

"Anyway, what he would do doesn't matter since we can't ask him. You'd better convince His Grace you want to marry him."

Before talking to Anthony, there was someone else Isabella needed to see—Lady Mary.

Her pulse was racing when she knocked on Mary's door in a secluded alleyway on the border with St. Giles. Rats scurried along the wet cobbles, and glass shards littered the ground. Someone drunk was singing at the top of their voice.

Lawson stood next to her. "If this place doesn't convince you that marrying the duke is your best option, then nothing will."

"I just hate deceiving a man who has been nothing but kind to me."

"Lady Isabella." Mary held the door open. "What are you doing here?"

She entered the small flat. The child slept in a corner among piles of clothes and baskets. Cold draughts sneaked inside from a window that didn't lock properly.

Mary smoothed down her worn apron and fixed a wayward curl to her chignon. "I apologise for the state of the house."

"Don't, please. I brought you something." Isabella put the envelope with the banknotes on the table. There were enough pounds for Mary to rent a better place.

"Thank you." Mary lowered her gaze. "The brooch you gave me helped me a lot. I have a nice sum aside now. Please take a seat."

"My visit has another reason." She licked her lips. "I'll be blunt. I'm with child, and I don't have a suitor."

Mary paused while sitting. "Dear me. If you came here for advice, I'm not sure what I can give you."

"The Duke of Gloucester showed interest in courting Lady Isabella," Lawson said. "I insist that marrying him with a special licence is the only solution. Lady Isabella isn't convinced."

Because that solution implied a lot of lies. "I would deceive him, and I don't know how to convince him to marry me quickly without raising any suspicions."

"Lady Isabella, please listen carefully." Mary took Isabella's hand. "Your life and your child's life depend entirely on your decision and your willingness to lie. If I had the opportunity to marry a gentleman and pretend the child belonged to my husband, I would have done it without a moment of hesitation. What awaits you is nothing but misery, at best. Death, at worst. The friends you have now will shun you. Your parents will send you away in the best of cases. You'll become nothing more than an embarrassment no one wants to talk about. I was lucky to find a job as a seamstress, but I earn so little I can barely feed my son. Ladies can't make mistakes.

Ladies can't break the rules. Ladies have no help when they need it."

"It can't be that dark." Isabella turned towards the crib when the baby let out a cooing sound.

Mary picked up her child. "Look around, my lady. It is that dark."

twenty-three

The day couldn't be more perfect for Anthony as he promenaded in his garden under the shade of the linden trees with Isabella. Lawson followed them.

Isabella wasn't as upset as she'd been the other day, but not as bubbling and cheerful as usual.

"I hope you don't mind walking in the garden," he said. "I'm not comfortable going out yet."

"The garden is perfect, but..." She pressed her lips together. "Never mind."

"Speak your mind. I've always liked that of you."

She gave him a small smile. "If you need company to go out, I'm happy to help. Sometimes it's easier to do things we're afraid of when we aren't alone. The more you hide, the harder it'll be to leave the house." Her gaze lingered on his scar but never in a horrified way.

"Thank you for your honesty."

She touched his arm, and the usual thrill coursed through him. "I try to be."

He stopped under the shadow of a weeping willow tree. "I always feel better when you're close to me. You bring me joy."

She beamed, a bright, full beam that brightened the whole city. The sun hid in shame behind a cloud. "Really? Even when I wrestled you to the floor?"

He chuckled. "The stairs. That was one of the best moments of my life."

"Coincidentally, one of mine too."

They laughed together, and he didn't care if his face twisted because of the scar.

"That's why I want to propose," he said almost without thinking, but then again, the words were true.

Her expression tensed for a moment before softening. "So you're really still interested in marrying me."

He hesitated only because he got lost in the depths of her dark eyes. "I am."

Her cheeks flushed a delightful colour.

"I don't want to make you uncomfortable." He touched her hand. "I should apologise for not having talked about my proposal again. After the shooting, I thought you might not want to be with me. Look at me." He flashed a bitter smile. "I'm hiding in my own garden while I look like someone who swallowed dynamite."

"I don't care about the scar." Honesty rang in her steady voice. "I really don't, Anthony. I care about you."

He couldn't believe the turn the day had taken. "I do want to marry you, but I thought you weren't sure."

"This period of separation made me think. And Helen has found other interests." She glanced up at him.

"I'm happy for her."

"Since she is no longer interested in being your duchess, I don't have to worry about hurting her feelings."

There were very few feelings to start with, according to Anthony.

"So, without competing with my sister, I would be happy to agree to your proposal." She flushed a deeper shade of pink.

He sucked in a deep breath because he didn't believe in his

good fortune. Isabella wished to marry him, despite what happened to him. He hadn't experienced such happiness in a long time. She wanted to marry him!

A jumble of thoughts and emotions overwhelmed him. He didn't know where to start. If he could, he would marry her today.

"When do you want to get married? Do you prefer a long or a short engagement? Where do you want to perform the ceremony? Oh, no, wait. Grandmama will insist on St. George Chapel in Windsor. I hope you don't mind." He forced himself to shut up.

"St. George Chapel is perfect."

"Would you be opposed to a special licence?" In for a penny.

"Heavens, no. It would be perfect."

That caught him by surprise. Again. A pleasant surprise, that is.

She caressed the crown of a flower. "My parents are going to leave soon for the Americas. They'll be away for a while as my father has business to attend to there, and my uncle lives in Boston. We could get married before they leave. What do you think?"

The option of having to organise a big wedding months ahead wasn't appealing. A special licence would allow him to get married quickly without too much fuss. Given enough time, Grandmama would plan a ridiculously pompous wedding with a flight of white doves at the exit of the church, a string quartet, and a banquet that would make the parties thrown at Versailles look like a quick repast.

Hell, no.

Just the thought of a wedding reception with two hundred guests from all over the kingdom and Europe gave him a fever. Not to mention all the dinner parties and balls he would need to attend before the wedding, showing his face to everyone in the country and enduring gossip about his looks. Even without the scar, he would hate the endless number of parties and the ceremonious hustle.

Enough reasons to buy a special licence.

"I agree. I'm not fond of frills and fuss."

As he glanced up at the house, he spotted Grandmama watching them from a window. She wouldn't approve of a quick marriage, but it was his wedding and his bride. And he was tired of not doing anything without a meticulous plan. Life was too short, as the duel had taught him. He wanted to be impulsive for once, and Isabella was the perfect reason to be.

"Is this what you want?" he asked. "Are you sure?"

"Yes." Her voice quivered, but her stare never left his face.

He exhaled, realising only then how much he'd wanted her to agree to marry him. He hadn't allowed himself to hope after the incident, but she'd obviously thought about him a lot. That humbled and pleased him to no end.

"I'll make the arrangements."

"Thank you." She rose on her tiptoes and hugged him, and for the third time, he was pleasantly surprised.

The hug felt too good. Her soft body pressed against him, and her sweet scent made him dizzy. He held her by the waist, incredulous that a wonderful woman like Isabella wanted to marry him. He felt guilty for all those times in his life when he'd been pessimistic or gloomy.

She blushed again, a delicious peach colour that exalted her black eyes.

"Thank you," he said.

"It's me who should be grateful."

Lawson politely coughed from the corner where she stood.

She withdrew quickly, cheeks red. "I'm sorry. I got carried away."

"Your spontaneity is one of the many qualities I admire about you." He kissed her trembling hand. "I might go to Doctors' Commons today. What better reason to leave the house?"

"Great." She seemed relieved.

He released her hand. The hand that soon would wear a wedding ring. "I'm looking forward to starting our new life together."

"So am I."

"Let's tell Grandmama."

"Let's elope."

He laughed. "Grandmama isn't as harsh as she seems."

Not even Grandmama's cold scowl could ruin Anthony's mood when he entered the sitting room. Grandmama was at the desk, writing letters. She removed her glasses and folded them carefully before straightening them.

"I have news, Grandmama."

"So I thought." She steepled her fingers on the desk.

He held Isabella's hand again. "Isabella agreed to marry me, by special license, and within the week."

Aside from her eyes becoming two narrow slits, Grandmama didn't show any emotion. "Absurd. You are the Duke of Gloucester."

Isabella lowered her gaze. "I promise I'll do my best to learn my duties as a duchess, and I hope you'll guide me."

Grandmama's expression softened a little. "There's no need to hurry."

"It's our wish." He wouldn't hear any objection to his choice. "I hope you'll be as happy as I am for the news."

"What about Patrick? He'll want to be here with you."

Isabella shifted her weight.

"I can't ask Patrick to return here in a hurry and risk offending von Gruner after his invitation. We'll lose Maiden Hill for good. At the same time, I don't want to wait months for him to be here. He'll tour the Continent before travelling to London. So no. I don't want to wait. We'll throw a ball when he's back."

Grandmama rose, looking like an executioner. "As usual, you present me with a *fait accompli*."

They shared one of their long, harsh stares.

"I do." He injected as much determination as possible into his voice. Not only did he not want to be preached to by Grandmama; he didn't want her to mistreat Isabella either.

"Then there isn't much else to say." Grandmama angled towards Isabella. "Welcome to our family."

He doubted Isabella felt welcomed at all.

twenty-four

Silence dropped in the sitting room when Isabella gave the announcement.

After Anthony had so happily agreed to marry her, she hadn't wanted him to leave his house and talk to her parents. He would arrange a meeting with Father to discuss her dowry and other things. Showing himself was a great sacrifice for him, and she didn't want to make him uncomfortable on top of lying to him. The fact she genuinely cared about him and liked him only made her feel more guilty. Although to her credit, he'd brought up the marriage.

Mother seemed frozen with her needle halfway through the fabric of her work. Helen's eyes remained wide and unblinking. Father watched her with his pipe hanging precariously in his mouth. They all seemed ready for a photograph.

Admittedly, she hadn't done a good job at giving the news. Guilt gnawed at her without rest, fuelled by the vision of Anthony's broad smile when she'd agreed without hesitation to his proposal. Also, her family weren't aware of Anthony's former intention of marrying her or of her secret meetings with him, so the news came unexpectedly.

"The duke wants to marry you." Mother lowered her needlework.

"Yes." Isabella summoned a bit of enthusiasm.

Father coughed puffs of smoke, putting down the pipe. "Why the hurry?"

"Because you're leaving for the Americas, and I would like to share the wedding with you. The alternative would be waiting for too long, and Anthony doesn't want a big wedding, given what happened to him."

Helen finally blinked. "I don't understand. He has never shown an interest in you, has he?"

It was time for a small confession. "Actually, he showed his interest in courting me before the incident, the night I danced the waltz with him. I meant to tell you, but then the incident happened. Anthony was recovering, and marriage was never mentioned again. I wasn't sure if he wanted to marry me anymore. So I stayed silent. But now that he's well and I don't have a suitor, we can go ahead. A week from now, we'll get married."

So soon, yet so far away.

"You never told me you liked him so much," Helen said, sounding hurt.

"You wanted to marry him. I didn't think mentioning my interest was appropriate."

Father arched his brow.

Helen rubbed her temples. "I don't know what to say. The Dowager assured us the duke wanted to marry me."

"Well." Mother exhaled. "The duke has the last word. He chose Isabella, and she said yes. That's all that matters."

"Do you want to marry him?" Father asked, suspicion in his tone.

"I do." Her hand covered her belly instinctively, and to be honest, Anthony was a good man.

She enjoyed his company and was ready to be a good wife to

him. Maybe their relationship didn't involve love or deep passion, but she couldn't ask for more.

Mother smiled. "I'm happy for you, but we have a lot of work to do in a short time. You have to decide if you want to marry in white as the queen did, or if you want to wear any other colour. Light blue is in fashion although white and lots of lace are becoming predominant. Your choice."

If only all her choices were that simple.

Helen slumped her shoulders. "You should be happy."

Mother tapped Helen's arm. "*You* should be happy for your sister and show her your support."

Helen narrowed her gaze. "I always do the wrong thing, don't I?"

"Not at all," Isabella said as Mother said, "Don't be sour. It's unappealing."

"Are you happy?" Father searched Isabella's face.

"Very much." Relieved, mostly. Guilty, surely.

Father rose to hug her. "I hope you're happy, darling."

She rested her head on his shoulder, a lump forming in her throat. "Thank you, Father."

~

MOTHER HAD BEEN RIGHT.

In the following days, Isabella had done nothing but get ready for her wedding, for her new life, for the biggest deceit she'd ever put up.

A life she hadn't planned, expected, or thought of.

There were so many things to organise, they postponed the wedding for another week. Lawson had assured her she wasn't showing, but she could swear a small bump had appeared on her belly.

The only good thing about the frenetic visits to the modiste, the endless writing of letters and messages to friends and relatives, and the discussions about the wedding breakfast was that she hadn't had time or energy to think about her situation. Or worse, about the fact she would lie in bed with Anthony in a matter of days to make him believe the baby she carried was his heir.

Every time her determination wavered, she thought of Mary in that horrible dark room and her small child.

She hadn't seen Anthony, which was good because she wasn't sure she wouldn't tell him the truth if he smiled at her and told her how happy he was. She hadn't seen the Dowager either, which was even better. The matron suspected the truth. Isabella was sure of that. The elder woman possessed the uncanny ability to see through people.

Lawson was her only anchor. The only one who knew everything.

The night before the wedding, Isabella kept tossing and turning in her bed. In the quiet of her bedroom—the last night she would spend in her bedroom—the doubts and guilt tormented her.

Perhaps she should tell Anthony the truth right after they were married. He would hate her, but she wouldn't carry the lie for too long. How awful. No matter how she considered the situation, she felt guilty.

Her wedding dress—a beautiful ivory gown made of lace and satin—stood in a corner of the room like a pale ghost haunting her.

She covered her face with the pillow, cursing again that night. If she didn't talk with someone, she would scream bloody murder. She left the bed to go to Lawson's room.

"Lawson." A sob escaped her. "What am I doing?"

Lawson stopped packing her clothes in a trunk and hugged her. "The right thing." She let Isabella cry.

"He was so happy when I told him I wanted to marry him. He has no idea. When did I become such a horrible person?"

"If he never knows, he'll never get hurt. Once you give him his heir, everything will be better. And the child is his nephew, his own blood."

"I feel despicable." She shivered, grabbing Lawson's shoulders for dear life.

"The alternative is death. Lady Mary was lucky to find a job and people to help her, and yet she's struggling. Other women aren't so lucky."

Lawson's words were of little consolation. But the wedding was going to happen.

The most difficult part would be to be in bed with Anthony. Not because she didn't find Anthony attractive, quite the opposite, but because she would need to lie to him again.

ODDLY ENOUGH, on the morning of the ceremony, Anthony wasn't terribly nervous.

He checked his reflection in the mirror after Wilson had finished helping him get ready and dressed—a rather long affair, for which he'd risen well before dawn, even though he'd travelled the night before to Windsor to be closer to the chapel.

The only matter that bothered him was whether he should let his hair cover the scars or not.

No hair, he decided. Isabella had told him she didn't mind the scar. As for the guests, he would endure the stares and mutters. With Isabella at his side, he would face the scorn.

He barely left his bedroom before Grandmama walked over to him as if she were ambushing him.

"You look elegant." She gave him a long, assessing glance.

"Thank you."

She straightened his collar and brushed an invisible speck from his shoulders. "Have you thought about what I told you last night?"

"I'm going to get married today. I haven't changed my mind."

"That young lady isn't ready to represent our family. "

"Neither am I." He covered the scars. He would leave that type of bravery for another occasion.

She didn't desist. "I couldn't invite all the people who should have been invited. Heavens, your brother is in the middle of the ocean. Not to mention that, given time and a proper strategy, the queen would have wanted to see you before the wedding. Her golden jubilee is coming soon. She's busy."

"Even if Isabella and I had a long engagement, I wouldn't have wanted to invite all the people in Burke's Peerage. I want a simple, quick ceremony with a small number of guests, and I want it now. And that's it."

She took his hand in hers. "I know I pressured you to get married, and I won't deny that you need to produce an heir and a spare, but the incident taught me your happiness is more important. Are you happy? Do you want to marry Isabella?"

"Yes." He kissed her forehead. "The incident taught me not to think too much about everything, and I like Isabella a lot."

Exhaling, Grandmama patted his hand. "Let's show everyone how proud we are to be the House of Beaufort."

"Of course."

The ride in the carriage and the pavement crowded with people triggered his anxiety. He fiddled with the collar of his shirt as the yells and bangs of that day, when he'd bled while stuck in the middle of an angry mob, echoed in his ears. He expected the people to assault the carriage at any moment. He wasn't sure what frightened him the most—showing his face publicly or being stuck in a riot again.

"Is something the matter?" Grandmama asked.

"The crowd reminds me of that day."

"You've been in a carriage after the incident and never had problems. Why now?"

"I'm nervous."

"I'm not going to tell you not to be nervous. You should be. I am nervous. Having an unprepared, wild duchess in our family is going to be a challenge. She'll humiliate us and cause trouble, mark my words."

"Please stop." He leant back into the seat. "Just for today, stop disparaging my soon-to-be wife." His tone was more forced than usual, and Grandmama didn't say anything else for the rest of the ride.

In the church, he couldn't stand still when he waited for his bride to arrive with the few guests. Every whisper or tap of the foot echoed off the high-vaulted ceiling of the chapel. The sunlight played with the stained-glass windows, casting a riot of colours on the Grecian columns. The sight was beautiful, but the guests had eyes only for him.

Apparently, his face was more interesting than the Panel of Kings.

His hair didn't completely cover the scar, and surely people had speculated on what he truly looked like after the rumours about him being disfigured. As soon as Isabella was next to him, he wouldn't care about anyone's judgement.

Lady Montrose and Helen were sitting on the right side of the aisle while the left side was reserved for his relatives. Not many.

The music began, and he straightened. A white silhouette came into view against the backdrop of the sunlight pouring from the door to the church. He hitched a breath.

When Isabella appeared dressed in an ivory silk gown that exalted her raven hair and black eyes, all his twitches and fidgeting stopped. Her beauty captured his attention, making him forget about everything else. Even her father at her side disappeared.

She looked ethereal and beautiful, like a ray of moonlight, as she walked towards him, holding a nosegay of small white flowers. Her plush lips parted when their gazes met, and her steps faltered. Her chest heaved. The closer she came, the faster she breathed. He doubted her nervousness was only due to the ceremony.

He couldn't say Isabella had the happy, bright countenance of a woman whose romantic dream was becoming true. She shivered, seemed to have lost weight in barely ten days, and had dark circles around her eyes. Her exhaustion might be caused by the intense two weeks they both had before the wedding and the fact her parents were about to leave.

But in case she had second thoughts about him, he wouldn't hide who he was or how he looked, so he tilted his chin up to let his hair fall back. Helen gasped, and Lady Montrose put a hand on her chest.

Grandmama shot them a glare filled with outrage. Had they not been on consecrated ground, he was sure Helen and Lady Montrose would have been burnt by that stare. They regained their composure.

Isabella, instead, resumed walking towards him with new determination.

When she took his arm and they both faced the altar, he stroked her hand with his thumb to tell her not to be afraid. She rewarded him with a smile.

He wouldn't hurt her. He wouldn't do anything to upset her. All he wanted was to take care of her.

twenty-five

The ceremony was done in a matter of minutes, or at least so it'd seemed to Isabella. As she'd walked along the aisle with her father to join Anthony, there had been a moment when she'd meant to flee, for Anthony's sake. But then he'd shown his scars to everyone, and Helen's gasp and Mother's mutters had bothered her so much she'd marched on to show him her support.

Her bravery hadn't lasted long. Not because she didn't believe Anthony was a good, kind man. He was, and exactly for that reason, he didn't deserve the deceit. However, if everything went well, her baby would grow up in a good, happy family and not in an orphanage, ending up in a workhouse when he was thirteen, or worse, being branded as an illegitimate child.

The wedding reception was brief as well. The Dowager barely spoke to her, and she was happy about that. When the guests left and she said her goodbyes to everyone, the frenetic whirlwind of activities of the past few days came to a grinding halt.

No more appointments, people to talk to, or things to do.

The wedding was done. She was Anthony's wife.

Now there was only her, Anthony, and her lies.

Since her parents would leave soon, she would travel to London in their carriage while Anthony rode with the Dowager.

Her hands trembled when she sat with Mother, Father, and Helen in the carriage, ready to go.

The footman opened the door. "My lord, Her Grace."

The Dowager swept into view, tall and proud in her austere gown. "I would like a word with my new granddaughter."

Muttering, "Of course," her family filed out of the carriage.

Father lingered for a moment before exiting.

Isabella stiffened when the Dowager sat in front of her in a swish of silk. The carriage suddenly turned small and crowded.

"Fear not," the Dowager said, "I only want to talk to you."

"Isn't that what highwaymen say before they thwack you?" She let out a nervous laugh.

The Dowager didn't crack a smile. "I expect nothing short of perfection from you. You will not put us to shame. You'll be the duchess my grandson needs."

She didn't say anything. As nervous as she was, she would say something silly. And the Dowager would find any reply inadequate, anyway.

"Remember my words." The Dowager left the carriage, taking her ominous words with her.

Isabella had barely time to realise the reality of her new life during the trip back to London. She didn't listen to the chatter about the wedding reception or the worst hat among the guests. Her mind was stuck on her imminent, unavoidable wedding night.

When Father hugged her in front of Gloucester House, she couldn't contain a sob.

He patted her back. "There, there, darling. Don't be upset. You're going to be a great duchess, and I'm proud of you."

His kind words only caused her to cry harder. If he knew the truth, he wouldn't be so sympathetic.

"We can postpone our journey," he said, "and stay here for a while with you."

"Oh, Benjamin, we can't." Mother wiped Isabella's tears with a handkerchief. "Everything is ready, and Isabella isn't a child. You'll be fine."

Helen hugged her as well in a surprisingly tight embrace. "I'll visit you."

After another round of hugs and kisses, she was ready to go. No, she wasn't. She kept tormenting her hands and her skirt.

Lawson sat next to her as she rode to her new home.

"Lying with a man is easier than it seems," Lawson said.

"I know." She touched her belly. "But this is Anthony. I've never been intimate with him."

"Don't complain and let him do everything, and remember a lady who rides regularly doesn't bleed on her first night. He won't suspect anything. Just lie back, and he'll do the rest."

An hour later, after a bath and a change of clothes, she lay in her new, enormous bed, caressing her belly. Everything about the room was large and impressive. Every detail—from the porcelain vases on the table to the expensive Sheraton furniture—reminded her she was now part of the ancient House of Beaufort. An intruder. Worse, a thief.

Her legs were sore, her head hurt, and guilt was killing her. Now that she was married to Anthony, instead of deceiving him further, she might tell him the truth. Or maybe not. She should wait a few days...no, waiting would be worse. She groaned inwardly. Her head would burst with doubts.

Lawson, finishing a few chores around the room, distracted her.

"It's done, Your Grace," Lawson said, folding a blanket. "For better or worse, it's done."

"What if I tell him the truth tonight?"

Lawson stopped folding clothes. "What good would it bring? His Grace will want to know who the father is, and how do you think he'll react knowing that his own brother is the reason for this hasty marriage? His Grace might decide to send you away, or worse, hate the child and send it away from you. Or he might ask for an annulment. After tonight, when the marriage is consummated, you won't need to worry. The baby will be safe from poverty or scorn. That's the only thing that truly matters. The child will become a duke or a respected lady, and above all, it'll be next to its mother as it should be." She squeezed Isabella's hand. "If you don't care about yourself, care about the child. For the child's sake, endure your guilt."

"Heavens." Isabella covered her face with her hands. "I'm not sure I can...seduce him."

"You won't have to do anything. He'll come to you tonight. All you'll have to do is lie down and stay quiet."

After Lawson left, Isabella slid under the covers and stared at the door that separated her room from her husband's. The light from the fire cast dancing shadows on the walls and the door, giving them a demonic look that sent a chill to her bones.

She wasn't afraid of the act itself. Quite the opposite. When she'd been with Patrick, the tumble had been extremely pleasurable. But tonight was different. Tonight, she had to guarantee a future for her child. At least after tonight, she wouldn't worry about the future of her child anymore.

She took a deep breath and waited.

ANTHONY HUGGED GRANDMAMA AGAIN. For a woman who rarely showed affection, she was particularly caring that night.

"You look pale." She searched his face. "You must be tired. I'm exhausted."

"It was a long day."

She kissed his cheek, the ruined one. He guessed she insisted on kissing his ugly cheek only to make a point and prove to him she didn't find him repulsive.

"Good night, darling." She paused at the door as if wanting to add something else. But then she waved at him and left.

When he was blissfully alone, he reclined in the armchair. The day hadn't been tiring *per se*, but the tension of being under everyone's scrutiny was exhausting.

Wilson came to help him out of his clothes, wash, shave, and don his dressing gown.

After that, he had no more excuses. It was in his right to visit his wife tonight. He wanted to. But there was no hurry, and he didn't know if she was ready. Still, he ought to visit her. Ignoring her was rude.

He loitered in front of the door, wondering if he should leave her alone, but he simply wanted to hold her. From the moment the reception ended, he hadn't been alone with her.

His pulse quickened when he pulled the connecting door open. The air in her bedroom was warm and smelled of roses like her. Only the fireplace and a lamp on her nightstand illuminated the room. She sat bolt upright on the bed. Her long braid fell to her waist.

"Anthony."

From her tone, he couldn't understand if she was relieved or worried.

He sat on the bed next to her, wishing to hold her. Just hold her. "Do you like your room?"

She pulled up the cover to her chin. "It's beautiful."

"You can decorate it as you want. You don't have to keep the old furniture or drapes. You can get rid of anything you don't like."

She nodded, shivering. "Thank you."

He scrubbed the back of his head. "I'm not ready for a honeymoon yet, but if you want, we can visit my estate in the north. It's beautiful in summer."

Another curt nod.

"Isabella." He gently took her hand; it was cold. "Please look at me."

She obliged, and there was no mistaking the fear in her wide eyes. She wasn't ready. In a way, neither was he.

"I'm not a beast. I'm not going to jump on you. Don't be afraid of me."

"I know. I'm nervous. That's all."

"No need to be." He kissed her hand before releasing it. No hug then. "Good night." He stood up.

She grabbed his hand with the desperation of someone drowning. "Don't leave."

Puzzled, he sat down again. She tugged at his hand until he leant closer to her.

"What is it?" he asked.

She slid her arms around his neck and hugged him. The cover slipped down, and the sweet softness of her body pressed against his. He held her, caressing her back until she stopped shivering.

"You can trust me," he whispered.

"I know."

"Why are you so scared?"

No answer.

"You must be tired." He straightened, getting away from her. "We'll talk tomorrow."

She gripped his hand again. "Can't you stay? Please."

There was a quiver in her voice he didn't like.

"Of course."

He tucked her in the bed and stroked her head. She snuggled closer to him, and he wrapped his arms around her. Even though he was tired, he couldn't sleep but listened to her soft breathing in the darkness. The turmoil bothering him was finally silent. He smiled because his wedding night couldn't be more perfect.

There was no hurry, and he could wait.

twenty-six

Anthony hadn't stayed with Isabella the entire night.

When she'd woken up, his side of the bed had been warm but empty. She'd hoped he would have stayed and lain in bed with her properly, so that her nightmare would be over. Her belly didn't attract attention, but it would soon do. Premature babies weren't rare, but she couldn't delay the consummation for long.

"Do not fret, Your Grace." Lawson helped her dress. "The duke will do his deed. Every husband does it. Are you ready to go to the dining room?"

"No, I'm not. The mornings are always the worst, and I'm afraid to feel sick in front of everyone."

Lawson nodded. "I'll have your breakfast brought up here."

A bitter taste filled her mouth when Lawson came back with a tray loaded with food. Her stomach categorically refused the kipper, bacon, and eggs. She had a bit of buttered toast and a cup of tea, which didn't last. The nausea hit her with the usual strength. No matter how deeply she breathed, or how much peppermint and lemon tea she drank, the nausea always won.

After her stomach was empty, she lay exhausted in the bed. "Is this normal?"

"I'm afraid it is, madam." Lawson handed her yet another herbal tea. "It'll go away in a few weeks."

"A few weeks? Great."

"The Dowager and His Grace asked about you when I met them on my way here."

"I'll go and see Anthony in a moment when I feel human again."

He'd been so sweet last night her guilt had increased tenfold. She'd believed he would have taken her immediately. She hadn't been ready for his kindness. But his kindness posed a problem at the moment.

After she freshened up, she found Anthony at his desk in his study, frowning while reading a letter. The sunlight formed a red-golden halo around him that suited his strong build. He radiated strength and safety, and she couldn't deny her need for both.

"Good morning," she said.

He stood up, smiling widely and genuinely. "Good morning. I didn't hear you."

"Apologies for not having come to the dining room for breakfast. I was tired." She cleared her throat. "You woke up early."

"I hope I didn't disturb you, but I had a few letters that needed urgent answers." He walked around the desk, and his expression was so sweet she couldn't remain still.

She rushed to him and hugged him, nearly jumping on him. He held her by the waist and made her twirl around. They both laughed for no reason.

She rested her cheek on his chest, finding the steady beat of his heart comforting. He kissed the top of her head.

"Thank you for your kindness," she whispered, feeling safe in his arms.

He gave her another kiss that melted her heart, also because he didn't let her go until she was ready to release him.

"I've just received a wire from Patrick," he said.

She stiffened. Had Patrick told the truth?

"He sends us his felicitations."

She hoped the relief didn't show on her face. "You seem worried."

He folded the piece of paper. "I'm always worried about Patrick. He gets easily in trouble and sometimes has little consideration for his actions although he has changed as of late."

No, Patrick got other people easily in trouble.

"Do you need anything?" he asked with a boyish smile she adored.

"I was just wondering..." *Why didn't you take me last night? Could we do the deed now?* "When we could spend some time together."

Her words must have particularly pleased him because his chest heaved with his deep breath.

"Of course. I want to show you something first." As his facial muscles contracted, the scarred part didn't move. "I look grotesque when I smile, do I? I've never been handsome. Patrick is the better-looking one. But now—"

"No." There was no hesitation in her voice. She touched his cheek with her fingertips, not sure if he would like it. "I've always found you handsome, and that hasn't changed."

He closed his eyes when she stroked his cheek. When he opened them again, she got lost in the gratitude in his large green eyes. Such a small gesture from her had caused such a big reaction from him. She lied about many things but not about her feelings for him.

He gently took her hand, lacing his fingers through hers in a move more intimate than she'd anticipated. A flutter started in her belly, and it had nothing to do with her child.

She tensed a little when he led her downstairs towards the conservatory. "What are we doing here?" She couldn't stop her voice from quivering.

"I have a surprise for you. Are you all right?"

"I'm still nervous."

A crease appeared between his eyebrows. "You don't need to be. I care only about your happiness."

She believed every word.

He opened the double doors and led her through the neat aisles towards the moonflowers. "I ordered some flowers that bloom at night—"

"The moonflowers." She realised too late her mistake. She should have waited for him to show her the flowers before talking.

"Yes. How do you know?"

"Not many flowers bloom at night." Which wasn't true. There were several species opening their petals in the moonlight. She was terrible at this game of lies. "Moonflowers are all the rage at the moment."

"I thought they were exclusive" He stopped in front of the beautiful flowers. Even closed, they were stunning. "For you. Although I should have waited for nightfall. I was eager to show them to you."

She touched the soft petals all wrapped tightly together. "They're beautiful."

Standing behind her, he caressed her cheek, and another shiver danced on her skin. Guilt had nothing to do with the sensation, though; it was his gentle touch.

"Did you order them for me?" she asked.

"A while ago. I wanted to impress you."

A lump of emotion swelled in her throat, along with annoyance at Patrick. He hadn't mentioned the idea had been Anthony's. "I spoiled your surprise."

He caressed her cheek again.

There was too much tenderness in his fingertips and the gesture for her heart to ignore it. She craved it. She craved his understanding, above all. Before he removed his hand, she took it and turned around to face him.

No space divided them. Her breasts pressed against his chest, and her body was flush with his. And now she didn't know what to do. She'd acted on impulse, and his emerald eyes were too intense; they didn't let her think. As she brushed a long curl of hair from his face, she touched his scarred skin with her whole hand this time.

He recoiled, stepping back from her.

"I'm sorry," they said together.

"Does it bother you? The touch?" she asked.

He put a hand on the scar. "The scar doesn't hurt anymore. It's not possible. I touch my cheek many times and feel no pain. But sometimes, when someone else touches it, it hurts. I feel the burn of the bullet again. I don't understand it."

"I guess a pain like that never leaves you."

"I hate it. The tension, the pain, the lack of control over my emotions."

"What happened?"

He leant against the door. "It was a duel."

"I thought duels were illegal."

"More or less. They're tolerated when the honour of a well-respected British officer has been soiled." He paused.

She couldn't believe he'd insulted an officer so harshly to start a duel. "I won't tell anyone. I promise."

He bowed his head. "The night of the ball, Patrick had an assignation with Lord McFall's wife in the library."

She was surprised she didn't feel anything. Not a sting of disappointment, jealousy, or anything else, really. Perhaps she'd turned into a cold monster. But she'd always known Patrick had a string of lovers. Besides, who cared? She had enough thoughts to keep herself busy.

"McFall caught him in *flagrante* and demanded satisfaction. The morning of the duel, Patrick was horribly nervous. He's never been a good shooter. He hates guns. When I saw him fumbling with the gun while McFall was ready to shoot, I pushed Patrick out of the way, and this is the result."

"Patrick," she whispered, shaking her head.

"That's why I worry about him. He doesn't think before acting. I can't protect him forever. He must learn to take his responsibilities."

She agreed. "Thank you for telling me what happened."

"Such a small thing." He smiled, and she smiled back. "Whenever you want to come here, this conservatory is all for you."

For now, she had trouble focusing on the plants.

"The moonflowers didn't overjoy you as much as I hoped," he said. "What can I do to make you happy?"

"You make me happy. A lot."

"I insist. If you could receive any gift, what would it be? I'm curious. What would you like to have?"

She had an idea. "If I could ask for anything…"

"Yes?"

"There's a woman I know, Lady Mary. Have you heard about her?"

"No, I don't think I have."

She cleared her throat. "She fell from grace after being with child, and her family sent her away. Now she lives hand-to-mouth in a horrible flat, working as a seamstress. I helped her in the past, and I would like to help her now in a proper way. If it's not much to ask, I want to donate part of the money for my personal expenses to her. I won't ask you for more money, I promise. I just want to help Lady Mary, and I won't buy anything extravagant for myself, anyway."

"Isabella—"

"She can have all the sum for my expenses. Or we can find her a job. Something paid better."

"I—"

"Her situation is so unfair that—"

He silenced her, pressing a finger to her lips. The gesture

became suddenly erotic, and his eyes ignited with unmistakable hunger. She couldn't deny a certain stirring in her chest as well.

He removed his finger. "You didn't seem to need to breathe. So, Lady Mary. No, you can't give her part of your money."

Her heart dipped to her stomach. "Oh."

"I'll set up an allowance for her without you having to cut your expenses."

Her heart soared back up, making her dizzy. "Would you do that for her?"

"No. I would do that for you."

She cried out in happiness and hugged him. "Thank you. Thank you." She scattered kisses on his face. "Thank you."

He laughed, holding her. "That's the reaction I hoped for."

twenty-seven

Two weeks had passed since Anthony's wedding, and he hadn't touched his wife.

Isabella was beautiful, but just slipping into her bedroom and taking her when they were getting to know each other better seemed wrong, although he enjoyed holding her when they slept together. Her reaction to his decision to help Lady Mary had left him incapable of focusing on his work for more than a few minutes. He wanted to make her as happy as she'd been again. He'd racked his brain to find something that would surprise her. Moonflowers obviously didn't mean much to her.

That was why he'd organised a surprise for her.

He entered her parlour, interrupting a hushed conversation between her and Lawson. He didn't grasp what they talked about, but whatever the subject was, they were passionate about it. They both straightened when he cleared his throat.

Isabella put a hand on her belly, cheeks reddening. "Anthony. I didn't hear you."

"I knocked twice."

"Your Grace." Lawson stood up and dropped a curtsy, her gaze on the floor.

"Are you busy?" he asked.

"Nothing of importance." Isabella set aside her peppermint tea. She drank gallons of it.

"I have another surprise for you." He stretched out his arm and smiled when she didn't hesitate to take it.

"What is it?" She glowed.

"I need you to close your eyes and follow me."

She did as told.

"I'll guide you. I won't let you trip."

"I know."

Her trust made him feel capable of lifting the house with a finger. She giggled when she tripped on a fold in the carpet along the corridor. He caught her to steady her and laughed too. Laughing with her was the most natural thing for him.

"The stairs," he said.

She clung to him, still laughing. When she was about to trip again, he had to admit defeat.

"Too dangerous." He gathered her in his arms, and she wrapped her arms around his neck.

"That's better," he said, checking her eyes were still closed.

"I agree." She snuggled closer to him.

"No peeking."

She rested her head on the crook of his neck, her soft breathing fanning on his skin. Her lips were half an inch from his jaw, so close he felt their warmth.

And he didn't laugh anymore. As she was in his arms with her eyes closed, the powerful need to protect her overwhelmed him. Their marriage might not have come from deep love—at least not on her part—but he would do his best to keep her safe and happy. The more he knew her, the more her presence filled his heart with happiness and hope.

He didn't put her down even though he arrived at their destination, wanting to enjoy holding her for a moment longer.

"I'm going to put you down, but don't open your eyes yet."

"All right."

He gently put her on her feet. She didn't let go of his hand while he opened the door to the glasshouse. He'd spared no expense, ordering the most unique and precious flowers from growers all around the world.

He knew nothing of gardening, but the colourful bunch of large flowers and the sweet scents were impressive.

She twitched her nose. "The conservatory again. The scent is lovely, but there was no need to make me close my eyes."

"Yes, there was." He led her in front of the workbench where the recently arrived plants sat. "You can open your eyes."

"What are you—Good Lord!" She clamped her hands on her mouth. She surveyed the collection with an expression that could be mistaken for sheer horror. "That's a leopard orchid. The one that looks like pouting lips is a psychotria, and those are cat's tails. That one is a middlemist red camellia. I can't believe it. It's the rarest flower in the world. A ghost orchid! A fire lily! It grows on the ashes after a fire and is considered a symbol of endurance and hope. They must have cost a fortune."

He could afford it, and the expense was well worth her smile. "All for you. The glass house is yours. And you can decide what plants you want to grow in our gardens."

She strode from one side of the table to the other, tilting her head to watch the plants from different angles and spouting bizarre names.

"There are seedlings as well." He gestured at the bags with labels on the floor.

"Thank you." She hugged him, pressing her body against his. "This is fantastic."

He wrapped his arms around her and inhaled her scent. "I'm glad you like them. I want you to be happy here, to feel at home. I know you don't love me, but perhaps with time, you won't consider me a terrible choice for a husband."

Sobs shook her, and the happy hug turned into her sagging

against him for support. "You aren't a bad husband. You're kind and generous, and I'm very happy to be with you." Her voice came muffled.

Yet she sobbed, her whole body shaking.

"Don't cry." He caressed her head. "I hope it's a cry of happiness." He handed her his handkerchief.

"Sorry, sorry." She wiped her eyes. "The gift is fabulous, wonderful. I'm crying because of the surprise. Beautiful surprise. Yes, it's happiness."

He cupped her face. "You're shaking."

"It's that..." She drew in a long breath. "You're wonderful while I've been horrible to you."

"No, you haven't." He wiped her tears with his thumbs. "You're one of the few people who are always honest with me."

She cried harder. "No, I'm not."

"Everyone has secrets, but I know you don't care about my scar or my title. I'm only Anthony for you, and that's all I want. Isn't that true?"

"Yes."

"Then I'm happy."

She hugged him again with desperation as if she were hugging him for the last time.

EMOTIONS TUGGED at Isabella in two different directions. There was absolute delight at her brand-new set of plants; they were more precious than the ones in her parents' house. But she found it hard to stop the tears.

Anthony had to think she was hysterical. One moment she laughed; the next, she cried.

Only the tenderness for Anthony remained though. Her heart burst with it. After she examined the plants again and made sure they were all right, she went upstairs to her room but came to an abrupt halt before entering it.

A couple of maids were emptying her armoire and chest of drawers, supervised by the Dowager.

Lawson clasped her hands over her chest. "I couldn't stop them, madam."

"What's happening here?" She stepped into the middle of her bedroom.

Trunks and boxes filled with her gowns were scattered around.

"There you are." The Dowager glanced at her. "It's time you dress properly as a duchess does."

"I don't understand."

The Dowager waved at a pile of pink gowns on the bed. "I'm getting rid of those awful pink gowns. You aren't a débutante anymore. You're the Duchess of Gloucester, and you'll dress accordingly."

"There's nothing wrong with those gowns, and I like them very much." She snatched one of the discarded dresses and put it back in the armoire. "I'm old enough to decide what to wear, thank you."

"Apparently not, since you have such childish tastes." The Dowager turned towards one of the maids. "Take that thing out."

She blocked the maid. "No. These gowns are perfectly all right, and I like them."

"Stop this fuss. You'll receive new gowns, of course. Better ones." The Dowager's calm tone irked her.

"No. I like these." A sob built up in her chest, and she couldn't contain it. Her emotions were all over the place. She sobbed in earnest, and the maid stepped back, glancing between the two duchesses.

"I beg you, madam," Lawson said. "Her Grace is happy with her wardrobe."

The Dowager radiated coldness. "Isabella represents the noble House of Beaufort. I will not let her ridicule us."

Isabella put a hand on her mouth to muffle the sob. She wasn't proud of her overreaction, but the more she cried, the louder the sobs. And tears welled up in her eyes so easily since she was with child.

"What is happening?" Anthony entered the room, carrying all his authority.

Everyone remained still.

The Dowager matched his harsh expression. "Nothing. It's Isabella who's making a fuss. I'm replacing some of her gowns."

He surveyed the room, and his gaze lingered on her. "Without discussing your plan with Isabella first, I guess."

"Well, she never has breakfast with us, and she spends her mornings locked up in her bedroom," the Dowager said. "She obviously doesn't want to mingle with us."

Lawson handed Isabella a handkerchief. "Pull yourself together," she whispered.

"Isabella." His tone changed from hard to soft in a moment. "Do you want to get rid of those gowns?"

She swallowed a few times not to sound like a kitten. "No."

"Then those gowns will stay." He faced the Dowager.

"She can't be seen around in one of those things."

"She's the Duchess of Gloucester, and she'll do as she pleases." He stepped aside. "Grandmama, please let Isabella decide."

Judging by how frosty the air became, the Dowager wasn't used to losing a battle. "I'll order new gowns anyway."

"Gowns that Isabella will choose." Anthony was as frosty as his grandmother.

A moment of uncomfortable silence filled the room; the false calm itched along her skin.

"I need a word with my wife." Anthony didn't lose eye contact with his grandmother.

To her credit, the Dowager left the room with grace and without arguing. The maids followed her. Only Lawson hesitated before leaving.

When the door was shut, Isabella twisted the handkerchief, feeling like an idiot. "I'm sorry about the scene."

"No. I'm sorry for how my grandmama behaved. She's used to controlling everything. She's always been like that. I'll talk to her and tell her not to make decisions for you."

She nodded, rolling her bottom lip between her teeth.

"I hate seeing you crying." He stood close to her, watching her with solemn eyes.

"I'm all right. It was mostly an angry cry. I feel rather silly now."

He caught a tear sliding down her cheek. "I think the only silly one was Grandmama." He picked up one of her pink gowns from the bed. "And I love this colour on you. You look beautiful in pink."

"You're just being kind."

"No, I mean it. I think you should ask the modiste to make only pink gowns for you."

She let out a chuckle. "Your grandmother would be horrified."

"Isn't that even better?"

She burst out laughing. "Thank you."

"I love it when you laugh."

His serious tone didn't leave room for jokes.

"I love it when you laugh, too."

They moved at the same time and hugged each other tightly. She had no idea what was happening. She didn't trust her feelings right now. Between her worries about lying, the child, and her constantly upset stomach, she'd lost control of her emotions. The warm flutter in her chest, starting whenever Anthony hugged her, could be anything.

Including something devastatingly deep.

twenty-eight

Isabella had to tell Anthony the truth, or she would feel guilty for the rest of her life. She would face the consequences of his anger, whatever they might be. Had he been cold or simply uninterested in her, she would have felt less guilty. But his kindness disarmed her of her strongest intentions.

When marrying Anthony had presented itself as the only solution, she hadn't foreseen the repercussions of her lies. She blamed her weakness and lack of judgement for everything she'd done. Although she hadn't foreseen the riot of sweet feelings for him.

But would he have married her knowing she was with child? Not likely. He would have forced his brother to marry her, but then again, what kind of future would that be for her child? Patrick had proven to be unreliable, and she wanted a proper family with a husband she trusted. When she'd wanted a tumble with him, she'd been aware of his libertine nature, and she wondered what he would have done if she'd had the chance to tell him about the baby.

The semidarkness in her room echoed her own thoughts. During the day, the endless discussions with Lawson sped time up.

Lawson insisted that she seduce Anthony immediately, but how could she?

At night, she was alone with her thoughts. She felt as if she were in a maze in which she couldn't find the exit.

She sat upright when the door connecting to Anthony's room opened. Her pulse thundered faster, and her mouth became dry. For the past nights, he'd come to sleep with her, and she'd enjoyed every moment. The sense of safety he gave her allowed her to sleep without waking up from a nightmare.

But tonight was going to be different. Tonight, she would tell him everything and so be it.

The light pouring from his bedroom formed a halo around him. In the dim light, he stood more imposing and threatening than usual. The dark-red brocade dressing gown gave him the look of a knight of old.

"Isabella." His deep voice reverberated in her stomach.

"I'm awake." She wished she didn't sound so weak.

He sat on the bed. "I wanted to know how you were faring. You burst out crying twice today, and then you ate very little at dinner. I won't sleep with you unless you want me in your bed."

Cold sweat dampened her back. Why was her heartbeat so quick? It had to be her guilt. She couldn't believe she was an easily frightened woman. "I'm tired. But otherwise, I'm all right."

He nodded, hands on his lap. "Do you want me to leave?"

"No." She straightened, but a cramp slashed through her abdomen. "Can we talk for a while?"

He smiled. "Of course." The bed dipped when he shifted his position. "If there's anything I can do to make you happy here, you have only to mention it. Lady Mary's allowance is all set. She lives close to Mayfair now."

"That's fantastic." She winced at a new pang.

"She sent me a letter to thank us. I forgot to tell you."

Another cramp lanced through her, but his words softened the pain. "You're so kind to me." She trapped her bottom lip between her teeth not to cry. "There's something I must tell you. Something that will make you change your mind about me."

He frowned.

"Anthony, I—" The rest of her confession was swallowed by a gasp. The pain clenching her belly was so excruciating she couldn't scream.

"Isabella." He put a hand on her shoulder as she sagged forwards.

Another cramp tore a groan of agony out of her. She gripped his arm, sinking her fingers into his muscles. It was like being slashed in two.

"I'll send for the physician." He went to stand up, but she tugged at his arm.

"Dr. Eileen Norris," she said among pants. "Please. Lawson knows where to find her."

"Immediately. I'll tell Lawson." He rushed out of the bedroom.

She curled up into a ball, rocked by muscular spasms that made her want to throw up. The room spun. She screamed in pain.

"Madam." Lawson swept into view and put a hand on Isabella's forehead. "I've sent for Dr. Norris. What is it?"

"The baby." Each word stole her breath.

Lawson shoved aside the covers. "You're bleeding."

She gnashed her teeth against another spasm. Minutes of complete agony passed. Sweat drenched her nightgown. Each spasm rocked her harder.

Lawson came and went from the bedroom, talking with someone. Another maid appeared. Isabella might have seen the Dowager but couldn't be sure. The whole household seemed to be up and about.

"Dr. Norris is here," Lawson said, but Isabella couldn't say anything.

Heavy footsteps approached. "My wife felt sick all of a sudden," Anthony said.

"I'll take care of her, Your Grace."

Hearing Dr. Norris's calm voice brought Isabella some comfort.

"I can help," he said. "Let me stay."

"Thank you, Your Grace, but Lawson will do."

There were mutters and footfalls, Anthony said something else, then quiet. Except for her groans of pain.

Dr. Norris rushed to Isabella's side. "What happened?"

"Cramps," Lawson said, "and she's bleeding."

"Let me see." The doctor pulled down the covers.

Isabella stifled a scream in the pillow.

Dr. Norris checked her pulse and touched her neck. "I know it hurts, but I need you to lie down and be still."

Tears blurred her vision, but she did as she was told.

twenty-nine

Anthony waited for Dr. Norris in the sitting room.

Isabella's terrified face and her screams of pain would forever stay in his memories. The ticking of the clock on the mantelpiece thundered. Each second without news about Isabella was a stab.

Not a sound came from the upper floor. The coming and going of the servants had stopped a while ago, and no one was telling him bloody anything. He should march to Isabella's bedroom and demand to know what the hell was happening to his wife.

"Being so nervous won't help." Grandmama was perched on the armchair, sipping tea as if it were a normal evening. "Bad news travels fast. I'm sure it's a case of indigestion."

"It seemed more serious than that." He paused next to the door, trying to catch any noises. A faint scream reached him, but he might be mistaken.

"She has had problems with her stomach for a while," Grandmama said in a voice that lacked confidence.

Rogers opened the door. "Your Grace, Dr. Norris is here to see you."

"Finally."

The doctor's short stature didn't diminish the aura of competence and authority she radiated. He tried not to look at what seemed to be a blood stain on her skirt.

Rogers shut the door once the doctor was in.

She bowed her head, cheeks flustered. "Your Grace."

"How's my wife?"

Dr. Norris put down her bag, her face tense. "I'm sorry to inform you that Her Grace lost her child."

"What the—" Anthony didn't finish the sentence, letting the words sink in. Or rather, one word.

Grandmama's eyes flared wide, but her lips remained pressed together in an expression that could be mistaken for deep sorrow and not shock.

Isabella had been with child. Anthony tried to contain the pang in his chest, the dark thoughts cramming his mind, and the need to get answers.

"I understand it's a shock," Dr. Norris said. "Unfortunately, there was a massive bleeding that—"

Lawson barging into the room interrupted her, pushing the door open hard enough to slam it against the wall.

"Dr. Norris!" she said. "You can't talk now."

Grandmama rose from the armchair, fists clenched. "How dare you come here like that? Leave this room immediately."

"Dr. Norris." Lawson shook her head, and wisps of her hair flipped around her flustered face.

"Leave," he ordered. "I must know how my wife is."

Lawson shot him a glare he returned. Finally, she dropped a quick curtsy before leaving as quickly as she'd arrived.

He exhaled through clenched teeth. "What were you saying, doctor?"

Frowning, Dr. Norris glanced from the door to him a couple of times. Then her eyebrows lowered as if she'd just realised something. "The duchess suffered a major bleeding that caused the miscarriage. Unfortunately, the first phase of a pregnancy is often the most dangerous. She's weak and might develop a fever in the next few days. The afterbirth is still attached, so I will apply warm tampons and change them every hour. That will allow me to remove the afterbirth tomorrow morning without causing further distress for the duchess."

"Is Isabella risking her life now?" Grandmama asked, sitting down again.

Dr. Norris hesitated before answering. "The bleeding stopped for now, and the risk of infection is low. But caution is of extreme importance."

He seemed to choke on his own breath at the thought of Isabella dying.

"The duchess is young and healthy," the doctor said. "This unfortunate incident won't compromise her ability to carry children in the future."

He nodded, staring at the flames in the hearth. If he asked more questions about the pregnancy—how far exactly was Isabella? Were the stomach problems due to the pregnancy? Did the doctor know who the father was?—both the doctor and Grandmama would realise he knew nothing about Isabella's condition.

She would be blamed for having deceived him, for deceiving everyone. Grandmama would ask him to send her away or even to get an annulment. More importantly, Isabella's life would be a nightmare. His reputation would recover. Hers wouldn't.

"What else does the duchess need?" Grandmama asked in a practical tone that masked her surprise.

"Meat, not overcooked," Dr. Norris said, "absolute rest for at least a week. The duchess must not leave her bed until I'm sure the bleeding won't start again. Plenty of soups and tea. Her room needs to be warm and dry at all times. The bedsheets must be changed every day. And of course..." She glanced at him. "Your Grace, no intercourse."

Grandmama arched her brow but said nothing.

"May I see my wife?"

"She's asleep now, but yes, as long as you don't tire her. The duchess was lucky. Many women die from a miscarriage like that. Please do take that into consideration in the next few days."

"What do you mean by that?" Grandmama said, letting her temper slip.

Anthony had a hunch. "My secretary will pay your bill tomorrow, and I'll have a room prepared for you for tonight, doctor."

"Thank you, Your Grace." The doctor picked her bag up and seemed about to say something else, but then she curtsied and left.

The moment Dr. Norris closed the door behind her, Grandmama sprang up to her feet and glared at him with such fierceness he expected the whole house to burn to the ground.

"She was with child." She clenched her fists, trembling. "How stupid of me not to realise that! The signs were there."

He leant against the wall. How stupid of him as well. The hurried marriage, the sobbing, the quick mood changes, the talk about honesty—everything made sense now.

She strode to him. "You took her before she agreed to marry you because, of course, she was already carrying your child during the ceremony. Otherwise the afterbirth wouldn't be such a problem."

He was about to protest his innocence, but that meant blaming Isabella, and while she was at fault, he needed to hear her side of the story first. Again, he chose silence.

"That's the reason for the hurry." Grandmama's eyes were ablaze with anger. The fact she was as tall as he was made her stare impossible to escape.

He scratched his chin. "Grand—"

"I haven't finished! So don't talk. I don't want to hear your pathetic excuses."

The harsh, angry tone caught him by surprise. She'd never given him an order without respect or affection.

"Isabella was forced to marry you. She had no choice." She pointed a finger at him. "You took away that choice from her. I thought you were better than that."

He swallowed hard, pushing down the urge to tell the truth.

"I've always thought Patrick was the flippant one between the two of you, but what you did to that poor girl is inexcusable." Her voice cracked with sobs. "I know she had a role in this. I know she has her share of guilt, but heavens, you're older than she is and have experience, and you should have controlled yourself. You should have been careful with her. Protect her."

He worked his jaw, struggling to keep his temper down.

Grandmama wasn't finished. "You're my grandson! You're a duke of the House of Beaufort, and you're going to take your responsibility."

"Of course, I'm going to," he gritted out. "That's what I've bloody done so far."

"Mind your language with me! You aren't the one lying in a bed, half dead. You don't risk your reputation and title. If the truth comes out, the blame will be on that poor girl."

He squeezed his lips together, gathering the patience to listen to a sermon he didn't deserve. But Grandmama was right, and Isabella needed his protection.

"By taking her before marriage, you ruined her. She had to marry you. When you told me you wanted a quick wedding, I didn't think, not even for a moment, that Isabella might be with child, because I trusted you. I was sure you wouldn't have taken her like a beast in heat. I was sure you would have never, ever deceived me by omitting she was with child. And as a consequence, she nearly died. How wrong I was. I shall never forgive you."

Clamping a hand on her mouth, she hurried out of the room, leaving him aching as if a dozen pugilists had punched him in the chest at the same time.

He took a moment to collect his thoughts. The evening was one shock after the other. First Isabella's pregnancy, now Grandmama's outburst. It was the first time he'd seen his grandmother losing her temper like that.

He rubbed the bridge of his nose and took a few deep breaths before going upstairs. A couple of maids were whispering in a corner but fell silent when they spotted him.

"Your Grace," they said together, curtsying.

There would be rumours, gossip, and blame thrown around, but he'd be damned if he tolerated them in his own house.

"Return to your rooms."

The maids almost tripped in their haste to obey.

He knocked on Isabella's door. "Isabella."

A teary-eyed, fierce-looking Lawson opened the door. She didn't greet him, and he didn't give a damn. He brushed past her, twitching his nose at the unmistakable smell of blood mingled with that of carbolic acid.

Isabella lay among cushions in the bed, pale and her breathing soft. Even without the doctor's diagnosis, he would have guessed she'd risked dying. It was as if the very essence of life had been sucked out of her body, leaving her bloodless.

Lawson was on him like a hawk. "What are your intentions, Your Grace?"

He was growing tired of being disrespected.

"She can't leave the bed," she said. "She might die if she does. I beg you, you can't throw her out now, nor tomorrow. The duchess is like a daughter to me."

Also, he was growing tired of people assuming horrible things about him. "I won't tolerate your tone any longer, Lawson."

"Your…"

"Leave or you'll search for new employment."

She lost some of her fierce attitude. She glanced at Isabella before dropping a quick curtsy and leaving.

Finally.

Once alone, he allowed his emotions to overwhelm him. He wasn't sure how he felt. There was worry about Isabella. He could have lost her. If she'd told him she was with child, a physician would have come regularly to visit her and perhaps she wouldn't have almost died.

On the other hand, she'd lied to him; she'd tricked him into marrying her. He would be lying if he said he wasn't angry and ashamed of how easily he'd believed her. How easily he'd believed she didn't care about his scarred face.

But he understood why she'd lied. Almost. The father of the child must have refused to marry her, was already married, or wasn't in her life anymore. Without getting married, she would have faced poverty and starvation. Like Lady Mary.

Everything made sense now.

He gently took her hand and held it, glad to find it warm. In front of her paleness and weakness, it was difficult to stay angry. She fluttered her eyes open, and for some reason, he felt like a thief caught red-handed. A quick breath escaped her, and her chest rose under the covers.

"Anthony. I'm..." She swallowed a few times with difficulty. "I know..." Her grip on his fingers lacked strength.

"You need rest. Don't talk. I only wanted to see you for a moment." He released her hand and tucked her arm under the covers. "Dr. Norris was clear. Absolute rest."

Tears welled in her eyes. "I'm sorry."

"So am I. But we'll talk when you're strong again."

She blinked the tears away.

"Sleep." He caressed the top of her head. "Don't worry about anything. Just get better."

He waited until fatigue overwhelmed her again and she fell asleep. He wanted to stay with her all night, perhaps sleeping on the chair or the sofa, but she might get too agitated, and he didn't want to cause her further distress or get in the doctor's way.

He found Lawson in the corridor pacing with her arms folded over her chest. She straightened when he closed the door.

"If you need help taking care of the duchess, ask Rogers and he'll send you the maids. If anything happens, call me immediately. Dr. Norris will sleep here tonight." He went to his room before she could talk.

He lay in his bed, suddenly exhausted. His pride hurt after Grandmama's speech.

And his heart was broken by Isabella's lies.

thirty

After a night of exhausted sleep, Isabella lay still in the bed as Dr. Norris worked.

The laudanum and the tampons had soothed the pain, but her whole body was sore and aching. Just bending her knees required too much energy. She winced as a sting hurt her.

Dr. Norris paused. "Apologies, Your Grace, but it needs to be done."

She put a hand on her empty belly. She'd been with child for a short time, but she missed it; she no longer carried a life.

"I've finished." Dr. Norris wiped her hands on a cloth. "You will experience more bleeding for a few days, but then it should stop. If the bleeding persists, send for me immediately."

She glanced at the heap of cloths stained with her blood. How could she be alive after bleeding so much? "How did the duke react when you told him about the baby?"

"Stunned." The doctor collected her tools and bottles. "Your Grace, it's not my place, but I guess the duke isn't the father."

She shook her head.

"And he wasn't aware of your condition."

Another shake of her head.

"The duke showed remarkable control of his emotions although I noticed the change in his expression."

"Do you think he'll send me away?"

"I don't know, madam." The doctor touched Isabella's forehead. "Many women, who suffered from what you experienced, get affected by melancholia. Should that happen, send for me."

If Anthony allowed her to stay.

After Dr. Norris left, Lawson fussed around the bed, adding pillows, cleaning, and changing the stained blankets. When she finished, she stood for a few moments watching her with teary eyes.

"The duke asked me to tell him when you were ready to see him."

"I owe him an explanation." Isabella propped herself up on her elbows.

"We can delay the meeting, though. I could tell him you need rest, which is true."

"No. I want to talk to him now."

"Very well."

Lawson helped her sit before leaving the room. There was a quick exchange outside of the door Isabella didn't grasp. She stiffened when Anthony entered, filling the bedroom with his intense presence.

He must have spent a horrible night too, judging by his dark-circled eyes. Even his jacket didn't stretch taut across his shoulders as usual, and the scar seemed more evident.

Emotion tightened her chest. He took a tentative step closer as if he didn't want to make brusque movements that might frighten her. Well, too late. She was scared to death.

"I hope you feel better," he said, sitting on a chair next to the bed.

"Much better. Just exhausted." She tugged at the lapels of her dressing gown for no reason.

Where should she start? An apology, an explanation, or a practical agreement on their future? Did he want an annulment?

He leant back, seemingly at ease, but the tension in his neck and hands betrayed his discomfort. He didn't push her to talk, though.

"I meant to tell you," she said, although the words sounded lame.

"Before or after the wedding?"

"After. The plan was originally to make you believe the child was yours." She chanced a glance at him. "I assumed you were eager to consummate the marriage."

His eyes were as cold and hard as emeralds.

"But the guilt was crushing me," she said. "I couldn't find the right moment to tell you the truth, and I was worried about your reaction. I still am. But then last night, when you were here, I did want to tell you. But the spasms became too painful, and I couldn't speak. I managed the situation poorly, and I apologise for having lied to you."

He rested his chin on his fist, but his movements were unnaturally slow. "You never meant to marry me."

She pulled the covers up. "Marrying you was the solution to a serious problem with few choices." It sounded awful, but there was no point in making it sound less awful.

"Who's the father?"

She closed her fists. How could she tell him it was Patrick? The truth would destroy him, and she wasn't sure how he would react. No, she knew. He would be furious, and rightly so.

"I can't tell you. Please don't force me to reveal his name. Besides, he isn't in London anymore."

He flexed his fingers open and closed. "Were you forced?"

"No." She turned towards him. "He was honest from the beginning and told me he had no intention of marrying me, that he wanted only to enjoy himself. He had rules about the quick affair."

"Such a gentleman." His tone was low and lethal.

"I agreed with his idea. I just wanted to try to be with a man and enjoy myself. I was curious and didn't want to marry him."

"Do you love him?" So much pain rang out of his voice.

"No, I don't. I never did."

He released a breath through clenched teeth. A long silence, heavy with her guilt, stretched between them.

She cleared her throat. "I guess you want me to leave. I'll leave as soon as I can travel. Do not worry."

"No." The brusque word was an order. "You'll stay here."

She was surprised. "Do you still want me to be your wife?"

He rose from the armchair to sit on the bed next to her. A whiff of his cedarwood scent reached her, covering that of blood. "I'm not going to lie. Your deceit hurt me. You tricked me into marrying you, and I'm angry."

She lowered her gaze because the glint in his eyes was hard to meet.

He took her chin and gently lifted it. "But you almost died, and that had me thinking."

It made her think as well.

"Think about what?" she said.

"The moments we spent together when we laughed and were happy, were they part of the plan?"

"No." She gripped his hand. "I enjoyed every single one. They were honest, happy moments."

If her answer satisfied him, he didn't show any sign. "Do you care about me at all?" Pain rang out in his voice.

"I do."

Again, his face remained unfathomable. "My grandmother doesn't know the child wasn't mine."

"Why didn't you tell her?"

"She wouldn't forgive you," he said. "She would want you to leave. Please don't tell her anything. It'll only start more discussions and arguments I don't want to deal with right now." He exhaled, rubbing his forehead. "I took an oath. I swore to be by your side no matter what, and I meant every word." He faced her. "No more lies. No more secrets."

"I swear it. I truly am sorry." Her voice cracked with emotion.

The only good thing about the terrible situation was that her chest felt lighter now that the truth was out.

"You're tired." He stroked her jaw with his thumb, and the kindness in his gesture calmed her quick pulse. "We'll talk again when you're better." He was about to say something else when the Dowager entered.

"Isabella." She narrowed her gaze at Anthony. "I didn't mean to interrupt. I'll be back later."

"I was just leaving, Grandmama." He stood up. The tiredness and pain on his face made her want to hug him and beg for his forgiveness until he believed her. "I'll see you later." He cast a long glance at her before leaving.

"How are you?" The Dowager lacked her usual haughty attitude.

"Tired. Sore. But alive."

The Dowager sat on the stuffed chair in a swish of silk and lowered her gaze. It had to be the first time Isabella had seen the Dowager so demure.

"Was it me?" the Dowager asked in a whisper. "Did I cause the incident?"

"Heavens, no. I'm sure you didn't."

"I upset you with my silly dislike for your pink gowns. You were distraught. I can't stop thinking your predicament is my fault."

"It's not." She touched the Dowager's hand.

The Dowager watched her with compassion. "Anyway, I do apologise for having upset you."

"Water under the bridge."

"Now tell me how you feel and what I can do for you."

She put a hand on her tender belly, and a sob came out of

nowhere. Maybe the Dowager's sudden kindness triggered her emotions. Or maybe it was guilt all over again because, during the past months, she'd worried about everything except her child. She'd only thought about how to find a solution for her situation, and now she would never hug it.

"I lost it. It's dead. I didn't have the time to realise how important it was for me, but the loss hurt." It was the first time she'd faced the enormity of her loss.

"Oh, darling." The Dowager held her in a surprisingly motherly embrace.

Isabella leant against her and cried as if the pain she'd kept inside needed to flow out. The Dowager patted her back, whispering something Isabella didn't understand.

"I know it hurts. And I'm not going to lie to you, darling. It'll always hurt." The Dowager rocked her gently. "People don't understand that losing an unborn child hurts deeply." When the sobs died down, the Dowager let her go. "You're young and strong. Time will help you. I promise."

"Aren't you angry with me for having lied?"

"I'm not happy about it. But what happened to you happened to me as well," the Dowager said so low Isabella barely heard her.

"Did you lose a child? Sorry, stupid question. Of course you did. Anthony's father."

"Not only him. I had a miscarriage a few weeks after my wedding, like you. At that time, doctors dealt with miscarriages in a more brutal way." Each word came out slowly. "Their practice was dangerous and so painful..." She waved a hand. "You don't need to hear me complaining, just that I know how you feel."

"I'm sorry." She couldn't believe she was holding hands with the Dowager.

"And of course, what Anthony did to you happened to me as well."

Isabella had no idea what she meant. Anthony had been nothing but kind to her.

"My husband took me before our courtship even began. I told him I wasn't convinced, but he said everyone did it. I was young and naïve, and afterwards, what we did left me no choice but to marry him. See, I discovered I was with child, too. George married me, but I felt my choice was taken from me."

"I'm sorry, but Anthony didn't...I mean I was happy. I agreed."

"At least he did the honourable thing and married you, but I shall never forgive him for his poor judgement."

"Oh, no, please." She squeezed the Dowager's hand. "Anthony is an honourable man. He treated me with nothing but kindness. He doesn't deserve your scorn."

"But he didn't risk bleeding to death, did he? He wasn't thinking with his brain when he was with you. And I don't understand what took him. He's always been such a sensible man. He wanted to court you, but then he got impatient. Irresponsible. Not to mention he didn't send for a physician to visit you regularly in the past weeks. Very poor judgement on his part."

No, only on her.

"He couldn't have known that a miscarriage would have happened."

"He didn't blame you for losing the child, did he?" The Dowager's tone promised a swift retribution if the answer were yes.

"Heavens, no. Did your husband blame you?"

"No, not George, but someone else. Those were different times. Women couldn't even speak of wanting to vote or go to the university. A woman doctor was unthinkable."

"Anthony is nothing but kind and responsible. I promise. He did nothing wrong."

The Dowager patted her hand. "I'm touched by your wish to protect him, but see, if he'd waited for the wedding, you wouldn't have felt pressured, ashamed, or worried. You wouldn't have been desperate to marry quickly. We can't exclude the tension of the past weeks caused the incident."

She hadn't thought about that. "It's not Anthony's fault."

The Dowager regained her composure. "Anyway. You will focus on getting better. That's the only thing that matters." She rose with her usual grace and walked to the door. "Needless to say, you'll keep all the pink gowns you want."

Isabella chuckled.

thirty-one

Anthony read again the letter Patrick had sent him from Cabo Verde. Usual chatter about the weather, business, and the beautiful Sophia. Patrick claimed to be utterly smitten with her. Not a word about Isabella. Of course, he didn't know about her condition yet.

Anthony lowered the letter on his desk and rubbed the bridge of his nose.

Patrick—a gentleman who thought only about pleasure, didn't seek marriage, and was out of London. The description of Isabella's mysterious lover fit his brother like a glove. Even the rules... Patrick had spoken about his rake's rules. Something about no gossip, no marriage, but only pleasure.

Not to mention that Isabella and Patrick had spent a lot of time together before he left for Cabo Verde. And she was looking for him that day when she'd fainted.

He exhaled. Patrick. Damn Patrick. Curse his bloody urges.

Fatigue more than anger flared up in Anthony's chest. The sleepless night had dampened his mood, and Patrick was lucky an ocean separated them.

He thumped the desk, causing the pencils to rattle. There was little he could do now, and Isabella was his wife. Patrick would be dealt with when he returned. This time, Anthony would not protect him.

He went to Isabella's room, his footsteps the only sound in the corridor. Since the incident, the house had been eerily quiet. The servants did their best not to make noises that might disturb her.

"Isabella?" He knocked on the door.

Lawson, who was now Isabella's guard dog, opened the door. "Your Grace."

"You may leave now. I wish to be alone with my wife." He walked past her.

For once, the maid didn't hesitate.

Isabella's pallor hadn't improved. Her lips were bloodless as well. He didn't remember the last time he'd seen her smiling. No, he couldn't confront her about Patrick. Not now. She needed to be fully recovered.

He sat on the bed next to her. "Are you bleeding again?"

"No." She tried to sit up, but winced.

"Let me." He slid an arm around her waist and gently pulled her up. She was as frail as a sparrow.

When she was up and resting against the pillows, he released her.

"Did you want to talk to me about something?" she asked after a moment of silence.

"No. I just wanted to see how you were faring."

"I'm improving. It doesn't look like I am, but I am."

"Do you need anything?"

"Yes." She shifted on the pillows. "I would like to know what you think. Have you changed your mind about your marriage to me? Do you want me to leave?"

"No." The answer came out quickly without him thinking. But it was true.

He didn't want her to leave. He didn't want an annulment, and not because an annulment or a divorce would tarnish the

House of Beaufort's reputation. She was his wife, and he'd sworn to protect her.

And he cared about her.

He closed his hand around hers as a new riot of opposing emotions waged war inside him. There was anger at having been deceived, disappointment at her lies, and a sense of defeat. But despite all that, he wanted her to stay with him because there was tenderness and care as well.

A knock came from the door. "Your Grace?" the maid said.

He removed his hand. "Come in."

The maid carried a tray with a steaming cup. "For Your Grace." She placed the tray on the nightstand.

Isabella sniffled. "Coffee."

"Just as you like it." He waved a hand. "With all the cream, milk, cinnamon...I hope I didn't forget anything. The list was quite long. But Dr. Norris said you could drink it."

Unshed tears glistened in her eyes. "Thank you." She inched towards him and hugged him.

The hug lacked strength, a reminder of how frail she was, but he had to swallow a couple of times. He held her, wondering how they could have a normal life after what had happened.

THREE WEEKS HAD PASSED since the incident, and Anthony was no less worried about Isabella.

While she'd left the bed and her health had improved, her mood remained gloomy. She was pale, quiet, and ate very little. Spoke even less. She worked in the glasshouse for an hour each day before getting too tired and sleeping for hours.

He'd caught her with puffy red eyes more than once, and he hadn't had the heart to talk to her about Patrick. Patrick could wait. Her health couldn't.

He observed her as she was sitting in front of him at dinner.

Her beautiful pale-yellow gown with its delicate satin sleeves left her shoulders half bare, but the dress did nothing to brighten her gaunt face. She fiddled with her white soup, twirling her spoon without using it. Her collarbone protruded too much for his liking.

"Would you like something different?" he asked. "Grandmama took care of the menu in the past weeks, but if you feel better, you can order everything you like from Cook."

"Absolutely." Grandmama nodded encouragingly.

She nearly jolted. "No, the menu is fine. The soup is delicious."

"You're eating like a bird." Grandmama's disapproving tone was sweeter than usual.

"I don't have a lot of appetite. I get easily tired."

"I think it's the lack of activity." Anthony didn't believe her tiredness had to do with the incident, not physically, at least. "Mrs. Fawcett is organising a public speech to raise support for the women suffrage. Would you like to go?"

"Heavens, no." Isabella rubbed her forehead. "Too tiring, and I haven't done anything for the movement in a while. I need to lie down. I'd better go to my room."

A footman helped her out of her chair.

"I'll have your dinner delivered to your room." Grandmama nodded at a footman.

"It's not necessary."

"You must eat, darling." Grandmama gave her a stern look.

She bowed her head. "If you'll excuse me."

He stood up as well and followed her with his gaze as she left, shoulders hunched.

"Melancholia." Grandmother shook her head. "Nasty condition of the soul. I caught her crying in the glasshouse the other day, clenching her belly. She didn't work at the plants at all. She sat on the bench and watched the fountain."

"Yes, the gardener told me he's doing the whole work." He

lowered his spoon, his appetite was gone as well. "I should take her somewhere. Go on a holiday. A change of scenery would do her good."

"Excellent idea. Where?"

"Our property on Bjørn Island. Plenty of green landscapes, and the sea is beautiful."

Grandmama gave him one of her incendiary stares. "You must be joking. That forsaken, rainy, gloomy island where the ground is frosted eleven months per year and it's so close to the North Pole you need five layers of clothes in August? Absolutely not. Perfectly happy people start to suffer from melancholia after spending a couple of hours there. Not to mention the uncomfortable sailing on a boat to reach it. A dark mansion isn't what Isabella needs."

"The cliffs are beautiful, and the northern lights are visible from the balcony."

"Pish. A sickening green glow that lasts fifteen minutes while you freeze to death. Some show. You can get the same effect by drinking absinthe while staring at a fire. At least you'll be warm." She wiped her mouth. "Take her to Mytos. The Ionian Sea, the hot weather, and the sunlight will be good for her."

He hadn't been on that sweltering, salty island in years. Not his favourite place. "We'll get ready to leave as soon as possible. You may start packing as well."

She paused eating her soup. Her pearl earrings stopped swinging. "I'm not going. The sun is too strong, the food is too spicy, and the locals are too friendly."

"Well, it was your idea, Grandmama. Isabella will appreciate your presence. I'll send Rogers ahead to get the house ready."

"But...I didn't mean to come." Her stunned expression would be comical if he weren't worried about Isabella.

"Thank you, Grandmama." He kissed her cheek. "If you'll excuse me, I have to see my wife."

Grandmama muttered something he didn't catch.

He went to Isabella's bedroom through the door in his room.

She was sitting on the bed in a pool of yellow satin, her shoulders shaking with sobs. The awful sounds tore at his soul.

"Isabella."

She wiped her face quickly, smearing the rouge on her cheeks. "I didn't hear you."

He took her face and searched her black eyes. They'd always been shining with mirth, but now they were two dark abysses. He could protect her from gossip but not from the sadness poisoning her.

"It's nothing." She sniffled. "I'm being silly."

"No, you aren't." He sat next to her. "You should admit you're mourning your child. That's the first step towards healing."

"I want to be strong. After all the lies I told you, I don't think I have the right to be sad. I want to do something to repay your kindness, but the more I try, the more tired I feel. Each day it seems the burden on my chest becomes heavier."

"You have the right to be sad. But the more you wallow in your sadness, the more difficult getting rid of it becomes." He held her hand. "I want to take you away from London. We have a house on the Ionian island of Mytos. The sunlight will cheer you up."

"I don't want to go."

"This house is filled with bad memories. You need a change."

"What about your work?"

"I trust my secretary, and I can work from there." He kissed her knuckles. "I want to start over. A new beginning for us. And I hope you'll agree."

"I don't want to cause you more trouble."

"No troubles. Think about all the new plants you might bring here for the glasshouse."

Her eyebrow spiked. "That's interesting."

He exhaled, and she rested her head on his chest.

"I'll do my best to be better," she whispered. "You deserve that."

"You must get better for yourself first." He wrapped an arm

around her shoulders. "My father suffered from melancholia, grieving for my mother. He never recovered. No matter what we did for him, he never got better. I think he didn't want to."

She shivered. "I'm sorry."

"I don't want your melancholia to get worse."

She snuggled closer. "May I ask you a favour?"

"Anything."

"It's selfish of me, but will you sleep with me tonight? I feel better when you hold me."

He couldn't refuse. "Of course."

She removed her silk slippers. "I don't want to call Lawson. She'll understand I cried and be worried. I just want to get under the covers and sleep." She stood up. "Do you mind helping me with the buttons? I'll do the rest."

He undid the back of her dress, noticing how her bones protruded from the skin on her back. No one knew how to treat melancholia with success, but staying in London and doing nothing but think about what had happened wouldn't improve her condition.

"Done. I'll get changed and be back."

"Thank you." Holding up her bodice with an arm, she stared at him. Her large black eyes had lost the sparkle that had attracted him to her. Now they were filled with pain—a sign of her ripped innocence.

After he undressed with Wilson's help, he went to Isabella's bedroom again. Wrapped in her dressing gown, she stared at the log fire in the hearth. The glow cast deep shadows on her gaunt face. She looked like a tormented soul Hell wanted to claim. She flashed an unconvincing smile when he stepped inside.

He waited for her to slide under the covers before tucking her in. She shifted closer to him when he lay next to her.

"Thank you, Anthony. I know I don't deserve your kindness, but thank you."

"Shush." He held her and kissed her forehead. "I care about you. You're my ray of sunlight."

"Some sunlight."

"Just passing clouds. It'll be sunny again."

She shivered and rested her cheek on his chest. He caressed her back, feeling her tense muscles. When her breathing became soft and regular, he kept caressing her, wondering if she'd ever care about him as he cared about her.

thirty-two

Isabella couldn't summon much enthusiasm about the imminent journey, and she didn't understand why.

Travelling and seeing the Mediterranean Sea and its flora had always been one of her dreams. It was summer, and the weather had to be lovely on Mytos. Yet an endless fatigue weighed her down, sucking her enthusiasm. Lawson had efficiently packed everything, stashing light-coloured gowns, parasols, and pretty large hats while Isabella finished a letter for Patrick. She'd postponed writing to him for too long, but he had the right to know what had happened. Although she didn't want Patrick to say anything to Anthony. That was her duty.

Her parents were drowning her in letters although they didn't know the truth. Only that she'd been sick. They'd wanted to return to London, but she'd persuaded them not to. She loved them, but they could be exhausting, and she was leaving, anyway.

Lawson served her a cup of tea. "Everything is ready, madam."

"Except my mood. Why do I feel so tired all the time?"

"Because you think too much about what happened. The duke is right. Fresh air and sunlight will do you good."

There was a knock on the door. "Your Grace, Lady Helen is here."

Not even her sister's visits had helped her feel better. Besides, like her parents, Helen didn't know the whole truth. Only that a disease had caused Isabella to stay in bed for a while. Time had changed since the Dowager had married, but miscarriages were still little understood.

Helen walked in, stunning in a tight blue gown that exalted her curves. Her cheeks were full and rosy, and her hair shone with a glossy hue. She seemed taller and stronger than usual, even happier.

Isabella caught a glimpse of her reflection in the mirror. She looked like the elder sister, aged badly after a bout of cholera.

"I'm so excited for you." Helen kissed her cheek. "An Ionian island. You must be thrilled."

She searched for a free chair for Helen, but aside from the stool at her escritoire, the room was crowded with boxes, trunks, and opened suitcases. "We can have tea in the sitting room."

"Do not worry. Don't stand on ceremony for me. We can have tea here." Helen sat at the escritoire in a froth of fabric.

Lawson bowed before leaving.

"How are you and the duke?" Helen asked, tugging at her gloves.

"I'm all right. He's wonderful. He does everything he can to make me happy."

"It doesn't seem to work. You're awfully pale."

"You look lovely."

Helen laughed, a deep, throaty laugh Isabella didn't remember having ever heard. "I'm so glad I didn't go to Boston. Since Mother left—" Her laughter died swiftly. "Sorry. How awful of me. I mean..."

She took Helen's hand. "Don't apologise for being happy."

Lawson returned. "I'm sorry to trouble you, madam, but Mrs. Stamell wants to know what Cook should prepare for tonight's dinner instead of the salmon. She couldn't find fresh fish at the market."

"Excuse me for a moment, Helen." Isabella left the bedroom.

She wasn't sure she enjoyed taking care of the menu and the other lady-of-the-house's duties, not at the moment, but the Dowager had insisted, claiming that keeping the mind engaged was the best remedy for melancholia.

After she talked with Mrs. Stamell and chose to replace the salmon with duck, she had to pause before returning to her bedroom. She was breathless as if she'd climbed over one of the hills in the Lake District. Her body wasn't used to exercising anymore.

When she entered, Helen jolted, a hand fluttering to her chest. She straightened on the stool. "All done?"

She frowned at her sister's fidgeting. "Yes, sorry."

She tried to focus on Helen's chatter about Gemma Bellincioni, an Italian soprano who had launched a new style of hats, but she simply nodded and sipped her tea.

When Helen left, asking her to write from Mytos, she felt guilty at the relief of finally being alone.

Perhaps going to Mytos was a good idea.

GOING to Mytos had been a terrible idea.

On the steamship *Adventure*, heading for the Strait of Gibraltar, Anthony was holding his wife as she cast up her accounts. The ship rocked right and left, slapped by a storm that didn't have any intentions of getting calmer. The rocking wasn't excessive, barely an inch or two per side, but Isabella's body overreacted, and he cursed himself for the decision to take her on this trip.

"You don't have to see this," she said, leaning over the handrail.

"Don't worry about me." He put a hand on her forehead as she emptied her stomach.

When she finished, she grabbed the handrail with both hands. Even though they were on the covered deck, the chilly rain splattered against them, and her hair was soaked.

"We need to leave." He put a hand on her waist. "I'm not sure we should be here during a storm."

"Here is better than the stuffy cabin." She leant against him, exhaling. "Where's Lawson?"

"Doing what you're doing but sensibly in her cabin." He helped her along the slippery passageway leading to their cabin.

First-class cabins lined the covered deck, guaranteeing a nice, open view of the ocean that was now boiling with rage.

"Is your grandmother all right?" she asked as he opened the door.

"She's in the dining hall, having dinner."

"Oh, goodness." She clamped a hand on her mouth. "It's her duchess power for sure."

He took a towel and dried her face. "I've never seen her feel sick. I don't believe she's human."

She sagged on the floor, paler and more exhausted than she'd been in London. "I'm so sorry, Anthony. I've caused you nothing but problems, and lots of unpleasant moments involving me being sick here."

"The first time I'd sailed on a ship, I wanted to die, so sick I was. I understand your pain, but it'll go away. And going to Mytos was my idea. I didn't know you suffered the sea so terribly."

She closed her eyes for a moment. "Neither did I. I've taken short trips on the Thames, but this ship and the sea are another matter."

He sat next to her. "You should eat something."

She scrunched up her face. "I'd rather have a tooth pulled out."

"Trust me, you'll feel better." He rose to take the tray with the food he'd ordered for her. "Hot, sweet tea and flatbread. Simple but effective."

"Are you absolutely sure it's going to make me feel better?"

"I am." He poured her a cup and broke a piece of flatbread. "The stomach needs something to do. And you can't be worse than how you feel now."

"I'm not sure, but all right." She did as told and sipped the tea.

He sat next to her, his back on the wall. "I like this gentle rocking. It lulls me to sleep."

"Gentle? I feel like the floor is going to swap places with the ceiling."

He laughed. "No, really. This is nothing. I've been on board ships when the sea was so enraged that all the cups fell to the floor and I was thrown off my bed. I couldn't walk straight, and the ship seemed about to capsize at any moment. That was rough."

"Why are you so good to me?" She chewed a small bite of flatbread. "You could be with the Dowager, having dinner. You could have sent me away. You could have asked for an annulment."

He brushed a sable curl of her hair from her forehead. "I am where I want to be. You promised not to lie to me again. That's enough for me."

She put aside the cup to hug him. "I care about you, too. I do."

"If you stop feeling undeserving of happiness, your health will improve tenfold."

"Easier said than done." She chewed another piece of flatbread.

"I want to ask you something."

"Anything." She paused drinking.

"Were you hesitant to marry me because you felt guilty or because of my face?"

"Heavens, Anthony. It was never your face." She put a gentle hand on his scarred side. "I'm so sorry if my behaviour made you believe that. I was conflicted about what to do. I was scared, and I knew I was being horrible and selfish. But your scar doesn't bother me." She traced the scar with her finger as if to make a point.

Hell, her touch.

He wasn't ready for the absolute shock going through him, so intense it was almost painful. He closed his eyes and leant into her soft palm, trying to remember when he'd last felt a woman's touch.

Not that he cared about being with any other woman other than Isabella, but the kindness of her touch was overwhelming. The sensation was equal parts pain and pleasure.

"I'll get better," she whispered. "I'll do everything to get better."

"I'm sure of that, and let's start with a change of clothes. Your gown is wet."

"I can wait for Lawson."

"We'll be on Mytos if you wait for her. Even my grandmother's lady's maid is sick. Wilson is passed out in his bed. It's a massacre."

He helped her out of the gown as the cabin rocked gently. She avoided his gaze.

"Uncomfortable?" he asked.

"A bit."

She unhooked her corset while he steadied her.

In her chemise and bloomers, she was simply stunning. Her smooth skin was the colour of the moon, and her dark hair fell like a silk sheet on her shoulders. He caressed her arm, amazed at how different it felt from his own—soft, smooth, and silky.

"I'm exhausted," she said.

"Time to go to sleep."

She circled his neck with her arms and rose on her tiptoes. He held her up from her waist. The ship gave a big jolt—even he couldn't deny it—and she gripped him for dear life.

"What was that?"

"A big wave." He laid her down on the bed, but she didn't let him go, so he went down with her.

Another mighty jolt.

"Is that normal?" She gripped him harder.

"We aren't going to sink."

"Honestly, my stomach frightens me more than sinking. I

don't want to be sick again." Her breath feathered on his neck, causing all sorts of emotions.

"Try to sleep. I'm sure the storm will pass soon."

As if to contradict him, thunder boomed overhead.

She laughed. He propped himself up on his elbow not to crush her, wanting to see her face while she laughed. She was so beautiful his heart stuttered.

"You need to sleep." He rolled off her and pulled up the covers.

She snuggled closer to him as usual, and he formed a protective cocoon with his arms around her.

He was happy just holding her.

Everything else could wait.

THE STORM HAD CALMED during the night, and in the morning, bright sunlight poured from the porthole. The sea was a blue slab of calmness, all innocence.

Isabella stirred in his arms.

"Good morning." He released her.

She stretched her arms over her head. "It seems like a good morning indeed. No more jolts, and finally sunlight."

"How are you?"

Her cheeks were cautiously rosy. "Better." She touched her belly. "The flatbread worked. I'm almost hungry."

He beamed. He didn't remember the last time she'd said she was hungry. "Excellent. We'll have breakfast together in the dining hall. The view is wonderful."

She stretched out again, yawning.

Her breasts pressed against the thin fabric of her chemise. He could make out her taut dark pink nipples. The temptation was too strong, and he ran a finger across her collarbone, touching the hem of her chemise. A flush crept over her neck to her cheeks, and her chest rose.

"Sorry." He started to withdraw his hand, but she stopped him.

"Don't stop. I like it. Please." She put his hand on her chest.

Heart pounding, he trailed his fingers lower until he brushed her nipple through the fabric. She let out a soft moan as her nipple hardened. He could spend the whole night just caressing her curves and hearing her breathing.

"I've never seen anything more beautiful than you," he said, brushing her breast again.

"Even now? I'm a scarecrow. Thin, pale, and wrinkled, not to mention chronically sad."

"Even now. I don't see what you see. I see a beautiful woman who charms me every time she smiles, talks, or simply exists." He cupped her breast, feeling its softness in his palm.

Her lips flushed red and parted as he rubbed her nipple with his thumb. He slowly opened the front of the chemise, uncovering her beautiful breast. When he touched her again, she arched her back. Little moans came out of her as he rolled her nipple. She squeezed her thighs together.

He could watch her for hours, listening to her moans. When he sucked her nipple into his mouth, they both groaned. He ran the tip of his tongue over the hardened peak, and she tangled her fingers through his hair, pulling it.

"You can touch me more." She took his hand again and placed it between her thighs.

He slid his fingers past the opening of her drawers to find her deliciously wet. "Does it hurt?"

She breathed hard. "I'm a little sensitive."

"We should wait." He went to remove his hand, but she stopped him.

"We've been married for a couple of months now, and we've never been together in bed properly."

He rubbed her nipple again. The temptation was too strong.

"You can...I mean, I'm ready. Dr. Norris said you won't hurt me." She stroked his jaw, starting a series of shivers down his body. "You've been very sweet to me, but I know a duchess must produce an heir and a spare, and that's the least I can do to repay you for your kindness."

He stopped touching her, a bitter taste in his mouth. Now he wanted to throw up. "I want to be with you. More than anything. But only if you're happy, and not because you think it's your duty as a duchess."

Her eyebrows knit together. "It came out wrong. It came out horribly wrong. What I want to say is I'm ready."

Yes, but he wanted her to be eager, passionate, and enthusiastic, not just ready as if she were talking about having surgery.

He brushed her chin with his thumb. "We have time. And I want you to be absolutely sure." He kissed her cheek and lingered for a moment on her soft skin.

Her eyebrows knit together. She didn't say anything, but he could almost hear her thoughts.

"We haven't consummated our marriage," she whispered.

"Trust me, I'm painfully aware of that. But I don't want it to be just an act. I want it to be meaningful and beautiful."

And he wanted her to desire him as much as he desired her.

thirty-three

Isabella had no idea the sun could be so strong and bright.

The white rocks and cliffs of Mytos multiplied the glow tenfold, causing her to squint. She inhaled the intense scent of the sea mingled with that of the wild flowers.

When Anthony had talked about Sirocco House, he'd described a modest building close to the sea. Instead, it was a palace made with tall white walls, terracotta tiles, and large verandas drowned in luscious bougainvillea.

After the storm and the darkness of her cabin, the day appeared incredibly bright. But the warmth in her chest was all for Anthony. She'd fallen asleep in his arms last night, surprisingly oblivious to the storm and the rocking of the ship. Whenever he held her, she felt safe, and a sense of calm suffused her. And his touch and kisses had left a trail of fire on her skin. The pleasure had been enhanced by the memory of the pain she'd endured.

She wanted to be the wife he needed and deserved. She wanted to make him as happy as he made her, and not out of guilt for having lied to him.

He could have easily sent her away after she'd recovered.

Instead, he'd been by her side, caring for her. And she loved every moment they shared.

At the base of the cliff where Sirocco House towered, she tilted her head back. The house was fit for a queen.

She panted by the time she climbed half the stairs that led to the front door. She was in terrible shape if only a flight of stairs had her gasp for breath.

"Do you want to take a break?" he asked, taking her elbow. "These stairs are steep."

"Yes, and I haven't exercised in a long time." She leant on the bannister over the sharp cliff. The sea lazily lapped at the rocks with a soothing swoosh while dark green bushes and purple flowers crawled up the house. "It's truly beautiful."

"My father loved it. Grandmama, not so much."

"This is murder," the Dowager said, climbing the stairs. "The sun and the climb are going to kill me." She paused next to them although her cheeks weren't red and her breathing seemed all right.

Lawson wasn't faring better, pausing every two seconds.

"I'm impressed you didn't suffer from seasickness," Isabella said to the Dowager.

The Dowager waved a dismissive hand. "Too undignified. No true lady should allow herself to be sick in that fashion. I'd rather force myself to be fine." Her composure slipped for a moment. "Not you, darling." She patted Isabella's cheek. "You do what you want."

Anthony smiled as if to say, '*That's unusual.*'

"Well, I'll proceed. Duchesses never cower in front of a challenge, nor do they whine." The Dowager went up in her slow but steady steps.

Isabella wrapped her arm around his and climbed the rest of the steps next to him.

"Better?" he asked, patting her hand.

"With you by my side, yes."

His eyes brightened. He beamed at her as if she'd paid him the best compliment ever.

The servants were lined up in front of the main entrance, waiting for them, and Isabella was so tired she didn't pay attention to Rogers introducing the staff and explaining who did what.

She sighed once inside the entry hall. Cool air caressed her hot cheeks, and the dim light soothed her eyes.

"The temperature is so different here," she said.

Anthony took her hand, going upstairs. "The walls are four feet wide. They keep the house warm in winter and cool in summer."

Her bedroom had a window overlooking the thick Mediterranean scrub. Cluster pine trees dominated the landscape, and other bushes she didn't recognise grew through the cracks of the limestone rocks, gripping them with stubbornness and defiance. The view had a rough wildness England lacked.

"I trust the room is to your liking," Anthony said.

"Beautiful." It was unburdened by the heavy furniture she had in London. No throne-like armchairs or large tables. Just a plain, wide space giving her a sense of freedom.

"My room is across that door." He pointed at a door on the other side. "Lawson has a room upstairs. If you need her, ring the bell."

"Thank you." She put her hand on his arm, and he smiled again.

"Do you want to take a walk through the gardens?"

"I think I'll rest for a few hours. The ship has tired me."

"Of course." He waited for the footman to drop her luggage and leave. "If you need me, don't hesitate to tell me. Grandmama can instruct the housekeeper if you want to rest." He leant closer and whispered, "I believe she enjoys giving orders."

She acted on impulse. Maybe because his kindness reached her heart and stayed there. Or maybe because she was tired of being sad. She rose on her tiptoes and kissed his lips. His eyes widened as he remained frozen. Shock? Surprise? Kissing him had seemed natural.

She stepped back from him. "Was I too bold?"

"Too perfect." His thick eyelashes fluttered.

She trailed her fingers over the scar. "Then I'll kiss you more often." She kissed him again, this time lingering.

He held her up by taking her waist and pressed his mouth against hers. They parted their lips at the same time. She darted the tip of her tongue out, stroking his lips, and he shuddered, his chest rising.

His fingers gripped her waist more tightly, and she put her hands on his chest, wanting to be closer to him. The fatigue that had never left in the past weeks vanished as he tilted his head to deepen the kiss. She expected him to be rowdy or dominating. Instead, he gently stroked her tongue with his, never pushing her for more.

The kiss was gentle and powerful, as he was. When he inched back, she was dizzy with tenderness and desire. Why hadn't she kissed him before?

"I'll see you later." He kissed her forehead before letting her go.

His fingers trailed over her waist, leaving behind a tingling path on her sensitive skin.

thirty-four

Anthony had let Isabella rest for a couple of days while he'd taken care of his correspondence, met his steward, and assessed which works the house needed.

After breakfast, she usually sat slouched on a lounge chair in one of the many balconies, coughing in her fist, and looking as miserable as she'd been in London.

If she kept to herself and sat in a chair all day, Anthony feared her health wouldn't improve. Although the kiss—the wonderful kiss they'd shared—made him hope for a change.

He smiled every time he thought about the kiss, especially since it'd been spontaneous and powerful.

He was looking at her from the window in the sunroom when Grandmama walked over to him.

"You ought to do something." She pointed at Isabella. "Nothing has changed. Unless you act, she'll do here what she did in London."

"I don't want to force her."

"Not force her but encourage her. And enough working for you. You barely rested yourself. Go and spend some time with your wife."

"You're right." He started to leave when Grandmama took his arm.

"I'm still angry with you for what you did. So take good care of her."

He nodded and kissed her cheek.

He was still debating if he should tell her the truth or not, but Patrick wasn't here to defend himself, and Isabella's health was a priority.

The warm, scented air teased his senses when he stepped onto the balcony. Despite the warm weather, Isabella's legs were covered by a quilt.

"Fancy a walk?" he asked.

"I'm too tired." And pale. The sunlight didn't prompt her to walk at all.

"You're too tired because you've been sitting on a chair for days, thinking about how tired you are. We'll take a slow walk with as many pauses as you like, and before you know it, your health is back. I want you to see all the flowers and plants here. This garden is bigger than it looks."

A little smile graced her lips. She stood up and wrapped her arm around his.

"I'm sorry I had work to do in the past two days."

"I needed the time to rest."

He wasn't sure about that.

He led her down a short flight of stone steps to the gravel path weaving through hedges, bushes, and flowerbeds with dozens of bees hovering around. In the background, the sound of the waves hitting the cliff resounded. No noises of carriages, no coal dust, and no grey sky.

She closed her eyes, tilting her head towards the sun. He spied on the gentle curve of her profile. When she opened her eyes and found him staring, she smiled, a bright, happy smile that lit her whole face.

They walked deeper into the garden to a remote part from where the house wasn't visible. The garden had a terraced, hanging structure where the plants grew across different levels, like the hanging gardens of Babylon. Tall trees and hedges also blocked the sound of the sea. Looking up, a tall wall of plants towered over them.

"We're alone in the world," she said.

"I wouldn't complain."

"The flowers are stunning." She paused next to a bush of peonies.

"Grandfather had a passion for flowers." Speaking of his grandfather...Anthony glanced at the last flight of stairs heading to the lowest terrace. A hidden wrought-iron door concealed the entrance to Grandfather's secret pleasure garden. If he wanted to show it to Isabella, he needed the key though. "Are you tired? Would you like to walk a little longer?"

"Yes. Where do you want to go?"

"Wait here a moment. I need to fetch something." He kissed her on the lips, and she laughed. So he kissed her again. But he had to go. "I'll be right back."

He raced up all the flights of stairs to the main balcony, startling the gardeners working on the hedges and a few maids sweeping the stairs.

Grandmama was drinking tea under a wide garden umbrella but sat bolt upright when she saw him. "Is Isabella sick?"

"No, all is fine." He rushed past her.

"Why the hurry?"

"Later. Later."

He barged into his room, scaring his valet who was arranging the suits in the wardrobe. He rummaged through the drawers of his desk. The key had to be...here! He snatched the large brass key and ran at breakneck speed towards the garden and again past Grandmama.

"But, really!" Grandmother dropped her cup, causing it to

rattle in the saucer. "This behaviour isn't dignified for a duke. Dukes never run."

"Sorry. Sorry." He nearly slipped as he shot down the stairs. "Bloody hell!"

"I heard that!" Grandmama said.

He raced down all the way to the last terrace.

Isabella was where he'd left her. She was bent over a bunch of pretty yellow flowers, her brow furrowed in concentration.

"Here I am." He was breathless.

She straightened and eyed him. "Goodness. What happened?"

He waved towards the house. "I've just terrorised half of the household and my grandmother."

She laughed. It was an enchanting sound. "For what reason?"

"A secret garden." He showed her the brass key. "Over there."

Her dark eyes brightened. "I'm intrigued."

"You'd better be. I almost broke my neck running down here."

He led her down a lateral flight of stairs hidden from view. One wouldn't find the secret path unless they knew where to look. The passage was so narrow Isabella had to walk behind him. Vines formed a green gallery with a ceiling so thick little sunlight filtered through.

At the end of the path stood a heavy-looking, wrought-iron door that time and the salty water hadn't managed to attack. The lock screeched when he turned the key. After a click sounded, he pushed the door, revealing yet another flight of stairs, rough and uneven. Purple wild passion vines climbed over a tunnel-like frame, forming a colourful ceiling over them. The flashy flowers nodded their crowns as if in greeting.

"It's lovely," she said.

"Be careful. The gardeners don't come here to clean often."

Brambles and other plants formed a thick tangle that blocked the passage in a few spots. He had to rip the plants to reach the garden, which wasn't in a better state but not as jungle-like as he feared.

"My grandfather had this garden built after Grandmama got furious with him. She refused to talk to him for days. They argued a lot." He held her hand as she jumped over a bush.

"Why was she furious?"

"Because he ordered sculptures of Greek heroes he wanted to place in the main garden upstairs, but Grandmama found them too scandalous." He paused. "He accused her of being too prudish and told her to 'unclench her pearls.' She told him he was a scoundrel and so on. Anyway, she won the argument, unsurprisingly, and he had to remove the statues. They should be here, buried under the wild plants."

The stairs opened to a wide, round area. Marble heads and graceful arms appeared through vines and tall grass.

"There." He removed a tangle of stems to reveal the statue of none other than Hero herself. "This is Hero."

The statue of a beautiful woman stood on the pedestal. Her tunic seemed ruffled by the wind as she stared at the horizon.

"She was a priestess of Aphrodite." He tugged at the remaining vines.

"She isn't scandalous at all." Isabella helped him clean up Hero.

"We're talking about my grandmother." He pointed at Hero's feet. "Bare ankles, bare calves, and suggestive curves. Too much."

She chuckled, and he would do anything to hear her laugh again.

"There's a pool!" She pointed to the other side of the garden.

"A natural pool, a small inlet."

She giggled when he helped her down the barely visible path to the cove. White stones formed a circle around a pool of turquoise water so limpid the bottom was crystal clear. The weather had smoothed and rounded the rocks around the edge.

"It's beautiful." She crouched to dip her hand into the water. "It's not too cold. Where does the water come from?"

"No idea. An underground connection, but the sea is right around this cliff."

She touched a few purple flowers around the edge. "There are small bushes of cistus here. They've been choked by weeds almost completely."

"My grandmother isn't fond of this garden. I think she's never been here, and after Grandpapa died, she asked the gardeners to ignore this place. She was angry with him for selling Maiden Hill."

"We should restore this garden to its original beauty."

He'd counted on her to say that. "I agree. I'll ask the gardeners to help clean it up."

She gazed around at the other statues before staring at him. "You know exactly how to make me feel better."

"No. But I try." He dipped his head. "I think I deserve a kiss for that."

She took his face before kissing him.

Holding her by the waist, he swept her off her feet and twirled her around. She wrapped her arms around his neck. When he put her down, her cheeks were deliciously flushed, and even her lips were a deep pink. He kissed her again, but this time, he couldn't contain his passion.

She opened her mouth and slid her tongue past his lips. And the kiss turned wild in a second. They kissed with their mouths open and their tongues stroking each other. It was a kiss that made him forget about who he was and where he was, and it was fantastic. Her hands wandered over his chest. Each contact with her palms and fingers shot desire through him. As if he didn't have enough of it.

He ran a hand from her waist up to her breast to cup it, tearing a gasp from her. He rubbed her nipple through the fabric of her shirt with more strength than the first time he'd touched her. Her reply was to graze his lips with her teeth. He pinched her nipple, and she bit his bottom lip, setting his blood on fire.

"Wicked," he whispered against her lips.

She smiled. "Only a little."

She was his wife, and he wanted to take her properly, but at the same time, he wanted to woo her.

She took deep breaths as he fondled her breast. "I like it when you touch me. And no," she added when he was about to say something. "It's not duty. It's not. So please don't stop now. I mean it."

She could read his mind because he'd been about to say just that.

Holding her with one arm, he unbuttoned her shirt. The more buttons he undid, the faster she breathed. Impatience won, and he opened her shirt, ripping a few buttons.

When her creamy skin was uncovered, he stared at the top of her breasts for a long moment. The corset pushed them up in the most enticing way. He unfastened the first hooks, just a few, to let the corset open. Underneath, only the thin chemise covered her. He tugged its hem down to bare her breast.

"Are you still sensitive?" he asked, brushing it lightly.

"Not anymore."

Still, he would be gentle.

He brushed his thumb over her pink nipple, watching it harden to a peak. She panted as he pinched it and rolled it between his fingers. When she sagged against him, he dipped his head to close his mouth around her nipple and suck slowly.

Her moan of pleasure was a sound he'd cherish forever. He tongued her breast until she squeezed her thighs together and breathed hard.

Slowly, he bunched her skirts up. Even in the hot weather, she wore several layers of petticoats, but he pushed them aside to find her bloomers.

More shoving and tugging got his hand between her thighs and over the opening of her drawers. They both stilled when his fingers were a mere inch from her heat.

At his first stroke, she drew in a sharp breath that ripped him apart, so intense it was. He demanded nothing but to make her feel beautiful, safe, and happy. He gritted his teeth when he touched her softness. Wetness soaked his fingers as he stroked her as gently as his desire allowed him.

Tension coiled in his body, and he suppressed the urge to go faster, deeper. He watched her face; she breathed with her lips parted and her eyes half closed. She gripped his waistcoat as he drew circles with his thumb. A quiver went through her, and she muffled her scream in his chest. Little pulses hit his fingers.

He let her enjoy the moment fully and rest against his body. When her breathing returned to normal, he reluctantly withdrew his hand. He made a mess of covering her again, wrinkling her skirt and fastening the wrong hooks on her corset.

When he finished, she looked like someone who had dressed in the dark while drunk.

"You'll have to take care of your clothes," he whispered, kissing her forehead.

She laughed against his chest. "Gladly."

If she let him, he would do everything to make her happy again.

thirty-five

Dusk had fallen slowly on the island as if the sun were reluctant to set on the beauty of the sea.

The night brought a fresh breeze to Isabella's cheeks as she stood in front of the open window in her bedroom. The lanterns shed a golden glow over the paths in the garden and the large terracotta amphorae filled with overflowing geraniums. She couldn't see the secret garden from there, yet it should be right in front of her.

That garden held more than one secret.

Anthony entered the room, and a whiff of his clean scent reached her. She turned around, smiling. Her body started to tingle the closer he came. Another man would sport a smirk of triumph or confidence after today. Instead, his expression was shy and adorable and started butterflies in her stomach.

"Can't sleep?" he said.

"I was wondering why I can't see the secret garden from here. I should."

"The secret garden is too close to the shore to be seen from here. I'll show you the perfect spot." He laced his fingers through hers and led her up the stairs.

They walked past the servants' rooms to go to the top floor. He opened a door, revealing another flight of stairs going up. The passage gave way to a veranda closed by glass walls. Dust covered the floor, and white sheets were draped over chairs and sofas.

He closed the door behind them. "Another place where the servants don't come. My grandfather wanted to turn the attic into a scenic sunroom, but he never finished the project, and Grandmama found the room impractical because of the steep stairs. But look." He turned towards a corner. "You can see the statues we cleaned up."

She craned her neck until she spotted the white marble of the statues shining in the moonlight. "Yes, how lovely!"

"Once the garden is all cleaned up, there will be a grand view from here." He hugged her from behind, wrapping his strong arms around her. "I like that this room isn't open to everyone so only we can enjoy the secret view."

She rested her head on his chest, savouring the warmth and sense of safety he made her feel. Those feelings were better than the deep pleasure of a tumble.

They stood there, watching the moonlight shining over the Greek heroes in the garden and listening to the sea's song.

"I want to give a ball here on Mytos," he said. "I want to invite all the guests Grandmama couldn't invite to our wedding."

She craned her neck to stare at him. "Why?"

He lifted a shoulder. "Celebration. I want everyone to know how happy we are. Would you like that?"

He looked so hopeful that she wanted to make him happy, and the idea of a proper celebration, without the burden of her sadness, appealed to her.

"Yes. Let's give a ball."

"We'd better start sending the invitations. Some people are spending the summer not far from Mytos, but others will need a couple of weeks to come here. The warm weather and the large garden will make for a spectacular night."

"It sounds wonderful."

She couldn't suppress a yawn. The day had been filled with too much excitement after the past dark weeks.

"You're tired. Let's go." He hauled her up and gathered her in his arms.

She loved it when he held her like that.

He put her down after the first flight of stairs, a mischievous glint in his gaze. He jabbed a thumb in the direction of the lower floor. "Look at that."

"What?" she asked.

"I want to try." Grinning, he mounted the bannister of the next flight of stairs backwards.

"Anthony, it's not a good idea. If you haven't done it before, you can get hurt, and this flight of stairs is quite steep."

"But a short one."

"You can't see properly."

"I don't need to." He released his grip on the bannister before she could say more.

"Anthony," she half-hissed, half-whispered.

He rushed down the polished bannister. Too fast. He let out a '*whoop*' that echoed off the walls.

She chased him down the stairs and couldn't shout a warning in time. At the bottom of the stairs, the Dowager stared at her grandson aiming at her.

"Anthony!" Isabella and the Dowager said together.

He managed to slow his descent but slipped to the side and ended up at the Dowager's feet with a loud thud. She winced when Anthony groaned, a hand on his back.

"Are you all right?" Isabella knelt next to him.

The Dowager's eyebrow was so arched it reached her hairline. "Have you lost your mind?"

He groaned again, sitting up. "A slight miscalculation. That's all."

Lawson, Rogers, and other servants came to the landing from different directions.

"His Grace fell," Lawson shouted over her shoulder.

"I'm all right." Anthony waved dismissively.

"What happened, sir?" Rogers helped Anthony up.

"Nothing, just insanity." The Dowager pressed a finger to her temple. "I don't even want to discuss what just happened. We shall never mention it to anyone."

"I want to host a ball, Grandmama," Anthony said with an air of triumph. "Everyone is invited."

The Dowager stared at him in confusion. "You? Hosting a ball? Did you hit your head?"

"Spare no expense. Let's invite as many as we can from London!"

The Dowager frowned. "We'll see if tomorrow you still want to host a ball. I've had enough odd things to deal with for one day. Good night." She headed to her bedroom, muttering under her breath but paused. "Isabella, a word?"

Swallowing, she followed the Dowager to her bedroom as Anthony instructed Rogers to send the invitations straight away.

When they were out of earshot, Isabella fiddled with her hands. "I know it wasn't appropriate, but it was a silly game Anthony and I played."

The Dowager patted her cheek. "I've never seen my grandson so happy. Thank you."

The shock made her speechless.

"I was worried about him," the Dowager said. "He's always been serious, but his brooding character has worsened since his parents' deaths. But you make him happy, and I hope you are as happy as he is."

"I am."

When the Dowager hugged her, she remained frozen. It was a quick, shallow hug, but still a hug. The Dowager released her and cleared her throat.

"A ball. Unbelievable. Now off you go. I need to lie down." The Dowager waved her off before retiring to her bedroom.

When Isabella returned to the landing, more servants crowded it.

"Are you all right, Your Grace?" Rogers asked.

Anthony scratched the back of his head, looking like a boy. "Yes, thank you. You may all return to your rooms."

After everyone left, he burst out laughing. "It was one of the most enjoyable things I've ever done."

"You could have hurt yourself. And your grandmother."

He kept smiling and gathered her in his arms. "Lovely night, innit?"

She closed her eyes while he walked down the corridor to her bedroom. He laid her on the bed and stretched out next to her, never leaving her side.

"We should change," she said.

"I don't want to call Wilson and Lawson."

"Fine. I'll help you, and you'll help me." She craned her neck to see his face. The naughty glint he had before rushing down the bannister was still there.

"Excellent suggestion. I'll start." He tried to unbutton her gown and tugged at her petticoats at the same time, making a mess.

"Wait. You're doing it wrong." She laughed when he didn't listen but managed to pull down her gown anyway.

With a lot of unnecessary tugging and pulling and her swatting his hands away, she was finally in her chemise and drawers.

"See? Easy." He ran a slow hand over her body.

"Easy? The room is a mess. My clothes are all crumpled, and I need my nightgown."

He exhaled dramatically. She chuckled again when he removed her chemise and drawers...and then she didn't laugh. He stared at her in the same way one would stare at a masterpiece.

He dragged one of his big hands down her body, leaving a path of fire on her skin. He paused on her ribs, a frown appearing on his brow.

"Don't look." She snatched the nightgown from the bed and covered the physical signs of the past months.

He let her cover herself before lying next to her. "You can't possibly be ashamed of your body."

"It changed, and not for the better."

"After you rest and eat properly, it'll return as it was before. You don't have a scar that will stay there forever. But you don't have to hide from me."

She gazed up at him and put her hand on his ruined cheek. He was right. His face was scarred for life. Her body would flourish again.

"I'm sorry. I always say or do the wrong thing with you."

"Not true. You taught me how to dash down a bannister. I won't ever forget that."

She felt all the bumps and edges of the scar with her fingertips. "Neither will your grandmother."

He let out a deep laugh. "Come here." He wrapped his arms around her and pulled her closer.

"You're still dressed."

"Right."

He sat up on the bed and started with his waistcoat. Just as he'd made a mess with her clothes, he tugged and pulled, discarding the clothes on the chair, or trying to. Half of them ended up on the floor.

When he was in his undergarments. The thin fabric of his undershirt showed his powerful body, and she pressed herself against him when he held her again. He stroked her head and removed the hairpins until her tresses were loose and free.

"You're beautiful," he whispered, kissing her forehead.

As he held and caressed her, she drifted off to sleep, aware she was the luckiest duchess in the world.

thirty-six

Isabella couldn't believe how beautiful the secret garden was.

After the gardeners had cleared the path and the statues of weeds, she had an idea of how wide the garden was. Green moss still covered the statues and the marble steps, and catchweed vines choked some beautiful flowers. But aside from that, the corner of the Mediterranean Sea promised to be a spectacular paradise.

"There's so much to do," she said as Anthony walked next to her, surveying the garden. "The ornamental plants need to be freed from the choking vines and brambles. Then we can plant everything we want." She turned around. He was staring at her, smiling. "Did I say something funny?"

His smile widened. "No. It's wonderful to see you happy." He took her face and kissed her lips.

She kissed him back. Kissing him had become a normal occurrence in a short time. Not just an occurrence, but she needed his kisses, caresses, and smiles. More than the physical contact, she craved his kindness.

"I'm so glad you forgave me." She took his hand and pressed his palm to her cheek. "I can't believe you were so generous to me, and I'm happy you gave me the opportunity to stay here with you."

"How could I not?"

"You didn't ask questions..."

She wasn't sure she wanted to talk about Patrick and ruin the beautiful relationship they'd built. But on the other hand, he had to know the truth. Or maybe she should wait to talk to Patrick in person since she hadn't had the heart to send him that letter. She rubbed her forehead, confused.

"We'll talk, but not now. Not here." Pain cracked his voice, and she felt his pain in her chest. "This is our corner of only happiness."

She hugged him, promising to do her best to repay him for his kindness.

~

AFTER HOURS OF WORK, during which a few more special flowers had been uncovered and freed from the weeds, Isabella sat on a picnic blanket next to Anthony. Cook had prepared a basket for them filled with fresh Mediterranean fruits, sandwiches, and cold drinks.

The shadow of a large cluster pine tree offered shelter from the sun, and the rhythmic song of the cicadas made her sleepy, especially after having pulled weeds and potted plants in the sun.

Anthony had dispensed with his jacket and waistcoat and rolled up the sleeves of his shirt, showing muscular arms. His hair was pulled back and held by a string because he'd complained about his curls ending up in front of his eyes while he worked.

The result was that the scar was fully exposed, and while she shivered as a phantom pain stung her, thinking of the agony he must have experienced, she liked it. The scar suited him. It gave him a wild look she found charming.

She removed her boots and stockings and wiggled her toes in the sun.

He drank from a flask of water. "It's so different from London here. So peaceful."

"I love this place. And we have our own private beach."

"It's spectacular at night. Tonight is Saint Lawrence's night. It's the night when the Perseids, the meteors of the Swift-Tuttle comet, come close to the earth and light the sky with shooting stars. Let's watch the stars together tonight."

"Yes." She fanned herself. "It'll surely be cooler than it is now. I wish I could take a bath."

"In our private beach? By all means. Go ahead."

"Anyone might come here."

"Not if I lock the door. Your wish is my command."

She trapped her bottom lip between her teeth and glanced at the inviting pool of water. "Yes."

As he went to lock the door to the secret garden, she studied the pool. It didn't have a visible opening to the sea. The mysterious underground connection with the sea worried her.

"Is it safe?" she asked Anthony. "I won't be sucked into a rocky pipe that will spit me out into the sea and splatter me over the rocks, will I?"

He frowned. "You have a rather morbid imagination. The pool is not dangerous, not when the sea is calm, anyway. But I'll go first." He started to unbutton his shirt.

She didn't turn around. After last night, her curiosity for his body had increased, and he didn't seem to mind she watched. His body could rival those of the Greek statues so well-defined it was. One sharp ridge after the other, the muscles contracted under his tanned skin. The sun had sprinkled freckles over his face, arms, and neck.

Her face warmed when he slid into the pool.

He was immersed up to his shoulders, and what was visible warranted a lot of appreciation. Drops of water trickled down his neck. His auburn hair had acquired a red-golden hue since he spent so much time in the sunlight, and the colour suited him. Even the freckles dotting his nose were perfect.

"See? Perfectly safe." He folded his arms over the ridge of the pool. "There's a crack through which the water comes in. I can feel the light current with my foot, but the opening is too narrow for a person—" He shouted before sinking and disappearing from view.

"Anthony!" She rushed to the pool and dived into the water without thinking. "Anthony!"

Perhaps the crack had sucked him in, and his leg was stuck. He would drown!

She was about to dip when he emerged in front of her, sending sprays of water everywhere.

"And here I am," he said, laughing. "Did you fall for it?"

She didn't crack a smile as she tasted the saltiness of the water on her lips. "I was scared to death." Her voice broke. "I thought you were stuck underwater."

"It was a joke." He brushed his wet hair from his face.

"It wasn't funny!" She swatted his shoulder and started crying for no reason other than the scare.

"I'm sorry." He hugged her, and she rested her cheek on his chest. "I didn't think you would take it seriously."

"I did. My heart stopped for a moment."

He caressed her head and back in slow circles until she stopped crying.

She sniffled. "I know I'm silly, but I was truly scared."

"No need to apologise." He kissed her temple.

She sagged against him, even though she didn't shiver anymore. Being hugged and cuddled was too nice, and the water cooled down her hot skin through her gown.

The weather was too hot to wear her usual layers of petticoats, so her skirt didn't weigh as much as it should. Still, she ought to remove it and let it dry in the sun before returning to the house. She fumbled with the ties until her skirt and petticoat were free.

"What are you doing?" he asked.

"I want a proper bath."

Removing the wet skirt required some gymnastics, but she managed. She propped her wet clothes on the ridge of the pool. Much better. He stepped back and faced the rocks while she removed her shirt, likely because she'd reacted badly the other night.

She paused to ponder if she should remove even her chemise and drawers. The fabric was all soaked through anyway. When she peeled off the wet undergarments, a sense of freedom made her feel lighter. And the water was deliciously cool. She let out a sigh of relief, dipping her head.

He craned his neck to glance over his shoulder. "Do you want me to leave?"

"No. Don't leave. Please. You were right. I've had enough of hiding."

He remained where he was, facing the rocks. His back was broader than she'd thought, and the water enhanced the shape of his body.

Maybe it was the beautiful garden and the lack of clothes, or the sudden sense of freedom she was experiencing, but she didn't care about many things at the moment. Not about being a duchess, nor about her sense of guilt and the truth she had still to tell.

She slipped her hand into his, feeling his strong fingers, and gently tugged it until he turned around. She had to tilt her head back to stare up at him, at his beauty.

She wanted to say many things, too many, so she didn't say anything.

His gaze slipped down for a moment before returning to her face. She ran her hand up his arm to his shoulder, neck, and cheek. Her strong, sweet husband. She caressed his broad chest and abdomen, and he let her explore.

When he put his hands on her waist, she gasped at the strong sensation of his hands on her naked skin. He lifted her to kiss her, his eyes darkening with hunger. She wrapped her legs around his waist and moved her hips against him. The feeling of him was ten times stronger than when she'd been with Patrick. She'd enjoyed herself with Patrick, but the safety Anthony radiated made everything stronger, more visceral.

"Am I going to hurt you?" His voice sounded strained as if he were in pain. "Is it safe?"

"Yes." She kissed him hard, surprising herself. She was desperate to feel him, to feel his body against hers, to be with him. "Make me your wife."

He matched her passion, devouring her mouth with dominating kisses. Heated flushes warmed her body. They fought to kiss and touch every inch of each other.

She panted, rocking her hips against him. His large hands took her waist and lifted her. Lowering her, he started to slip inside her. A moan escaped her as he stretched her slowly.

"Are you hurt?" He paused, stroking her buttocks.

"No. It's wonderful."

Still, he inched deeper gently, watching her face with awe.

Her body was tender and sensitive, or maybe she was simply nervous, but the tenderness became sheer pleasure. When he was sheathed in her, a low groan rumbled from his chest. He held her still for a long time before kissing her savagely. And she loved it.

She did her best to move her hips with him. Water splashed around as he thrust faster and deeper. She sank her fingernails into his back as a combination of maddening need and burning pleasure overwhelmed her. She rocked her hips faster.

He became more urgent until her body shook with a powerful release. She cried out and sagged against him. He roared his pleasure, quivering against her.

Just like the vines she kept weeding out, she clung to him as if her own existence depended on that. She felt that, if she let him go, she would never find him again. Or herself.

The water lapped at their bodies lazily in stark contrast to the frenzy that had taken them.

He kissed her neck and breasts without hurry, trailing his soft lips over her skin. Each gentle brush of his lips and tongue left her breathless and her skin tingling.

Where did all that pleasure come from? It must have been hidden inside her body, lingering, waiting for this perfect moment to come out like a torrent engorged by a summer storm.

"I love you, Anthony." The words flowed naturally out of her because they were true.

He hugged her tightly, swallowing before answering. "I love you, wife of mine."

thirty-seven

Isabella couldn't stop giggling as she and Anthony made their way to the house.

After their dip into the pool, they were both drenched. Her clothes were soaked and wrinkled by the seawater, and her hair was a mess, but she'd never been happier.

He pulled her to a dark corner from which one of the French windows to the ground-floor sitting room could be seen.

"If we get in through one of the secondary entrances, we'll avoid being seen and questioned."

They waited until the maid sweeping the terrace left. They stole across the path to the window. He peered inside before pushing the window open. The smell of beeswax and lemon polish made her giggle again for some reason.

"Shush," he said, smiling. "We'll get caught."

They crossed the sunroom, leaving wet footprints on the terracotta tiles. He paused again before stepping into the corridor. Then they went up a secondary flight of stairs.

"Could you imagine my grandmama's face if she saw us now?"

"You don't need to imagine anything. You have only to turn

around." The Dowager's voice came from the other side of the hallway.

Isabella gasped, and Anthony shoved her behind him as if his grandmother were an assassin.

The Dowager stood with her arms folded over her chest and her eyes narrowed to slits. She raked a slow, assessing glance over them. The lower the gaze went, the more her lips thinned.

"What is the meaning of...this?" She waved at them and the wet patches on the floor.

"We fell into the pool," Isabella said at the same time as Anthony said, "We took a bath."

"Which one of the two versions is true? For heaven's sake, you didn't even agree on telling the same story." She pressed two fingers to her temples. "What if the servants see you like that? Wet, dishevelled, sneaking into the house like thieves!"

"Exactly," he said. "We must change. I'll see you later."

"I agree." The Dowager waved him away. "Go to your room. Now. I'll help Isabella."

"But—"

"Now, Anthony."

Before leaving, he kissed Isabella on the lips, tearing an outraged gasp from the Dowager.

"Go. Shoo." The Dowager hurried to Isabella's bedroom and opened the door. Before letting her in, she peered inside. "No maid. In you go."

"I can change alone."

"I know." The Dowager tossed her another glance. "What happened?"

"We were working in the garden, and it was so hot we decided to take a swim." She peeled her drenched clothes off her body.

"Is that all?"

"What do you think happened?"

"I just want to make sure he didn't do anything to upset you."

The Dowager helped her remove the skirt, twitching her nose. "There's mud on the fabric."

She towelled herself dry and put on a fresh chemise and her dressing gown.

"Sit, I'll brush your hair." The Dowager patiently untangled Isabella's long tresses with expert moves. "Was he kind to you?"

"Very. Anthony is gentle and caring."

"I'm still upset with him for what he did to you."

She trapped her bottom lip between her teeth. The fact the Dowager blamed Anthony hurt, but he'd told her not to say anything.

"We did it together. Please don't blame him. I was happy to be with him."

"Are you happy now?" The Dowager's tone became suddenly low. "Does he make you happy?"

"Yes. Anthony is the best man I've ever met."

The Dowager ran the brush down Isabella's long hair with gentle strokes. "I love him dearly. He was a shy boy while Patrick was the cheeky one. But Anthony was always ready to protect his brother from every danger or a well-earned scold. He wants to protect those he loves."

"He protects me, too. From myself as well. I'm happy with him."

"I was happy with my husband as well. Our marriage was an arranged one, but we liked each other from the beginning. That was until our son died, and he sold Maiden Hill. I haven't forgiven him, either."

"Are you sorry we're restoring the secret garden? It was your husband's project."

The Dowager smiled. "How can I be sorry when the garden is bringing so much joy to you and Anthony? No, don't worry about me. Instead, you should be worried about Patrick."

"Patrick?" She did her best not to gasp.

"That boy." The Dowager released a long breath. "He wants to court Lady Sophia von Gruner, marry her. He has lost his mind."

"That's good, isn't it? If he marries Sophia, there are good chances Maiden Hill will return to you."

"You don't know Patrick. He has a good heart, but I've heard him declaring his undying love for a lady more times than I care to count. He'll seduce Sophia and leave her."

No, she knew Patrick a little.

THE NIGHT SKY was clear and with no moon when Anthony got ready to watch the stars.

He was eager to show Isabella the beauty of the night on an island where there weren't lights. Holding her hand and a lantern, he led her down the stairs to the secret garden.

The fragrance of jasmine rose from the bushes, and the rocks cooling down in the night released a salty-metallic fragrance he found intoxicating. They stretched on a picnic blanket next to the pool, in a spot where the tree branches didn't cover the starlight.

"It's so beautiful." She laced her fingers through his, watching the dark velvet of the sky, and his pulse gave a kick.

"A shooting star." He pointed at the flash of silver crossing the sky.

"I missed it."

The crickets replaced the cicadas at night and sang their soft tune, but his heart beat louder.

"I saw one," she said.

"Have you expressed your wish?"

"I have." She pouted. "But it's not coming true."

"What did you wish for?"

"For a kiss from my husband."

He propped himself up on his elbow and dipped his head.

She tasted of summer and roses, of hope and good dreams. He

moved his lips slowly as she tangled her fingers through his hair and pulled him closer.

Only the stars witnessed their kiss in the secret garden.

He slipped his tongue past her lips and deepened the kiss. The gown she wore was thinner than the others, and the warmth of her body easily reached his skin. He caressed her breast. She drew in a deep breath as he teased her nipple with his thumb.

Her legs spread wide, allowing him to nestle between them. He held himself up not to crush her, but he had to feel her skin. A battle started as they fought to unbutton, untie, and strip each other's clothes. The sound of a piece of fabric being ripped came, but he had no idea if it was his shirt or her skirt.

Garments were pushed aside none too gently by impatient hands. Sighs and moans mingled with heat and breath. The more he got undressed, the more his temperature rose. Then the bliss of feeling her smooth, naked skin against him stopped time.

He stilled to savour the sensation of her breasts against his chest, her leg around his hip, and her black eyes filled with awe and starlight.

They stroked each other slowly without necessarily meaning a tumble. It was a slow exploration to simply enjoy touching. He kissed her neck, and she reclined her head. A shiver pebbled her skin when he closed his mouth around her nipple and sucked gently.

He slid a hand between them to find her wet. Her hips rocked and ground against him. He drew circles, rubbing her while scattering kisses on her skin.

He pushed her legs further apart. The slit of her drawers parted and showed him all her beauty. She gasped when he ran his tongue over her. Incoherent words came out of her as he kissed her deeply, tasting her wetness. She writhed under his tongue, and he had to hold her hips still to deepen the kiss. Her release came with one of her shouts. He loved it when she shouted.

He loved hearing her wild and unrestrained, and he loved that he was the reason for her pleasure. When she sagged on the blanket, he made his way up her body. She was stunning in the soft light from the lantern and the starlight kissing her skin. She gripped him and urged him inside her.

He undid the falls of his trousers. Then it was sheer bliss. She was silk and velvet all around him. He started moving in and out of her, watching her biting her bottom lip. He felt that bite on his skin. They found their release together and held each other, sharing their breath. He lay next to her.

"It was perfect," she whispered.

Right then, a bright, large shooting star crossed the sky, and he had only one wish—that she was happy.

thirty-eight

Anthony hated gardening, but working next to his wife in the secret garden had its perks. After the gardeners had cleaned up the patch, it was only he and she among the scented flowers, butterflies, and the sound of the waves. They had the pool all to themselves, and no one ever bothered them.

Four weeks of hard work had turned the wild place into a lovely, manicured pleasure garden with the marble statues shining in the sunlight. The plants Isabella had chosen needed to grow and bloom, but overall, the work was worth it.

He was sitting under their favourite tree with her after a particularly pleasant dip in the pool. She rested her head on his lap, her hair wet. The sunlight and the gardening had turned her skin a lovely shade of brown and gold Grandmama found outrageous, but he loved it. Her body was supple again thanks to the delicious food and the exercise, and the dark shadows in her gaze had gone.

"We have to return to London, don't we?" she asked as he caressed her hair.

"Not yet, and I want to return here to see all the flowers growing, and of course, I'll have a gardener take care of all the work we've done."

"It's so beautiful what we did together."

He caressed her cheek and neck. She'd gained weight, returning to her flourishing form, but above all, she smiled more although she wasn't the completely careless woman he'd met. Maybe she would never be again.

"I want to give you an heir," she said.

"Isabella." He shook his head. "You listen to Grandmama too much."

"I mean, I want a child with you. I want our love to grow as it grows here."

He kissed her, tasting the salt on her lips and the sunlight in her laugh.

"Your Grace?" Rogers's voice came from the other side of the wall closing the garden. "I'm sorry to disturb you."

Scoffing, he opened to the butler. "What is it?"

"Lord Patrick is here, sir." Rogers wiped his forehead with a handkerchief. "He brought Lady Sophia with him."

"What? Without telling me?"

"Patrick is here?" Isabella walked over to them. "I didn't know he would come."

"I ordered him to," he said. "When I sent the invitations for the ball."

"Why?" Her eyes widened with unmistakable fear.

He didn't want to reveal he knew the truth in front of Rogers, so he remained silent. But words weren't needed. She paled.

"Rogers, you may return to the house. I'll be there shortly."

"Why didn't you tell me?" she asked the moment Rogers was out of earshot.

"I didn't want to upset you. You were recovering so well."

She brushed a few leaves from her gown. "How did you…"

"It was obvious."

She lowered her gaze. "All this time, you knew the truth, but you didn't tell me."

"Again, I wanted to protect you."

"I felt guilty all this time, torn between telling you or not, and you already knew everything."

He raked a hand through his hair. "Hell. I didn't mean to make things worse."

She brushed past him. "I need a moment."

"Isabella."

"Please." She started up the stairs without looking at him.

THOUGHTS PILED up too quickly in Isabella's mind for her to keep up with them.

Anthony had meant to protect her, but at the same time, he could have spared her a lot of misery by talking to her. On the other hand, she hadn't mentioned Patrick either.

Speaking of the devil. She came to a stop on the veranda where Patrick was talking with the Dowager. The stunning blonde woman at his side had to be Lady Sophia. Her pristine blue dress matched her large eyes, and with her slender, elegant figure, she looked like a princess out of a fairy tale. Patrick was the perfect Prince Charming next to her.

Isabella patted her hair; it had to be a disaster between sweat and salty water. Her gown wasn't faring better with wrinkles and grass blades. Instead of proceeding to the veranda, she took the side path and headed for the French window. She met Lawson along the way to her bedroom.

Lawson gave her an alarmed look. "Lord Patrick is here."

She tugged at her gown. "I know."

"Do you need help to change, madam?"

"I do." And to hide.

"He wasn't supposed to be here," Lawson said once they were in the bedroom.

"Anthony ordered him to come. He knows."

Lawson paused with the comb in her hand. "Since when?"

"Since it happened. He didn't tell me anything."

"That's...good, isn't it?" Lawson brushed Isabella's hair.

"I guess so. I'm not sure. I think he should have told me."

"Maybe His Grace didn't want to upset you."

"But what's the point of inviting Patrick here then?"

Lawson worked in silence to make her presentable again.

Was she overreacting? After all, Anthony had been kind to her, even though he'd known the truth all along. But she was emotionally drained and physically tired of worrying.

He had forgiven her. Maybe he hadn't forgiven Patrick.

Maybe she had to talk with both of them.

DURING THE PAST DIFFICULT MONTHS, Anthony went through different emotions regarding his brother.

At first, he'd been furious. Then his worry for Isabella had taken over his mind, and then he'd found a sort of peace or acceptance.

Isabella was healthy again, they were happy together, and the past was the past. But the moment he found himself face-to-face with Patrick, who showed off his usual nonchalant attitude, something ugly stirred in his chest.

He forced a smile, bowing to Lady Sophia. She had none of her father's harsh lines and unforgiving gaze. Tall and blonde, she had a soft face and a sweet voice. He wasn't fool enough to let her looks deceive him. The von Gruners were proud and cunning.

"It's a pleasure to meet you, my lady."

She bowed her head, her golden curls bouncing over her cheeks. "Patrick told me everything about you." Her gaze swept swiftly over the scar in a calculating way as if she were assessing his weakness.

He could bet Patrick had instructed her not to look alarmed at the scar.

"Alas, we know very little about you," Grandmama said. "We didn't even know you were coming."

If Sophia was annoyed by Grandmama's tone, she didn't give any sign. "My fault. It was a last moment's decision, and I insisted on coming here. After all, if we want to discuss the negotiation on Maiden Hill, we ought to see each other."

Patrick kissed her hand and stared at her in awe. "Sophia has our cause at heart. She's so compassionate and lovely, she understands our struggle."

To his surprise, Sophia returned the lovey-dovey stare with matching devotion. For a moment, they got lost in each other's stare as if they were alone in the world.

Grandmama exchanged a glance with him. He could hear her thoughts. Was it the first time Patrick had fallen in love?

He'd endured the usual pleasantries and polite exchanges with Sophia and Patrick, controlling his need to speak to his brother for almost an hour until he locked himself in his study with Patrick.

Not to mention Isabella was angry with him. He'd planned to tell her about Patrick at the right time but hadn't found it. Or maybe he hadn't wanted to. Speaking about the truth meant to bring tension and unhappiness between them.

"I hope you're as happy as I am, brother." Patrick sprawled on the armchair and stretched out his long legs. "Maiden Hill will return to our family soon. With a bit of luck, we might celebrate Christmas there. Imagine, our house restored. And hell, Anthony, Sophia is everything for me..." His voice turned serious. "She's as strict as Grandmama, fierce as a warrior, and gives me a sense of purpose, a direction. Does that make sense?"

Anthony propped himself on the desk, too restless to sit. "Right now, I care only about one thing. Isabella."

"Of course. I understand." Patrick snatched a glass of lemonade from the table. "Grandmama told me Isabella was terribly sick but didn't specify anything. Not even you told me exactly what happened."

"She suffered a miscarriage." He did his best to stay calm.

That got Patrick's attention. "Dammit, Anthony. I had no idea. I'm sorry."

"You should be because the child was yours." He couldn't completely remove the tension from his voice.

Patrick stopped sipping. He remained frozen in shock for a moment before letting out a nervous chuckle. "Not possible."

"Do you deny having had an encounter with Isabella?"

Patrick placed the glass on the table and stood up. "I did have an encounter with Isabella. It was nothing serious." He glanced at Anthony before continuing. "But it was well before you and she got married. I had no idea you were interested in her. Hell, it happened before you decided to get married."

"Exactly."

"What do you mean by—" Patrick paled and scratched his chin.

"She married me because she was with child, your child, while you vanished, leaving the chaos you caused behind."

Patrick held up his hands. "I had no idea she was with child. She didn't tell me anything."

"Should she have told you everything in a letter or a wire?"

Patrick swallowed a few times. "Anthony, I didn't know. Had I known, I would have done something."

"Marry her?"

"Yes!" Patrick straightened. For the first time, Anthony saw a strong resemblance between them. "I'm not completely despicable. If she was sure the child was mine—"

"What the hell do you mean by that?" Anthony moved before he realised he did. All the frustration he'd bottled up in past months burst out. He grabbed Patrick by his jacket. He'd spent his life protecting his little brother, and he didn't regret it, but this time, defending Patrick wasn't possible. "She nearly died."

Patrick parted his lips, but before he could speak, there was a quick knock on the door.

"Anthony, I wanted—" Isabella swept into view, cheeks flushed. "What's going on here? Anthony, release him immediately."

He did as told but didn't step back from Patrick.

"Is this why you asked him to come? To manhandle him?" She gazed from one brother to the other. "What's happening?"

"Tell her," Anthony said.

Patrick straightened his jacket. "Anthony told me about...the incident, and I told him that, had I known, I would have taken my responsibility if you were sure the child was mine."

Her eyes flared wide with horror.

"I'm sorry," Patrick said. "I didn't mean to imply anything."

Isabella's cheeks flushed. "You were my first and only one before my marriage. I know you didn't mean to cause me trouble, and I agreed to everything we did together, but you ought to take your responsibility. You were the father of my child and..." She swallowed hard and left the room.

Anthony went after her.

As he followed his wife, Patrick shouted, "I'm sorry."

"Isabella." Anthony chased her up the stairs.

When they'd arrived on Mytos, she hadn't been able to climb the stairs without taking a breather. Now she went up faster than a deer. She raced past her bedroom and went further up to the unfinished sunroom.

"Isabella." He followed her.

She faced the window from where the secret garden was visible.

"Darling." He put a hand on her shoulder.

"I didn't have anyone else. I was with Patrick once, and then you. And no one else."

"I don't care how many lovers you had before me. I don't care about who your first one was either, as long as I'm the last one."

"What was the purpose of confronting Patrick?"

"He's my brother. He must face the consequences of his actions and grow up."

"You could have told me you knew the truth."

"The truth doesn't change how I feel about you. I love you. Nothing is going to change that."

"I love you, Anthony."

There was a knock on the door. "May I?" Patrick stood on the threshold of the dusty room. "I want to apologise." He bowed from the waist. "I caused both of you a lot of suffering, and I'll make amends. I promise. I say stupid things when I'm agitated, and I take every single stupid thing I said back. Please forgive me, Isabella."

She stared at him for a long moment before nodding her head once.

"What can I do to make amends?" Patrick asked, his voice cracking.

Anthony held her hand. "Let's start with taking Maiden Hill back."

THE GUESTS they'd invited for the ball kept arriving at Sirocco House for three days. Wave after wave of sweaty and panting lords and ladies flooded the house.

Isabella had to neglect the secret garden to welcome the guests and take tea with them. Their quiet corner of the Mediterranean Sea had become crowded in a short time. But she smiled when Helen climbed the stairs to the main entrance, cheeks red and sweat glistening on her forehead. Her maid and footmen followed her.

"Helen." She opened her arms to hug her sister. "Thank you for coming."

Helen hugged her back. "I wouldn't have missed this ball for anything in the world, and I'm happy to see you fully recovered."

"I'll show you your room. You'll love it."

As they went upstairs, Helen gazed around with interest. "This palace is magnificent."

"The gardens are beautiful." She entered Helen's bedroom where the footmen were leaving the luggage. "You have a spectacular view from here."

Helen removed her hat, pacing around. "Worthy of a princess."

"I'm glad you think that." Anthony entered the room, and Isabella's heart gave a silly thump. He kissed her cheek. "Isabella is my queen." He stared at her in awe before facing Helen. "Welcome."

Helen bowed her head. "Anthony."

"I hope you love Sirocco House as much as we do." He lifted Isabella by the waist and made her twirl, tearing a laugh out of her.

"What are you doing?" She chuckled when he put her down.

Helen averted her gaze and focused on the four-poster bed.

Isabella caught a glimpse of a scowl but could have been mistaken. Perhaps Helen was simply tired.

Anthony laced his fingers through hers. "We'll let you rest. We'll see you later at dinner."

"Later, Helen." When she left the bedroom, she could have sworn Helen had a forlorn expression on her face.

thirty-nine

Weeks ago, Isabella would have been exhausted by the preparations of such a grand ball. Instead, thanks to Anthony's love and her work in the garden, she was excited and full of energy when the ball began.

She walked through the crowded room, smiling and nodding at her guests. Some of the guests' smiles might be fake, but she didn't care. Anthony loved her, and with him by her side, she would face anything.

The room couldn't be more different from the one in Gloucester House. The large windows and pots of flowers made it look wider than it was, and the scent of wild jasmine was a feast for the senses.

She paused when she spotted Helen standing alone on the balcony in a dark corner.

"Helen." She closed the French window behind her, cutting off the sound of the music and the chatter. "What is it?"

Helen wiped a tear quickly. "Nothing."

"It can't be nothing. You love balls, and the room is full of eligible gentlemen. I'm surprised you're hiding here in the dark."

"You'll be angry with me."

"Tell me everything."

Helen shivered and took a few deep breaths before answering. "I failed."

"At what?"

"I had one job, marry the duke, and I wasn't good enough for him. I did everything Mother asked me, but he didn't like me."

Isabella was puzzled. "You didn't fail. You and Anthony weren't meant for one another. That's all."

"It's that I saw you here in this beautiful house with Anthony, and I couldn't help but think it could have been me." Her whispered words were like a slap.

"You weren't interested in Anthony after his incident, and you've never cared about him. You were only interested in his title, and you have many suitors to choose from."

"You weren't interested in Anthony, either." Helen heaved a sigh. "I read the letter you wrote to Patrick. I know about your affair with him and your child."

Another moment of stillness went through her. "I was with Patrick only once, but I don't understand what my miscarriage has to do with anything."

"You married Anthony only to hide your pregnancy. You didn't like him, but you married him to cover your lies. While I did everything to please him..." Helen pressed her lips together.

An echo of the guilt struck Isabella. "Yes, I married Anthony in a moment of need, but do not think, not for one moment, that I don't love him. I love him very dearly, and he loves me. Our marriage started with deceit, but trust me, I'm aware of how lucky I am, and I much appreciate everything I have. You don't have to be jealous of Anthony."

Helen sat down slowly on the bench as if moving were an effort for her. "I'm not jealous of Anthony. It's you." Her words were barely audible.

"Me?" She huffed. "You're jealous of me?"

Helen took her time to answer. "You've always done what you

wanted, enjoying every moment, while Mother expected me to be quiet and always do as I was told. I've never had the courage to pursue my own desires or talk back to Mother, as you have. I wish I were more like you."

Shock silenced Isabella. The idea Helen had been envious of her all that time was ludicrous. Helen had received nothing but praise from their parents, tutors, governess...everyone.

"I know my own weakness isn't an excuse," Helen said. "I should have been more determined, but I constantly felt the pressure of being perfect in everything."

"Have you been unhappy all this time?"

Helen swallowed a couple of times. "I wouldn't say unhappy. That wouldn't be fair to our parents, but I was overwhelmed. And seeing you so happy and free..." She shook her head. "I'm sorry. I know it's awful of me."

Isabella did awful things too, and the signs of Helen's unhappiness had been there, but she'd been too busy with her own drama to take note of them.

She sat on the edge of the bench next to her sister. "I had no idea you felt that way. I thought you wanted to marry a duke, not just because Mother urged you to."

Helen gave a little shrug. "I wouldn't mind marrying a duke, but I don't want to be forced to." A sob shook her. "I'm sorry my selfishness hurt you."

"If you'd told me how you felt, I would have helped you."

Helen pressed a hand to her mouth. "As I said, I'm not as brave as you are, and I hope you'll forgive my words one day."

She reached out and squeezed Helen's hand. "I still love you."

Helen hugged her, whispering, "I'm sorry."

Isabella held her back. If there was one thing she'd learnt from the horrible experience of losing her child, it was to keep those she loved close.

~

ANTHONY WATCHED as the guests for the ball moved into the ballroom. But as he greeted the guests, and too many stared at his face, he couldn't deny the discomfort bothering him. The guests had already seen him, but apparently, his face was a constant source of shock and attention, judging by the mutters, gasps, and looks.

Grandmama instead was radiant, almost jubilant. She showed a broad smile and fanned herself with a certain energetic flair.

The idea of giving a ball at Sirocco House had been his, after all. It was a way to show himself to society after his absence from London. and once his brother was there came with the added bonus to make sure Patrick didn't have a change of heart regarding his love for Sophia. Once they were seen together at the ball, Patrick couldn't easily change his mind. But above all, he wanted to celebrate his marriage and his wonderful wife.

"Why are you so happy?" he asked Grandmama.

"Waiting for all the guests to arrive here from England or other parts of the Mediterranean has been annoying but very rewarding. Look at Lady Acton. She's panting. Her face is all red. She isn't used to the hot weather, and I asked Rogers to have the path to the house lit with large braziers. It's unbearably hot there. A sauna." She smirked. "Lord Gully has sweat patches under his armpits. Lady Howe is so overheated she can't even speak, thank goodness. She doesn't say anything worth hearing anyway. She looks like she might have a fit at any moment. And Lord Lambton hasn't recovered from the seasickness. He's all green."

Anthony frowned. "Grandmama, did you invite these people to watch them suffer in the heat?"

"I didn't tell you anything so as not to upset you, but each and every one of them made cruel comments about your face after you showed yourself in the House of Lords." She snapped her fan closed. "I replied to the comments with polite remarks, but they didn't stop. A lady never makes a scene, but she doesn't swallow insults without reacting, either. This ball in the middle of the Ionian Sea is exactly what they deserve."

"Remind me never to upset you, Grandmama."

"Your Grace, Gloucester." Lord Lambton bowed, huffing. "Wonderful house." He dabbed his green face with a handkerchief.

"I trust you had a pleasant journey." Grandmama stopped a passing footman carrying a tray of canapés. "Would you like a canapé, Lambton?" She selected one with creamy cheese and watercress on top. "They are delicious. Some of them are made with smoked fish. You can taste the sea. Nothing like a rich meal after a long journey across the sea to restore the spirits."

Lord Lambton pressed the handkerchief to his mouth. "If you'll excuse me." He hurried out of the ballroom.

He exhaled. "Grandmama."

"What?" She had another canapé. "Lambton said you could find a job as a circus freak. Serves him right."

"Stop torturing our guests."

"No, I'm having too much fun." She fluttered her fan and stared at a young lady who was whispering behind her gloved hand.

The whispering ceased immediately, and the young lady composed herself.

How Grandmama could do that was a mystery.

Anthony instead couldn't take his eyes off his wife as she entered the ballroom from the balcony with Helen at her side. The trip to Mytos had healed her both in body and spirits.

"Isabella is enchanting," Grandmama said.

"She is."

"Even in that pink gown."

"Please, Grandmama."

"Well, tastes are tastes."

Sophia came from the balcony as well a few moments after Isabella and Helen.

Even from across the room, he could tell Sophia's cheeks were flaming red. She lifted her chin and marched towards them, her eyebrows drawing together.

"Something must have upset Sophia," Anthony said.

"My, a von Gruner being upset by something. Why am I not surprised?"

Sophia stopped in front of them, clenching her fists. "You all lied to me. My father is right. We can't trust the Beauforts."

Anthony exchanged a glance with his grandmother. "About what?"

"Patrick had an affair with your wife, she became with child, his child, and then she lost the baby while she was married to you, but no one told me! I've just heard a conversation between Isabella and her sister about Patrick. I know everything."

Anthony narrowed his gaze at her.

Grandmama regained her cold composure in a moment. "I must ask you to stop talking. We don't want to make a scene."

"I don't care about making a scene when I'm surrounded by liars." Her Austrian accent became heavy. "You're a disgraceful family as my father says." She turned towards the door and marched away in a flutter of blue satin.

"That little, unbearable brat," Grandmama said, and he didn't scold her.

Isabella fell silent, as did everyone else when Sophia crossed the ballroom with angry strides. She hadn't understood the brief conversation Sophia had shared with the Dowager and Anthony, but something must have troubled her.

Isabella followed her among mutters and whispers. "Sophia?"

Sophia went down the stairs in the garden, quick in her slippers.

"Sophia."

Sophia faced her. Anger flashed red across her cheeks. "You had an affair with Patrick," she said without a preamble.

The accusation shouldn't surprise her, but the tone hurt her.

"No. We were together only once. It was a mistake, but it didn't happen again, and it was before he met you."

"You carried his child and lost it."

She had nothing to apologise for with Sophia. "Why are you so upset?"

"Not one of you told me anything." Sophia raised her voice.

"Because it was none of your business." Isabella matched the lady's tone. "Besides, Patrick didn't know about the child until a few days ago."

"But he knew about the quick affair with you. I think I have the right to know that the man who wants to court me had an affair with his brother's wife."

"It's up to Patrick to tell you about his escapades, but we all suffered through the incident and eventually moved on, and what happened between Patrick and me doesn't affect you."

"How can I trust a man who doesn't take his responsibilities? How can I trust a family who keep secrets?"

That was a good question to which Isabella had no answer.

"Your family is corrupt," Sophia said. "You don't deserve my help. You can forget Maiden Hill. My father will do whatever he pleases with it. Even bring it down brick by brick." She resumed walking away, but Isabella followed her.

Since Sophia wanted to throw the blame around, Isabella could do the same. "Maiden Hill isn't just a house. It's a precious memory. Your family have been nothing but cruel towards my husband by neglecting Maiden Hill. He grew up in Maiden Hill. His father died there. Yet you and your father don't care. All for what? Revenge over a spite that happened decades ago. Perhaps your family isn't as innocent as you think."

Footsteps approached, and Isabella composed herself.

Patrick walked over to them. "Sophia. Please."

"I don't want to see you. The Dowager said the Beauforts have never faced any scandals. Well, enjoy your first one. Because I'll make sure everyone, in every European court, will know who you are, Patrick—a libertine who got his brother's wife pregnant." Sophia marched away.

The threat hung in the night air like a ghost.

He exhaled, rubbing his brow. "I ruined everything. And the ironic thing is that I love her."

"Give her time." Not that Isabella thought Sophia needed only time but also a good dose of discipline. "How did she learn the truth?"

"Anthony told me she eavesdropped on a conversation between you and Helen."

"And now?"

Patrick shoved his hands in his pockets. "And now the negotiation on Maiden Hill is over."

forty

After all the chaos and questions had ceased and the guests had retired to their rooms, Anthony withdrew to his study. Sophia's threat risked ruining his family name. Gossip might go away after a while, but the Beauforts' reputation would be soiled.

Not just his family's reputation was at stake, but also Maiden Hill would be lost with his parents' souls.

Isabella paced behind him. "There must be something we can do to change Sophia's mind."

"A von Gruner? In a few decades maybe, but the von Gruners are bloody vindictive."

"We must talk to her again."

He didn't turn around when the door opened. He kept staring at the lanterns in the garden. Even without looking, he knew Grandmama had entered. The sharp sound of her heels gave her away.

"May I talk to Anthony alone?" she asked.

He shared a glance with his wife, having a hunch about what Grandmama wanted to talk about.

"Of course." Isabella left.

There was a click when she shut the door, and he was alone with his formidable grandmother.

Her soft hand touched his shoulder. "You let me believe you were the father. You took the blame."

"If I had told you I had no idea Isabella was with child when I married her and that I suspected Patrick was the father, you would have demanded I throw her out."

"I'm ashamed to say you're correct." She sat on the armchair in a swish of silk, looking defeated for the first time. "I wasn't fond of Isabella at first, but after the tragedy, I couldn't help but love her. She's a strong, compassionate woman, and she loves you. She makes you happy. You've changed so much since she's been in your life. Yes, if you had told me the truth, I would have wanted her out of the house. You were brave and honourable, and I apologise for having shouted at you."

"There's nothing to forgive, Grandmama. I only wanted to protect Isabella."

"From me." She hung her head in a dispirited pose that worried him.

He held her hand. "You've changed as well."

She regained some of her usual confidence. "I wished Patrick had changed, too."

"Patrick." He shook his head. "Once again, he caused irreparable damage."

"Do not fear. I will give him a scold he'll remember forever. I don't think I can forgive him."

"Please, Grandmama. I only want to move on. We'll be stricter to Patrick, but no more arguments. I can't bear them."

She smoothed a fold on her skirt. "If anything, Patrick is distraught. Sophia broke the engagement, and the guests are already gossiping about the incident. This is a rather upsetting string of disasters, even for someone like him."

"We must find a way to convince Sophia to stay quiet. And even if she does, I don't think we'll ever get Maiden Hill back."

She rose to look out of the window next to him. "Isabella told me the secret garden is lovely. You two worked hard on it." She tilted her head in the direction of the secret garden although it wasn't visible from there.

"Grandfather would be proud."

She flashed her smirk, hooking her arm through his. "Well, the easiest solution to our predicament is that she marries Patrick, as it was planned. And we might have the perfect way to make sure she says yes."

~

TWO DAYS HAD PASSED since Lady Sophia had stormed out of the ball, and Sirocco House had been in a flurry of activities for Isabella. Or rather, the activities had been focused on the secret garden, and Patrick had nearly done the whole work under her directions. He'd moved heavy pots, dug, and trimmed plants relentlessly, obeying every order he'd received without complaining.

She was standing in the middle of the garden, surveying the work they had all done. Anthony, the Dowager, and Patrick paced around.

Anthony checked the orchids draping a marble bench, the Dowager studied the statues with a disapproving look, and Patrick seemed to have aged ten years.

The garden was stunning now, restored to its former glory. Colourful flowers bloomed from every corner. The statues had been scrubbed to star-brightness, and the pool was a turquoise jewel against the backdrop of the limestone rocks.

Budding red roses, pink orchids, and lilac lilies formed a scented frame for the bench next to the pool. The path to it was adorned with all the white flowers she could find, from daisies and white roses to white tulips and stars of Bethlehem. Shining terra-cotta pots were overflowing with scented jasmine and white orchids. If Sophia's heart didn't melt in front of such beauty, then she wasn't human.

Anthony slid an arm around her waist. "Anyone would fall in love."

She kissed him. "Even a von Gruner."

"I think I've learnt my lesson," Patrick said. "With all of you here as my witnesses, I swear I'll change. I'll become a different man. I caused you nothing but trouble, and I was punished, too, by losing Sophia."

"You aren't the only one who needs to change," the Dowager said, wiping her hands with a handkerchief. "Anthony must stop protecting you and taking the blame for things he didn't do. Isabella should be less naive, and I should..." She tapped her chin with a finger. "No, I can't think of anything I need to improve."

They laughed.

"Everything is ready," Anthony said. "Show Sophia you love her, convince her to marry you, give us Maiden Hill back, and stop this nonsense."

"Woo her," Isabella said.

Patrick raked a hand through his hair. "I'm not used to wooing anyone. I'm just straightforward and say what I think."

"And how did this strategy work for you?" Anthony asked.

"Not well, admittedly." Patrick massaged the small of his back. "The garden is breathtaking. Thank you."

"Have you memorised the speech you wrote?" the Dowager asked.

"Of course." Patrick had an expression of hurt innocence.

"Then we need to get ready for Sophia." She brushed dirt from her gown. "She should be here soon."

They rushed back to the house, and Isabella dismissed Lawson. Since she and Anthony had already undressed each other, she meant to put that into practice.

They laughed and stole kisses while tearing at each other's clothes before donning fresh ones. The breeze carried the salty scent of the sea mingled with that of the flowers. Her worries vanished when she was with Anthony, when they both cared for each other.

He held her by the waist and scattered kisses on her face. "If Sophia weren't coming here, I would stay in bed with you."

"But we have a mission." She turned around. "Button me up."

He obliged but gave her a kiss on the neck every time he fastened a button.

Once they were ready, they hid behind a tall hedge in the secret garden, waiting for Sophia to arrive.

The Dowager joined them, scoffing. "Why should I hide? It's most undignified."

"This moment is only for Patrick," Anthony said. "It's his mission to convince Sophia."

"We're only witnesses."

The Dowager edged closer to the bush. "I can barely see anything through these leaves."

Footsteps sounded, and Sophia came into view. Her tight burgundy dress was a stark contrast to the white flowers lining the path. The sight looked like blood on snow.

Sophia gazed around, seemingly with a lack of interest. If she found the secret garden stunning, she didn't show it.

"What did you want to tell me?" she asked, removing her gloves with snapping gestures.

Patrick swallowed hard. "Sophia, my life has changed since I met you, and I..."

"He's forgotten the words," Anthony whispered. "The fool."

"I..." Patrick stroked his chin.

The Dowager pinched the bridge of her nose.

"Yes?" Sophia's tone was sharp.

"Hell." Patrick ran a hand through his hair. "The truth is that I'm a shallow, despicable man."

"What is he doing?" Isabella whispered.

"I've never had to work hard or take anything seriously because my elder brother has always been there for me, to protect me. I had the money and power but not the responsibility of being the next duke. Yes, I treated Isabella beastly. I'm a scoundrel, a rake, and a cheat, but I'm not lying when I say I love you. I know that because your happiness is essential to mine, because you hold my soul, and that's the beginning and the end of my world. I want to be a better person for you, and I want you to be next to me when I make a mistake because I know you'll help me correct my ways."

Sophia's composure slouched a little. "How can I trust you?"

"Try me. Ask me to do something for you, and I will do it."

Isabella held her breath. That was a bold statement on Patrick's part.

Sophia tilted her chin up. "Would you renounce Maiden Hill for me? Marry me but never, ever see Maiden Hill again?"

Anthony muttered a curse the Dowager didn't chide.

Isabella shook her head. That was a low blow. Whatever Patrick said, he would lose Maiden Hill.

Silence as thorny as the firethorn's spikes spread.

Patrick shifted his weight and attempted to glance over his shoulder to where they were hidden. But then he straightened and faced Sophia.

"No." His determined reply cut through the silence. "I love you, Sophia, but Maiden Hill belongs to my family with the precious memories it holds for us. I can't give it up. Not even for you."

Anthony grinned, nodding. The Dowager remained unfathomable, as usual.

Even through the leaves, Sophia's sudden pallor was evident. Either she was angry or disappointed.

"Then you don't love me," Sophia said, turning around.

"She's leaving." Isabella clenched her fists before coming out of her hiding place. "Sophia!"

Sophia stopped right next to Hero. "Isabella. Were you eavesdropping on my conversation with Patrick?"

"As you eavesdropped on my conversation with Helen."

Sophia had the decency to blush.

"I won't interfere with your personal relationship with Patrick, but I don't want to lose Maiden Hill because of your personal quarrel with him."

Sophia folded her arms over her chest. "Patrick is an indecisive and weak man."

"Patrick has just shown you he's ready to sacrifice his feelings for you to honour his family. This isn't the act of a weak man. You should have been appalled if he'd agreed to your blackmail."

"It wasn't blackmail." Sophia lost her confident attitude. "It was…"

Isabella arched her eyebrows, trying to imitate the Dowager. "It was blackmail. Maiden Hill might be simply a house to you, but for us, it's the place where the memories of our loved ones are resting. It's part of our family, given away in a moment of extreme pain." She took a step closer to Sophia. "Anthony's grandfather sold it because he was heartbroken. He was hurt, and your father took advantage of that pain for revenge, acquiring the house with a stratagem. Your father behaved dishonourably, causing more pain to the late duke. Tell me, Sophia, are you proud of that? Of the way your father took advantage of a man's broken heart to spite him? A man who was grieving the loss of his son and daughter."

Sophia lowered her gaze. As the sun set, the shadow of Hero crept over Sophia, turning her burgundy gown into a dull grey.

Isabella continued. "You have the power to right a wrong that has tormented my family for too long. It's your choice. You can end this quarrel right here, right now."

Hero's shadow fully engulfed Sophia who looked tiny compared to the tall and proud statue.

"I don't believe you're so flippant not to realise what pain your father inflicted upon us. Make a choice." Isabella let her words sink in. Anthony and the Dowager had left their hiding place as well, and they were standing behind her.

Sophia wiped her cheek so quickly Isabella wasn't sure there had been a tear at all.

Sophia bowed her head. "You're right, Your Grace. I'll do my best to convince Father to return Maiden Hill to your family."

She didn't dare show her happiness but remained composed, as the Dowager would do, fighting a smile threatening to break on her lips. "Thank you."

Sophia gazed around the garden, looking like a simple young woman. "This garden is beautiful, a truly magical place. Patrick chose well."

He hadn't, but never mind.

"Thank you, Sophia," Anthony said.

Sophia nodded. "Patrick, I wish you well."

Patrick bowed and didn't beg her to stay.

After another graceful bow of her head, Sophia left. The moment Sophia disappeared up the stairs, Isabella let out a whoop.

Anthony hugged her. Patrick smiled although a hint of sadness lingered on his face. The Dowager showed the biggest, happiest smile Isabella had ever seen.

Anthony crushed his brother in a tight hug. "Well done, Patrick."

Patrick didn't react with the enthusiasm she would expect. He stared at his hands covered in cuts and bruises as if seeing them for the first time. The hours of manual work had taken their toll on him.

"I haven't done anything well," Patrick said. "I hope one day you'll tell me that again when I deserve it."

The Dowager hugged Isabella. "Wonderful. The way you held yourself together while confronting Sophia was wonderful."

She laughed, but the laugh turned into a quick sob. "I'm so happy I might cry."

"Absolutely not." The Dowager wiped Isabella's eyes with a silk handkerchief. "You're a duchess."

Anthony was in trouble. Huge trouble.

He stared at his two sons, George and William, his two identical twin sons, wondering which one of the two he'd just fed. One had eaten more than the other. Or worse, the other hadn't eaten at all.

He ought to be quick because when Isabella came from her meeting with Mrs. Fawcett, she would want to know if the boys had eaten.

And to think he'd insisted on spending more time with his children, instead of letting the nanny take care of them.

"Now, be nice to your papa." Anthony searched those pairs of black eyes the same colour as Isabella's. "Which one of you had the rice pudding twice?"

He tried to get clues from their clothes, searching for a grain of rice on them, but the clothes were the same colour, the same fabric, the same cut, and they were equally crumpled. The twins' small hands were sticky with who knew what substance, and their curls were styled in the same way. He should have paid more attention.

Footsteps approached, and his heart gave a quick kick.

"Good afternoon." Isabella hurried towards the children in her lovely dark pink gown. "Did you miss Mama?"

"How was the meeting?" he asked.

"Excellent. We recruited more ladies to our suffrage cause. The petition is gathering signatures quickly. And you'll be surprised to know that Helen has done most of the job. She's become quite passionate about our rights. Of course, Mother isn't too happy, but Helen's betrothed agrees with her and—" She eyed the plates on the table and then him. "You tried to feed them again."

"No."

"Anthony."

"I did."

"Why didn't you let Lawson do it?"

"Because my father loved sharing food with us, and many modern scientists claim the relationship between children and their parents is important and develops through bonding with food. And because I want to do it."

"All right. You're passionate. I just hope you didn't make a mess, as usual."

"Mess? Me? How insulting."

She kissed the twins who cooed in reply. "I missed you too, darlings. So, no mess?"

He cleared his throat. "There might be only one teensy problem."

Isabella narrowed her eyes in the same fashion as Grandmama would. "I knew it."

He shrugged. "It's not my fault. They were crawling across the room while I gave them the rice pudding, and I got distracted for a moment, and I'm not sure which one ate more."

"How can't you tell them apart?"

"I told you they need to wear different clothes and hairstyles."

Isabella huffed. "They are. William is the one with the pilgrim collar, and George has the bishop one." She pointed to the wide white collars of the twins' shirts.

"What?" Honestly, he didn't see any differences.

"One collar is rounded, the other is pointed."

"For Petes's sake!" He threw a hand up. "From now on, I want different colours. William will wear only green, and George only red. And they'll have their names embroidered in clear letters on every piece of clothing."

"It's outrageous that you don't see the differences. William's nose is different from George's, and William's curls are less bouncy than George's."

He gave up and sat on the carpet with her and the twins crawling around. "I admit defeat."

Grandmama entered the room, and her pinched expression softened the moment she saw the twins. "My beautiful great-grandsons." She joined them on the carpet, and William and George squealed in delight. "Patrick sent a wire. Everything is going well in Maiden Hill. The restoration is on schedule."

"Is he still thinking of Sophia?" Isabella said.

"No, thank goodness. He's too focused on working in Maiden Hill. I knew that working hard would cure him of his heartache. Besides, who needs that stubborn, unforgiving woman?" Grandmama huffed. "Patrick has truly changed. He isn't pursuing any lady."

Anthony arched his brow. "Sophia reminds me of someone I know."

"Tosh. I was sceptical about Patrick's change, but I'll admit he did change, and he's doing an excellent job in Maiden Hill."

"I hope we can spend next Christmas there." Anthony wrapped an arm around Isabella's shoulders and the other around Grandmama's. "After Maiden Hill has a new façade, windows, and a new roof, the only thing missing is love."

about me

Love stories have always captured my imagination. What's better than two people falling in love with each other? I write steamy romance, usually with a paranormal twist in an historical setting. Add a touch of suspense and mystery and a pinch of darkness. I love stories with  strong, sexy heroes and mischievous heroines who pull no punches.

I live in the City of Sails, New Zealand, drinking tea (coffee gives me anxiety) and devouring books.

Join my newsletter for exclusive content and the chance to receive an ARC copy of my books. Just copy and paste this link into your browser:

Barbara's Newsletter: https://bit.ly/39yZ4Lw

also by barbara russell

If you want historical romance:

<u>Victorian Outcasts</u>

If you love steamy paranormal romance set in Victorian London, my
Royal Occult Bureau series is for you:

<u>The Royal Occult Bureau Series</u>

Are you into shape-shifter romance? Check out my da Vinci's Beasts
series, set in WW2:

<u>da Vinci's Beasts Series</u>

For more Victorian paranormal romance with witches and sexy warriors,
see the Knights of the White Blade series:

<u>The White Order Series</u>

www.ingramcontent.com/pod-product-compliance
Lightning Source LLC
Chambersburg PA
CBHW050506110726
47899CB00005B/1341